Cats Can't Shoot

Books by Clea Simon

The Theda Krakow Series
Mew Is for Murder
Cattery Row
Cries and Whiskers
Probable Claws

The Pru Marlowe Pet Noir Series
Dogs Don't Lie
Cats Can't Shoot

The Dulcie Schwartz Series
Shades of Grey
Grey Matters
Grey Zone
Grey Expectations

Nonfiction
Mad House:
Growing Up in the Shadow of Mentally Ill Siblings
Fatherless Women:
How We Change After We Lose Our Dads
The Feline Mystique:
On the Mysterious Connection Between Women and Cats

Cats Can't Shoot

A Pru Marlowe Pet Noir

Clea Simon

Poisoned Pen Press

Poisoned Pen Press
6962 E. First Ave., Ste. 103
Scottsdale, AZ 85251
www.poisonedpenpress.com
info@poisonedpenpress.com

Printed in the United States of America

For Jon

Chapter One

When I first got the call about a "cat shooting," I assumed the worst. People can be evil, and I've seen the damage they can do. But when I got to the house, I realized that no feline had been brutalized, at least not the way I had feared. The longhaired white cat I found cowering in a cupboard was apparently unharmed, aside from shock and some singeing where the powder had marked her silky white coat. It was the person who was dead.

The house was anything but, buzzing like a beehive. I didn't know what the brouhaha was about at first, just that the call that summoned me had sounded serious. So, for a change, I'd come. In general, I don't do summoning well. As independent as any lone female, I prefer to name my terms. The phrase "cat shooting" had caught me, however. When an animal is in danger, I'm willing to bend the rules. And while I wasn't given the details, as soon as I pulled into the long semi-circular drive, it was clear something was up. With their coveralls and protective booties on, those technician types didn't fit with the detailed woodwork or the spacious porch that wrapped around two sides of the restored Queen Anne. Two of the techies, carrying in some kind of plastic case, left the carved door ajar, so I'd followed them in. So many people were filtering in and out by then nobody seemed to care if I tramped in on a crime scene. In fact, despite the ominous words I'd heard on the phone, I wasn't entirely sure that I was in one. Until I saw what was left of him.

Downstairs office—probably the grand house's sitting room in a prior incarnation—with a view of a lawn that must have stretched down to the river, and a body that had been dead long enough to really look it. Donal Franklin, if the letterhead scattered across the desk was any indication. I certainly couldn't tell. I'd met Donal—Don, he'd called himself—at a black-tie Valentine's Day dinner I'd been duped into attending. But the cold, still thing that lay in a pool of blood bore no resemblance to the dapper socialite I'd danced with not six weeks before. This thing was white, fake looking against the darkening blood. Plastic. Like another dead body I'd seen, not that long ago.

"Pru—Pru Marlowe—over here."

The sound of my name snapped me back to the present, and I managed to turn away from the mess that had been a man.

"You okay?" The question came from Jim Creighton, Officer Jim Creighton. He wanted to know if I was going to be sick all over his evidence, not if the sight of a less than fresh corpse made me weepy. He's sentimental that way.

"Dandy, Jim." I swallowed. A fly buzzed by. Someone must have opened a window, and the stationery fluttered slightly, rearranging itself by the body. I had probably turned a little green, but the breeze—cold, harsh—did me good. Besides, Creighton knew me well enough to know that I'm tougher than I look. Not girly at all, despite the long dark hair that I keep tied back while working and what have been described as dangerous curves. We'd had some contact, the good officer and I, in the past. Right now, he had his hands full without worrying about my tender feminine side. "What's up?"

Despite the magnetic pull of the corpse, I kept my eyes on Jim Creighton and even managed a step in his direction. In truth, it wasn't hard. Even in his drab brown uniform, our local peace officer was a looker. But any urge I had to ruffle that too short, sandy hair was muted by our surroundings—and the technicians who hovered, photographing and cataloging everything on that desk or on the floor, where the blood had begun to congeal.

Next to the puddle lay some kind of gun. With its sleek, dark barrel, maybe nine inches long, and a trigger like a flower petal, it looked more decorative than deadly. The filigree pattern on its side—silver gone tarnished, I was guessing—and the beauty of the grain drew me. Could this pretty toy have done all that? I reached for the polished grip.

"Uh uh." Jim Creighton was as fast as he was smooth, and his hand closed over mine. "Over here." He led me to a bay window where a built-in window seat held oversized art books. *Flayderman's Guide to Antique Guns*, I crouched down to where he'd pointed and read. *The Art and History of the Duel.*

"Light reading, Jim?"

"No, Pru. Over *here.*" He nodded to his side of the shelf, empty and dark. "Be careful."

I leaned over. There, as far back as she could go, was the cat. A Persian, by the look of her, one side of her white ruff spattered with black powder. The whiskers on the same side looked singed. I wouldn't be able to assess any injuries until I had her out of her hiding place, though, so I held one hand out and let her sniff. She squeezed back further and hissed.

"Watch it." A plump tech had seen me. His arms above the gloves showed scratch marks, beaded with blood. I hadn't been Creighton's first choice. "That's a killer kitty."

"Seriously." Creighton heard me start to laugh. "That cat— looks like it set off the gun that killed its owner. There's a tuft of fur in the trigger housing, and paw prints all over."

I sat back on my haunches. Not many men can take my stare; Creighton only shifted slightly. "Look, Pru, I can't get into it. Just take it on faith, for once. Okay? Call it an accident. A real freak accident."

So that's what he'd meant by a cat shooting. Death by feline. That's when the relief swept over me, the kind I've learned not to show. Some people, they think human life matters more than other kinds. Not me. Besides, I didn't know the man, not well, and anyway, he was beyond my help. That Persian, though, she was terrified, and for all I could tell, burned or injured. Usually, when people and animals interact, the animal gets the worst of it. Usually, the person is to blame. I'd get more out of Creighton later. For now, I turned back to the cat.

"Well, then, we'd better check this out. All right, kitty?" I lowered my eyes to appear nonthreatening, all the while reaching out with my thoughts. I visualized the gun, that pretty, deadly toy. A loud noise. A man falling. Something had happened here, and I was hoping for images. Pictures of what had gone down. None of it made sense to me, though the black powder dusting the cat's side did imply some kind of involvement with the prone and silent man. "You didn't kill him, did you?" It seemed impossible, no matter what Creighton had said. "Kitty?"

Usually, I can tell these things. It's not only that I prefer animals to people. It's a sensitivity I have, what some people—not me—would call a gift. Usually, I can pick up something. Hear a thought—a memory. Whatever. This time I was getting nothing.

"You want a broomstick or something?" The plump tech had come up behind me. Just what this traumatized animal needed. I silenced him with a look that made him happy to return to his corpse and crouched back down to floor level.

"So, kitty, you want to tell me what happened?" The gun was gone, secreted away in some evidence bag, but I tried to remember the pattern. The way the cold metal would feel on a paw pad. The man on the floor. There were a million possible stories here, and in most of them, a person was at fault. "Did you do it?"

The cat just hissed.

Chapter Two

I finally resorted to the gauntlets, the long leather gloves that protected me up to the elbow as Ms. Kitty lashed out and bit. I'm not a fan of the gloves. Last thing a scared animal needs is the smell of hide and a force without the sense to withdraw when slashed. The situation wasn't getting any better, though. And between the noise and the aroma of her dead person, I couldn't see the white cat relaxing any on her own. Besides, those powder marks worried me.

I'm not a vet. Not even an animal behaviorist really, although I've nearly finished the certification program. What I am isn't that easy to understand, but as I drove to the county shelter—the closest facility around that has a decent animal hospital attached—I tried to make myself clear to the freaked-out feline in the carry box beside me.

"Listen, kitty, I may be the only friend you've got left." From the carrier, a drawn out cry, half wail, half whine, made me wonder if she'd understood me. "I'm trying to help you here, okay? You've got to work with me."

The whine continued and I switched on the heat. Late March in the Berkshires and spring has pretty much arrived, though the optimistic green on the trees would mean little to a housecat. I had to consider that she might be injured. At the very least, she was in shock. Sure enough, as the monster engine in my Pontiac GTO warmed up the car, the low-pitched whine subsided, and I considered my next step. We had twenty minutes, more or less, before the shelter, and I was hoping to get through.

That whine, I figured, was the Persian's way of telling me off. Tuning me out, blocking the sound of my voice with her own white noise. Maybe it helped her block my thoughts, too, as they prodded and probed for something in that fur-covered skull.

I should explain here: I'm not what they call an "animal communicator." I can't tell you what Bootsy wants for dinner, usually, or how Spot is doing over the rainbow bridge. But I have a strange skill. I can hear what animals are thinking. What they're experiencing, really. It's not that they talk to me, or not most of them. It's more like I pick up what's on their minds, what they're smelling or hearing or want to do. See the world through their eyes, kind of, though for most of them sight is the least of it. Sometimes, it works the other way, and I can reach out with my voice and my thoughts. That part's iffier, and I was willing to bet the white Persian wasn't getting anything from me; the whine had returned, becoming more of a growl. That could have been her choice. Those leather gloves are never a great idea.

All I knew for sure was that I had a traumatized animal riding beside me. While I hadn't noticed any obvious injuries—it's hard to examine a spitting, slashing cat—all four claws had seemed to be working when I lifted her out of her hiding place and maneuvered her into the carrier. I was betting that shock was the primary concern, but shock can kill an animal. And no matter what Creighton said, I didn't see what relevance any household accident would have on the animal's care. It wasn't like he was going to charge the cat. What mattered to me was getting the animal calmed down and examined. Then we could figure out the next step.

The next step. For a lot of animals, that would be a problem. A shelter looks nice, and you can throw in a few white lies for the kids. I knew better, that it's usually the end of the line, and it didn't improve my opinion of my own species. I wondered if she'd matter to anyone left in that house. There's no way of telling at one glance, but she looked like the real thing. Short, heavy body. Face like a bookend. Besides, nothing else in that house had looked random—or inexpensive. And with that great logic that only we humans have, those that are worth more are usually given the best. As I've said, there are reasons I prefer animals. No, I didn't see euthanasia in this cat's future. The only question really was, now that her main person was dead, what might her value be.

◇◇◇

"No kids, but there's a wife," Creighton had told me. "We're still trying to reach her. She's off on a shopping weekend." He didn't have to add the obvious: only a certain class of people buys things for recreation. The house had already let us both know who we were dealing with. "She'll be making the decisions, most likely."

I tried to picture her. Polished certainly. Suave. I didn't remember who Don had been with that night at the dance. I don't know if she'd been there. We'd met at the bar. My date had gone off to sweet talk another dude with money. It wasn't romantic; it was business. He was the type who always had a plan. And I'd been pissed—in both senses—when Don had come by. Maybe the one drink, that one dance had been charity. I'm not proud, and I had wanted to make sure that I was busy by the time Mack came back to collect me. But the dance had been good, old Don light on his feet and sure with his hands even as the tempo picked up. He was used to this, not like me and certainly not like Mack, and I'd said as much, as he glided me right up front by the band.

"My wife," he'd explained, as he dipped me low. "She's after me to try new things." He didn't have to reference her again; it was never going to go any further. We'd both smiled and backed away as soon as the song ended, and I ended up dancing with one of his friends. That didn't mean I didn't wonder who he had at home. I'd hoped she was classy, at least as much as he was. At the very least, I figured, she was generous.

The thought of the corpse on the floor and the man it had been chilled me. Wealth, class—it didn't matter that much. No matter how much platinum the widow could flash, she'd be coming home to a tragedy, and it might be a while before she was ready to deal with a skittish animal again. I pictured a silver fox, slim and tailored, and could all too easily imagine her understated makeup cracking under one more burden.

"Tell her the cat is in good hands." I'd said to Creighton. "Tell her, the cat is safe." Times like this, I fall back on my training. Repeat your command. Keep your voice even and low. The tone, as much as the words, carry your message.

"I'm sure she'll be broken up about the kitty." Something in Creighton's voice made me want to reiterate the command, but he caught himself quick. "Hey, who knows?"

"She's going to have other things to worry about." I gave him that much. The Persian was in the carrier by then, and I was pulling off the heavy leather gloves. "Still, it might help to know something is being taken care of. A pet can be a comfort."

"Some comfort." He had turned from me by then, but he had heard the howling and the hissing. He'd kept his distance as I donned the gauntlets. Besides, a technician was packing up the loose papers, all the random knickknacks of the room. The body would be next. "Let me know when I can examine the cat. She's evidence."

Chapter Three

"So this is the infamous creature."

Doc Sharp talks like that. It's part of his Yankee persona, along with the pipe smoke and an inability to speak directly to adults. But he's the head vet at the county shelter and a competent practitioner. Plus, he's responsible for a large chunk of my income, so even as he placed the carrier on the examining table and opened the top, I nodded—and kept my mouth shut.

"What have we here?" The low growl had started up again. The good doctor glanced at me quickly, then back at the cat. "Who's an angry pussums?"

"She's been like that since I first saw her." He'd obviously gotten the basics from Creighton. "I didn't notice any blood or open wounds. Still, with fur that thick, who knows?"

He looked toward the door. I'd seen Pammy, his vet tech, out at the front desk, flirting with some meathead. It was her job, not mine, to assist Sharp, but if she got pissed at me I didn't want her taking it out on the cat.

"Let me get my gloves on." I turned back to my bag.

"Maybe that won't be necessary." The cat had gone quiet, and Doc Sharp reached into the green plastic box.

"Wait—" Too late, one claw had lashed out, quicker than either of us could react, and the vet staggered back a step. "You okay?"

"Of course, of course." Doc Sharp walked over to the sink. I could see his hand trembling as he poured the disinfectant on the wound. So much for baby talk. "Anxious little creature, isn't she?"

"Well, she's been through a lot." I couldn't tell him what I really thought. That I should be getting something from this cat—something beyond the low whining growl. "And we don't know if she was injured." I paused, unsure how to phrase what had happened. "In the accident."

"Accident." Doc Sharp muttered as he wiped his hands on a paper towel. I'd lifted the white cat out of the carrier by then and kept both hands on her as he returned to the metal table. This might be Pammy's job, but I didn't want to be blamed if more blood was drawn. "Let's see what we've got here."

I knew the routine and held the cat facing me. Through the gloves, I could feel the low rumble of that growl, quieter now, almost like a purr. It didn't get any louder as Doc Sharp came up behind her, and I took that as a good sign. This cat was making her intentions clear, but she wasn't looking to escalate the situation.

"Let's start with the heart." The gray-haired vet chuckled a bit at his rhyme as he adjusted the stethoscope earpieces. I made sure my hold was solid, but the white Persian didn't move as he approached. The kick startled us both, and for a moment I thought I would lose my grip.

"Whoa, kitty." I didn't want to hurt her, but the cat was scrambling to get away. And as she squirmed, I felt it—something pushing at my consciousness. A sense memory. Hands. Hands holding her tight as she struggled to break free. I sighed. I finally get something and it was this. Those hands were mine, no doubt. The image her impression of what was happening now, as she tried to get away. She was hating this. Fighting. But I couldn't let go. Not now, not here.

"Never seen that before." Doc Sharp had stepped back and was doing his best to recover his cool. "I thought she'd settled down."

I was holding the cat by her sides and she strained her head around, to the left and then to the right. The growl was loud again, easily audible, and spit was already darkening the long cuff of my glove. I looked down at her and she stared up at me. Her blue eyes were wide, wild. And suddenly I heard it. A noise so loud I nearly jumped. A bang like a boulder hitting concrete. Or, no, an explosion. It must have been the gun firing—wild and terrifying. Deafening.

"Wait a minute, Doc, I think I've got it." Sometimes, being sensitive means I miss the obvious things.

"What?" He didn't come any closer.

"She started when you touched her, not as you approached. Could she be deaf?"

"You mean, because she's a white cat?"

I could have kicked myself. Of course, the genes for white fur can carry a recessive trait for deafness, particularly in blue-eyed cats. I'd been out of school too long. But that wasn't what I had meant. "Or because of the blast." She'd heard something, I was getting that from the terrified feline, even if I couldn't explain it to Doc Sharp. "You know, maybe a temporary deafness?"

Even as I said it, I wondered. While I can "hear" what an animal is thinking, it's not like they're talking to me. Most often, what happens is I pick up on what they're noticing. Sights, smells, and, yes, sounds. It was a strange skill, and one I'd only recently acquired. It would be easy for me to read it wrong. Whoever had been responsible for the shooting, the cat had been close by. Maybe she had been too close to the blast—and the volume had knocked out her hearing. Or maybe she was deaf and had experienced the firing of the gun in other ways—a blast of energy or a smack of heat—and I in my simplistic human fashion had misinterpreted. What I needed was time alone with this cat and enough peace so that she could calm down. I wasn't going to get it here.

"Let's see, shall we?" Doc Sharp had regained his cool. "Head, please." I automatically moved one hand up to the back of the Persian's skull as Sharp used his otoscope to look inside those velvet ears. "No visible damage."

He moved onto the eyes, and another hiss, complete with spraying saliva, gave him the opportunity to examine what looked like fine strong teeth.

"Young animal. She seems to be in good shape."

If that were true, why wouldn't she let me in? Unbidden, the image of the dead man came to me. She'd been there. She was, at least, a witness. What had she seen?

I kept my questions to myself and continued to hold the white cat. Doc Sharp ran his hands down each hind leg, then started on the front. At his touch on her front right paw, she started again. "Some sensitivity," he noted, his brow wrinkling in thought. "Could be from the accident." His wide mouth set at that, but he kept on with his exam. Doc Sharp was a pro.

"I'm going to palpate her belly now." It was as much a warning as a request, and I moved into place automatically. Sliding my hands back down that muscular little body, I stepped out of Doc Sharp's way.

"Help me."

There are a lot of noises, people and animals in other rooms, at a shelter. This voice came so sudden and so soft that I wasn't sure I'd heard it. "Excuse me?"

"I didn't say anything." Doc Sharp looked past me. "But there might be something wrong here. I'm feeling some mats in her fur. Can you reach that muzzle?"

I didn't like it. The muzzle, a cone of canvas that would strap over the cat's face, would not help calm her down. Then again, he had already looked at her teeth—and I had no excuse. Shifting my weight to keep the cat secure, I stretched behind me until I felt Velcro.

"Help. Please." The voice was quiet, but clear. I turned back and found myself staring right into those blue eyes. Round, rimmed in that perfect white fur, they lacked the expression that human eyes have—a quality actually provided by our dozens of facial muscles. Still, I got a sense of sadness from them. Sorrow and—was it regret? *"I'm sorry."*

"Kitty?" I murmured, unsure of how this rattled creature would want to be addressed or if she could even hear me. This wasn't, I was sure, her fault, no matter what Creighton said. Communicating—that was a problem. Concentrating, I waited, hoping for something—some clue—that would help me proceed. But then Doc Sharp's large hands scooped up the muzzle and the khaki canvas came between us, turning the white Persian once again into a struggling beast. The connection had been broken.

Chapter Four

"Deaf." Wallis snorted, a ladylike little sniff. *"Dumb is more like it."*

Wallis is a tabby, a regular shorthaired cat, and so she has a bit more of a nose with which to sniff than the white Persian. Which may have been the point. I'd come home looking to bounce some ideas around with her, but she doesn't like it when I get too interested in another animal and she has ways of making this clear. *"And I am not referring to her vocal chords."*

I didn't respond. Not out loud, anyway. I wasn't sure of what, exactly, Wallis had already picked up from me. All the questions ricocheting around my head must have transmitted something. She sauntered into the kitchen soon after I arrived, and jumped to the windowsill as I reheated the coffee that I'd been called away from hours before. There she sat, back toward me, and I waited, aware that in my non-feline way, I'd given offense.

For a while, we were quiet together. Her watching the birds; me watching her. Neither of us said anything, as the mood gradually shifted toward something almost friendly. We've been living together for years, and even when we're at odds, I trusted her judgment more than most creatures'. Whatever her take would be, it would be worth putting up with a little snit of jealousy. Cats are independent, sure. That doesn't mean they want us to be. So I tried to enjoy the quiet before I mentioned the Persian again. Then, once my coffee was hot, I brought her up as a challenge—just another puzzle in an odd morning.

"There's just so much I don't know, Wallis. And, yes, it's true, I don't know how intelligent this creature is." Wallis flicked her tail. "Persians can get a little inbred."

That was a sop to her ego. Being a tabby, Wallis is quite clear on what geneticists call hybrid vigor. It seemed to sate her, because she turned away from the kitchen window to take me in with her cool green eyes. Midday and the sun streamed in through the bare branches, backlighting the guard hairs on her tiger-striped torso. Tabbies are considered common. At that moment, I couldn't see why anyone would prefer a Persian.

"Vain, too," she said, stretching out one snowy white mitt as if to admire her pedicure. She had heard my compliment—or sensed it—and it took me a moment to catch on that she was talking about the Persian. That moment, however, was enough to tick her off. *"And you care—why?"*

I hesitated. To start with, this was no ordinary conversation. Although I think of the communication that Wallis and I have as "speaking," there's rarely any audible sound involved. In the year since my so-called gift manifested, I've learned that she can read my mind, more or less. It's only out of courtesy that she responds to my most clearly voiced thoughts. The fact that the conversation is all in my head, though, often makes me wonder. Did I in reality just field a question from Wallis, the tabby who has shared my home for the past seven years? Or am I talking to myself?

"If the question is intelligent, then it's from me." Wallis jumped down from the sill. I held my tongue. After years of being ignored, she could be a little sensitive. Instead, I closed the window; despite the bright sun, the air was still chilly, and found myself staring at the sticks and mud in the yard of what I now call home.

"Huh." Another small, derisive snort let me know that although the cat had walked off, she still held me in her thoughts. This time, I completely understood. I'd come back to Beauville, my childhood home, out of desperation. Two winters ago, that was. I'd not been taking care of myself, and I'd gotten sick—very sick. And somewhere between the fever and the dehydration,

Wallis had started to take care of me. She'd bullied me into drinking water, then into seeking help. And although she hadn't wanted me to freak out and check myself into the hospital, it was her attentions that kept me from dying, another single statistic in the cold-hearted city. When I'd gotten out, we'd had words, such as they were. The city had become too much for me; the regular clamor and bustle suddenly augmented by the whines and cries of every nonhuman creature around. Leaving seemed a good option, and I'd packed up my old car—and Wallis—and headed back to the one place where I knew they had to take me. Beauville, Massachusetts. A picturesque little town nestled in the Berkshire mountains, home to my aging mother, this big old house, and every variety of evil known to man.

"So, this is home now? Good to know." I turned from the bleak scene. Within a month, the view would start to get better. Wallis sat in the doorway, fixing me with those cool eyes.

"Sorry, Wallis. It just seems, well, right for now."

She turned away. Nobody can ignore you like your cat. She wasn't done, however. *"You said we'd reconsider. We'd get through the winter."* It was as close as she had ever come to asking.

"I know." I took a breath, tried to gauge my own reaction. The city. Life. Was I still afraid?

"That's no reason to stay, you know." She had begun to wash. She does that a lot when she wants to appear nonchalant. *"In fact, it sounds like a coward's reasoning."*

"But now I've got another reason." The sound of that small voice—*help*—came back to me. So quiet, and yet so clear.

"Oh, lord help me." Wallis' voice cut through loud and clear. *"Here we go again."*

◇◇◇

"It's not that—" I caught myself. Arguing with a cat is difficult. Arguing with a cat who is walking down the hall away from you is near impossible. "I'm not turning into a soft touch, all right?"

The twitch of her tail let me know she was listening. But as I followed her into the living room, I knew I had only seconds to make my case.

"Look, Wallis, it isn't just sentiment, okay? There's something going on here. Something strange. And nobody else around here is going to figure it out." The image of Jim Creighton came to mind. He was sharper than I'd originally given him credit for, but he had no reason to investigate.

"And you do?"

That got me. "I'm curious. I mean, I want to know what happened. That cat knows more than she's telling me. The cops think she killed her owner, and I think she believes she did, too."

"Really?" Wallis drew it out. *"Interesting."*

Forget what you think about cuddly kitties. Wallis and I are a lot alike, and that meant we could both be a bit barbed. This, however, was too cool, even for me. "Wallis?"

She eyed me and, without a word, turned away again.

"Admit it," I called as she sashayed back down the hall. "You'd miss me."

The only response was something very much like a purr.

◇ ◇ ◇

I swallowed whatever urge I had to call her back and poured myself another cup of joe. No use going soft now. Instead, I sipped the bitter black brew and tried to piece together what I'd learned that morning—and why I even cared.

It's not that I felt that much for Donal Franklin. He seemed like a nice enough guy. He knew how to dance, and he had been kind to me when I was in a mood. I remembered him complimenting my hair, simply done but glossy as a raven's wing. It was a nice touch, since my dress didn't come close to most in the room. I had responded with a joke about the band, and he'd laughed lightly. He'd made me part of things, for a few minutes anyway. But people die. If I hadn't learned that in the city, I'd have picked it up back here, watching my mother fade away the previous spring. She'd not been a health nut; still, she'd been the kind who did everything right. Didn't drink, didn't smoke. Tried her best to keep her only child out of trouble. She'd struggled to keep us together after my father had taken off, and she hadn't stopped me when I wanted to leave. That says something. Still, she was so fragile by the end that even turning her in bed hurt her. And then she was gone. Hard to be sentimental about something so common.

Maybe living with Wallis had worn off on me a little, too. She didn't hunt. Not really, and I know that if I ever neglected to feed her I'd hear about it. But she was a predator, and her view of her fellow creatures was pretty basic. Foxes ate birds' eggs; coyotes ate foxes. Ate cats, too, if they could get them. And whenever I got touchy about her outdoor exploits, she'd point out that birds were no better. Not just the hawks, but the bluejays. Hell, even cuckoos could be deadly to those poor suckers who let them into their nests. Donal Franklin died because that's what happens.

What I didn't like were the questions around it. Okay, so maybe there had been some kind of freak accident—I'd pump Creighton later for details. And just maybe the Persian was deaf from birth; a majority of blue-eyed white cats were. But the combination was unusual—and the not letting me in? My special communication had never relied on hearing before, more often than not it was silent. Besides, that cat had experienced something that had traumatized her. Something that was rattling around in her smooth white pate and making her feel culpable, and I wasn't any kind of a behaviorist if I didn't want to help the animal find some peace.

And, oh hell, someone had asked me for help. I looked up from a mug of coffee grown cold to the empty spot where Wallis had sat. Maybe she was right. Maybe I was becoming something of a pushover. As I knew from experience, the soft ones died first.

Chapter Five

It wasn't like I had a lot of spare time to worry about other people's troubles. One year back, and my business—such as it was—had picked up to the point where I was considering raising my rates. I still didn't have my certification—I didn't see how I was going to write a thesis on what some little bird told me—but that didn't seem to bother the clients.

The notoriety was only part of it. Sure, some people liked hiring me because I'd helped figure out a murder a few months back. It made me a celebrity in a morbid kind of way. Others liked that I was a local kid who'd thought she'd gotten away, then came back from the big city with her tail between her legs. Fame works both ways. Whatever their reasons, once my clients hired me most of them picked up on the connection I had with their animals.

"She's a miracle worker!" Old Nancy Pinkerton raved to her neighbors. In reality, her Siamese's litterbox problems had been caused by her own inattention to hygiene. I came by once a week, clipped the kitty's claws and changed the box. In exchange, the velour-clad matron talked me up to her bridge group and book club. And the Siamese, who introduced herself to me as Her Most Serene Highness, the Princess Achara, got both the attention she felt she deserved and a bit of gossip. Not that Nancy knew the half of what was going on when I sat down with the regal beast she called "Pickles."

"My cat knows things," the old lady had bragged. "Like, that she deserves the best." I'd smiled and taken the chocolate-point royalty onto my lap, bowing my head ever so slightly in the deference Her Highness expected. In some ways, old lady Pinkerton and the Siamese were perfect together.

It wasn't the life I'd imagined when I'd set out to become a behaviorist. And as I got ready to head out again, I had to admit Wallis had a point. A constant cycle of such basic pet care wasn't what you'd call exciting. But the claw clipping and dog walking had kept the heat on through the winter, and spring was still new enough that I couldn't see changing up just yet.

"Wallis, I'm heading out." I put my empty mug in the sink and reached for my jacket. "Back by six."

"As if I couldn't hear everything you do a mile away." A low mutter from the other room reached me. *"Two miles."* I shouldn't have mentioned a time. Wallis can't read a clock and that always sets her off.

As I eased onto the road, I mulled the question further. There were other incentives to stay in Beauville. For starters, there was my car: a 1976 Pontiac GTO. I'd not thought about driving all those years in New York. Out here again, I realized how much I loved it. The freedom, the power. Things get bad, and you go. And so when my old Toyota had died in a midwinter storm, I'd indulged myself. The vintage muscle car was a work in progress, its baby blue paint job and 455 cubic inch engine the smoothest things about it. That was fine by me. I needed a hobby, and the price was right. Besides, I loved how it ate up the road, that big motor purring like a cat.

There were other benefits as well. As the crisp, fresh air reminded me, I'd come for the quiet. Midday, and all I heard were some bird calls—the usual "I'm here, I'm here, I'm here" as returning species searched for mates and nests. Even these weren't too obtrusive anymore, more background noise than anything.

City life was louder. That was its nature, and at first, I'd accepted that. After I'd discovered my new sensitivity, however, the constant noise had rubbed my nerves like sandpaper. Too many voices, on all the time. Not just the people and their neurotic city pets, but all the urban wildlife—rats, raccoons, squirrels—had crowded into my consciousness till I thought I would go mad. One nest of pigeons, in particular, had nearly driven me over the edge with their familial inanities, day in and day out.

Plus, after more than a decade in the city, I'd soon gotten used to having more space. And with our newfound communication, Wallis and I got along much better if we could each retreat during the day. Though recently, with my various clients, I wasn't around as much, and she seemed to be growing a little more sociable. I didn't know if she missed me, if she'd begun to forgive me for uprooting her, or if age was making the tabby a little needier. Still sleek and plump as she neared fifteen, Wallis no longer went out much at night. She said that was to keep me from worrying, and I didn't question that—not out loud, anyway. Whatever she read in my thoughts, she kept to herself. We were learning how to get along.

As I pulled my blue baby into the parking lot of China Pearl, I mentally organized the week. I'd rushed my morning walk with Growler, a bichon frise and one of my regulars. A summons from the cops will do that, but I also knew that my notoriety—and a first crack at the local news—would keep me in the good graces of most of my clients. My stops this afternoon were all routine. Cleaning the filter of the big tank at the Chinese restaurant was pretty much brain dead work. I'd offered to teach the owner's son, but Mrs. Chen was having none of it. It wasn't so much that she wanted her boy to study, though that would have fit the stereotype. It was more that she knew the value of the huge tank and didn't want to risk it. More than the oversweet moo shi, the angels, tetras, and their ilk drew families from across the county. And her son, well, she knew he didn't need any distractions. She didn't know that he'd found a major one in his gym teacher, and that the two were carrying on hot and heavy when Joe Jr. was supposed to be cramming for his MCAS. I knew because a little bird had told me. Literally. Unlike the chickadee, I kept my beak shut.

Forty minutes later and I had done my wet work for the day. Metaphorically, too, as I'd disposed of an ailing suckerfish who had outlasted his prime. I felt for the skinny beast. He'd done his best for the tank, and I'd have let him live. But Mrs. Chen knows her business, and the sight of the little sucker as he floated to the top and then struggled to regain his equilibrium had been putting some diners off their eight delights.

"Sorry, little fellow." I could hear his confusion, his growing panic, and I apologized under my breath, as I netted him from the tank. Wallis would have had a field day with that. Then again, she also would have wanted to play a bit before I dispatched him with a quick blow and then flushed his corpse down the toilet. Maybe it's just as well we have a little space.

I was thinking about Wallis as I drove to my next gig, a bridge partner of Mrs. Pinkerton's. For all our disagreements, it has been Wallis who has helped me most with this strange skill of mine. She's the one who explained to me how it works, as best she could, anyway.

"*You might call it mind reading.*" She spoke as she would to a kitten; that was the level she was dealing with. "*What goes on, I hear. And you hear me, more or less. Always have.*"

I'd started to protest at that, but she'd stopped me before I could form the words. She was right. I've always sort of understood what my cat was thinking. We all do.

"*Only difference is, you used to ignore it. Like most of them.*" Wallis had a life before I found her at the shelter. She doesn't like to refer to it. "*Now you're back at square one. With kittens it takes a while to learn what to tune out. You'll learn.*"

I never did, not really. It had been a year, and the best I could manage was to not be overwhelmed each time I walked into the shelter. Maybe part of my longing for the city was really a fear of what was coming. May, June…this place was going to become a madhouse.

"*Wow! Wow! Out! Out!*" Going to be? As I cruised into the Genslers' drive, I could hear my next client, voicing her discontent. "*Out!*"

"Lucy! Quiet!" Poor Eve Gensler. She didn't have a clue. Everything about her, from her tentative tone of voice to her physical response, was designed to egg her dog on. "Lucy!"

The woman who let me in was wearing a faded housedress and flapping her arms ineffectually. The miniature poodle she addressed was leaping in the air, her nails clicking on the linoleum flooring as she danced in circles around her person.

"Now, Lucy." I kept my voice low, my arms by my side. Body language is key to animal communication, especially when you're stuck using some poor creature's human-given name. "You know that's not how we behave in the house."

The dog calmed enough to sit, although her tail wagged frantically.

"Nancy's right. You have a gift." Faded and gray, Eve Gensler looked as worn out as her dress. I kicked myself for bumping my visit till midday. Poodles are smarter than most people give them credit for. That also means they get bored quicker, and my three times weekly visit was probably all the excitement she got.

"It's nothing special," I lied. "You remember what we talked about?" I smiled as wide as I could. By all reports, Eve Gensler had raised a son. The polar opposite of her gregarious bridge partner, this pale remnant of a woman seemed incapable of disciplining anything. She needed my training skills more than her dog. "Tone, body language. Control?"

"I know, I know." She shuffled off to get the leash. "I try, I do. But she's just so full of life."

"May we go out now?" More jumping, the poodle up on her hind legs like a circus dog. *"I can't keep this up much longer."*

"I know," I answered them both. "She's young. She needs her exercise." Some fresh air might do her person good, too. "I'm sorry I couldn't get here this morning. Would you like to come out with us?"

"No, no, I can't." Her eyes widened, as if afraid of the prospect. "My niece is coming by."

I snapped the tawny toy's lead on with a sigh of relief. I'd asked in a moment of weakness. I don't get paid enough to walk them both.

"Besides, I heard what you were doing." Eve was still talking. "Nancy called me and gave me the details. Robin—that's my niece—was friendly with the Franklins." She shook her head. "Makes me glad I never had a daughter."

"Sorry?" I hadn't really been listening. After Mrs. Gensler's poodle, I had two more appointments—and I wanted to get back to the shelter, see that Persian again.

"Don't be." The way Eve was already heading back down the hallway. "According to Robin, the marriage was as good as over. Still, it makes one wonder."

I stood there, staring at her. So small, her voice so quiet. And yet…the level of gossip in our small town continued to surprise me.

"Cats," the faded old lady was talking to herself now. "Horrible creatures. Nasty. A dog would never do that."

Chapter Six

The poodle relaxed as soon as we were out the door, which made my job easier. Her person had given me food for thought, and I was chewing it over as I took the little dog on her rounds. What I wanted to know, basically, was whether the gossip was true. Was the Franklin marriage on the rocks? If so, did Jim Creighton know? It would be all too easy to stage an accident, and I had no idea why my friendly neighborhood detective seemed to be so sure the Persian was to blame.

"*Out! Out!*" While I was musing over the possibilities—and whether I should alert the hunky cop—the small dog was greeting the world. "*Wow, wow.*" Some things were the same in any language, but as we turned a corner I began to wonder about the poodle's intellect. Poodles may be one of the brainier breeds in general, but there are always exceptions.

"*Wow?*" Some of it, I knew, was suggestion. Eve Gensler encouraged the worst kind of behavior—the jumping, the dancing, claws on the floor—even as it overwhelmed her. I'd been hired to train the tawny toy, as well as exercise her a few times a week, although most of our time together was spent simply walking. Lucy should have known better; any dog past puppyhood would. To some extent, she was simply bored and full of pent-up energy. Then again, any animal who willingly accepts a name from a human is probably not the sharpest tool in the woodshed. Lucy, of all the animals I'd come in contact with in

Beauville, was the only one who had blinked at me when I'd asked her, in a moment of privacy, her real name.

"Lucy, non?"

"You're not French. And—are you sure?" I didn't know what I'd expected. Grimaldia. Fluffanella. Even Quiche Lorraine. Something that fit the little dog's exuberant personality. But Lucy?

"Why not? Oh, oh. Wow!"

We didn't have the most scintillating conversations, and I had come to accept the truisms about toys. Small dogs, small interests. Now I watched her snuffle and explore, her eager nose reliving the visits of other canine visitors as we made our way down the block. She'd found one particularly interesting place to sniff and soon after relieved herself. City training dies hard, and I reached to retrieve her waste.

"Merci."

That was unexpected, and I looked up to find the shiny black eyes considering me carefully, the fluffy blonde head tilted slightly.

"What?" It came out as a typical short, sharp bark. For a moment, I wasn't sure how to respond. *"Toy?"*

The acid in her tone called me back to myself. "I'm sorry. I didn't mean to…" I shook my head. Sometimes there was no winning. "Look, I've got a lot on my mind."

The little dog kicked at the ground, a gesture I knew well. Wallis used it as a catchall. Waste, bad food. Whatever she wanted to dismiss. "And I'm not your person, okay? She's not a bad sort."

"Rrrough."

"Yeah, she looks the worse for wear." I didn't know Eve Gensler's past, but I found myself wondering about her parting comment. It, too, had had a bit of an edge. "Does she always gossip like that, or is this something she picked up from that niece she's talking about?"

"What is this 'niece'?" The answer came so fast and clear, I stopped in my tracks. Lucy came up short on her leash and turned on me with a look. *"Walk?"*

"Sorry." I was lucky she wasn't a cat, and we moved on while I tried to formulate my next question. "The niece…" It would have helped to have a face. Instead, I visualized Eve Gensler, trying to add some color to the cheeks and hair. "Robin?"

"Oh!" The little dog half barked, half snorted, and I looked over to make sure she wasn't choking. She wasn't, but the way she batted her eyes up at me made me wonder what else was going on. *"Nice coat."*

"Excuse me?" The poodle was proving more talkative than I'd expected. Just not in any way I could use.

"Nice coat." Lucy looked up at me again, waiting. *"But!"* Poodles, I don't know.

"But what? She wasn't trained? She wasn't well bred?" I was reaching. Trying to put myself in the vain little dog's mind.

"We are pretty girls. Pretty. But we are more than a nice coat." That could've been a statement about Robin or me. More likely, the poodle was referring to herself. *"Non?"*

"Oui," I caught myself. "But can we cut out the bad French?"

With a canine shrug that shook her torso, Lucy trotted forward. Whatever point she'd wanted to make, she had made, and I was left to interpret. Still, she'd tried, and as we headed back toward Eve Gensler's dimly lit house, my heart went out to her.

"Lucy, want to walk another block?"

"No!" Lucy's bark was shrill. Decisive. She'd crouched down, ever so slightly. The posture was classic submissive. It also allowed her to look up at me through her lashes. Ears perked, the look was pure flirtation, leading me on. *"Maybe the river, perhaps?"*

"You've been down to the river?" Somehow, I couldn't see old Eve making it that far.

"Non." Those eyes, so large and liquid, would have filled with tears, if they could have. *"She always promised…"*

It was fast, so fast I almost missed it. A flash of something— irritation. Intelligence. At any rate, something neither flirty nor faux French.

"Robin." It was a statement, not a question.

"She said." The little head hung down now, the bright eyes hidden. *"Said."*

And didn't follow through. Even I could see that. "Could have been, she was nervous." We weren't exactly in the wild here. There had been talk about wolves, though—about Eastern gray wolves coming back into the area. I doubted it, but, then, I'm not the type to be scared of a rumor.

"No! No! No!" Each bark grew more assertive. *"No!"*

"I don't think so either," I said. So I led her back toward Eve Gensler's house and, checking to make sure we weren't being watched, opened my car door. Despite the weak sun, it was chilly out. More like late winter than spring. But it was dry and the cold air would clear my head. I needed to think, and Lucy deserved a treat. Wolves or no, we were going to the river.

Poodles are water dogs, and Lucy was quivering with excitement as she smelled the damp, rich smell. With snowmelt and the various spring thaws, the little river had thrown up enough silt to dampen the banks damp and leave them frankly fishy. The water itself looked muddy and fierce, a far cry from the clear stream that would draw the kayakers in July. Still, Lucy strained toward it.

"We can't." I took a preemptive step back. I didn't know if this little toy would want to dive in, see what she could retrieve. The water level had retreated to something like normal, but if I couldn't see the bottom, I didn't trust it. Besides, I'd never hear the end of it if I brought back a wet dog. "I'm sorry."

Lucy whimpered, her tail momentarily stilled. Then she was off again, sniffing everything. Watching her in this setting, I could forget that she was a toy. Lucy was pure dog here, with none of the affectations of the bored house pet. I'd never seen her so happy.

"Growler?"

I thought I'd misheard her.

"How is he?"

"Fine." I was taken aback. It was easy to forget the complex world of smells that connected the canine world. The tawny toy must have picked up some scent of the white puffball I'd walked that morning. I doubted the two little dogs had met.

"Fine dog. Fine." Her snappy bark accented the thoughts. I nodded.

"You've been neutered, right?" The thought sprang to mind before I could stop it. Wallis would have words with me for that.

"Huh!" The little dog barked back. Wallis would have words about that, too.

◇◇◇

By the time we got back, Eve Gensler was beside herself with worry.

"Lucy! Where *were* you? I was—I was—" Two red spots appeared on her cheeks, and while the color should have been a welcome addition, I felt a twinge of guilt. She was such a timid creature.

"It's such a beautiful day." I took the offensive. "The first day that really feels like spring, doesn't it? So we went for an extra-long walk." She was still sputtering, so I threw in my *pièce de résistance.* "No extra charge."

"Well, all right." She bent to pick up the little dog, whose tail was wagging hard enough to make her body shake. "No charge?"

"Nothing extra." I smiled. In a previous life, this woman must have been a doormat. She smiled back. I had my opening.

"So, your niece? Robin, is it? She's a friend of the Franklins?" I trusted the poodle's take more than her person's. Still, it would be good to know.

"Mrs. Franklin took to her. She didn't spend that much time at their club or anything. Something about her health, and Robin's always been a bit of a loner anyway. Poor girl." I wasn't sure to which woman my client was referring.

"Ha!" said the dog. I didn't need any translation for that.

At this point, I wished I were free. I'd have loved to have bounced this new information off Wallis. Maybe even called Creighton. In an unofficial capacity, of course. We'd had one or two pleasant run-ins over the winter. A few nights that made us both wonder, and that made us both back off when we realized just how small this town is. Opposites attract. Always have. And it didn't exactly hurt to have the law on my side.

As far as that went, anyway. Jim Creighton might look schoolboy fresh, but he was smarter than he was pretty, and I had to be careful not to give up too much when I thought I was doing the questioning. I was curious as to what he had, though. More curious because of that brief flash from the cat—*"I'm sorry."* How could he tell if the Persian had pulled the trigger? Was it even possible?

Thoughts of killing, accidental or otherwise, seemed particularly apropos as I pulled up at Mrs. Pinkerton's little bungalow. Even before I climbed the stoop, the strangled howls reached me, paused, and then started up again.

The noise was unearthly—like the cries of the damned. Nancy Pinkerton's husband had taken off years before, if rumor ran true. Gone to help with a daughter's ongoing renovations and never come back. Probably right around the time the bouncy lady of the house had welcomed this din into it. There were neighbors, too, less than thirty yards to the right, and I wondered what they made of the ungodly sound.

"Mrs. Pinkerton?" I knocked, unsure if she could even hear me. A fresh wail started up. "Mrs. P? You there?"

"Just one minute!" Her jolly tones seemed at odds with the howling. As did her next words. "Please stand back."

I'm used to people. They are much less predictable than animals. So I did as requested, and heard what sounded like the door coming unlatched. Then, nothing. "Mrs. P?"

"Pickles!" A stage whisper came through the door. "Pickles, now!" Another howl. I wasn't worried about the cat. I was used to her vocal exercises. Besides, the lithe Siamese knew how much her caterwauls annoyed most people. She enjoyed it. The closed door was a different story.

"Do you need help?" I pictured Nancy Pinkerton lying there in one of her pastel tracksuits, hip broken but determined to "not be a bother." I wondered if she had fallen on her cat. "Nancy?"

I reached for the door. And just as I did, the knob started to turn. A little at first, then completely, and the door opened just enough for me to see Nancy Pinkerton standing several feet away, beaming like the proud grandmother she was. Taking her place by the door, Her Most Serene Highness Achara stood on her hind feet. Stretched to her full length, with her cream belly exposed, she still held onto the doorknob her chocolate brown paws had successfully manipulated. And here I was, wondering if a cat could shoot a gun.

Chapter Seven

Could those little paws bring death? I pondered the possibility as I started on her Highness, hauling the slim, self-satisfied Siamese onto my lap. And did Nancy Pinkerton have some kind of insider knowledge?

"Heard you were talking about the Franklins." I watched the old lady from under lowered lids. The Princess was aware of my inattention, but I held her firmly. "Did you know them?"

"Knew *of* them." The old lady, in pink today, leaned in. "My lord, I certainly didn't see this coming."

"Oh?" I had my clipper out. The Siamese had delicate paws, the fur smooth and short. That Persian's would be like catcher's mitts by comparisons.

"Well, everyone knew she played around." Her cheeks colored to match her outfit. I liked her for that. "I mean, so I'd heard. He never seemed to take it seriously, though."

"Maybe he should have." I clipped. The cat pulled back.

"You don't think—" Her color was deeper now, more like last week's magenta. "Oh, my lord."

My phone saved her from more of a grilling. My phone and her Highness—who kicked free of my lap with a claws-out push off that left puncture marks in my jeans. Like many beauties, she could get annoyed when she wasn't the center of attention. Which probably explained my tone of voice when I finally called Creighton back.

"What?" I was in my car by then, rubbing the sore spots on my thigh. Next time, I'd start with her hind paws, get them before she could get me.

"Good afternoon to you, too." He was laughing. Despite starting his day with a stiff. I figured it had to be me, and I softened a bit.

"Sorry, you caught me with a client. She didn't like the phone ringing in the middle of an appointment."

"I thought you never got bit." Before I could explain, he went on. "Anyway, I'm sorry. You said you wanted to know what was up with that cat."

"I do," I waited. Jim Creighton and I had an odd relationship. Despite the occasional intimacies, we really were on opposite sides of the fence, and we both knew it. That was probably what made things so hot. It also made me hyper aware of him, of the games we both played. Now he was in cop mode: he wanted something in return. I could almost smell it.

With anyone else, the silence would have been awkward. Not Creighton, though. As I sat there, rubbing my leg, he started to laugh.

"Pru, you're a piece of work. You know that?" It didn't seem like he required an answer. "I really did want to fill you in."

"Uh huh." I'd give him that.

"It turns out, it is entirely possible for a cat to have fired that gun." Thoughts of those bulky paws came back into my mind, but I kept my mouth shut. Creighton kept talking. "The kind of gun it is, it's a wonder it didn't happen sooner."

He was teasing. "Okay, shoot." I started to smile despite myself. "If you'll pardon the expression."

"The gun was some kind of antique dueling pistol. A museum piece, really. It only held one shot—a ball and powder—so it wouldn't have been obvious that it was loaded. And because it had a fancy attachment to hold the, hang on a minute—the fulminating compound." He shifted and I could hear papers rustling. "A scent-bottle, they call it, it wouldn't have been clear that it was primed to go off."

"You'd still have to pull the trigger, wouldn't you?"

"I was getting to that." He must have closed his notepad. "It was a dueling pistol, Pru. They were fighting guns, quick-response weapons. This one had a hair trigger. Didn't even need to be pulled. The cat could have stepped on it. Pushed its head against it. Almost anything could have set it off."

Creighton's explanation should have been a relief. He was right: this gun sounded like an accident waiting to happen. The questions it raised, however, were just as volatile.

"Donal Franklin was into these guns, right?" I thought about the study. Tried to remember if there had been any other weapons in the room, maybe framed on the wall. I couldn't picture any. *New things…* I heard an echo of the dead man's voice. There were books, though. I'd seen them. "Wouldn't he have known all this?" I couldn't tell Creighton about the small voice I'd heard—the soft, clear cry for help. I had to get at my suspicions another way. Before he could answer, I added a third question. "Could it have been intentional?"

Suicide. Not that rare when there's a marriage on the rocks. That poodle had cast doubt on my source, but in a case like this common sense seemed more reliable than a nervy miniature.

"Forensics is looking into it, but I'd say it's unlikely. It looks like he was too far away, and there's no powder on either of his hands. Which means simple human error, Pru. I know it's less interesting, but, hey, that's the downside of this job." He was sounding like himself again. Death or no death, a man relaxes when his work is done. I wished I had his confidence.

"I've made contact with a dealer out by Amherst," Creighton was still talking. "He's quite excited about the gun and walked me through all this. He thinks Franklin might have been examining the mechanism, or even starting to clean it. He might have been going to fire it—some collectors do, though it seems a little foolhardy with a two-hundred-year-old relic. The guy out in Amherst was horrified by the idea, even though he was the one who brought it up as a possibility, but I think he was more concerned with value. And Donal Franklin wasn't an expert, just an interested amateur. Maybe he didn't know about the "scent bottle" thing, that it could hold a charge. Maybe he never checked to see if the pistol was loaded. What we do know is that he got a phone call, and he must have put the gun down on the desk to talk. We found his cell. It fits."

"A little neat, don't you think?" That quiet voice. *Help*. A marriage that wasn't working. A spouse who was encouraging dangerous new hobbies. "You talk to the wife?"

"That's who called it in, Pru. She was the one who had called her husband—from the road, outside Northampton. We have someone staying with her now. She heard it all."

In a way, it was a relief. I felt bad for the cat. Bad for the wife, too, of course. Even assuming things weren't that great between them, nobody wants to hear her spouse shot. But I was out of it. A day or two for the paperwork to be filed, and this would be labeled a clear-cut case of death by misadventure, or whatever our county coroner would call it. Of course, our coroner was a former GP, so for all I knew, he'd label it alcohol poisoning. Anyway, it wasn't my problem. My leg hurt. I was tired. One of the great things about my mother's failure to renovate is that, along with a heating system that could be cranky on these cold March nights, I inherited a huge clawfoot tub. I envisioned myself neck deep in hot water, assuming we had hot water. I added a tumbler of bourbon to the picture, and that was enough inspiration to start the engine and enjoy the ride home.

Only things never work like that. Not in my life. So when the phone buzzed again, bouncing around on the seat like a rabid rodent, I tried to ignore it. I had no family left. No man regular enough to worry about, and Wallis couldn't use the phone. Late afternoon, and the light was fading. I could build a fire in the living room. There was something in the freezer, as I recalled.

The phone buzzed.

"Hello?" This had better be good.

"Dear Prudence. Long time, no contact." The voice was male and familiar. Not local, though. I pulled over to the curb to better sort through my mental Rolodex. Whoever it was knew me well enough to know how I worked. He chuckled, and that did it.

"Tom?" The laugh had been low and sexy. It went with muscles, dark hair, and a scar that pulled at the side of his mouth.

"And here I was, thinking you'd forgotten." Like I'd forget Tom Reynolds, all danger and nighttime excitement. Tom had given me the switchblade I always carry. "And not want to have dinner with me."

"Tom, I'm not in the city anymore." I tried to remember when I'd seen the big guy last. Two years ago? Two and a half?

"I know, babe. What kind of a cop do you think I am?" So he was still on the force. The way Tom had played it, close to the edge, I wouldn't have been surprised if he'd switched over. "I'm looking into something for someone, and I found your new number."

"You're in Beauville now?" I couldn't explain why this creeped me out exactly. I like my breaks to be clean. Maybe I'd come to like my cops clean, too. "For how long?"

He chuckled again and I visualized his mouth, the way the scar pulled. "So you did miss me. I don't make plans, Pru. You know that. But I'm thinking it might be fun to get together again." He was pushing too hard, sounding a little strained. A little tired. "Maybe we can help each other out. What do you say? Eight?"

"Look, Tom, I've had a hell of a day." I didn't want to get into it. Talking about Donal to Tom felt dirty somehow. "I don't know if I'm up for anything."

"Seven, then." He wasn't waiting for an answer. "Look, Pru. I'm not sure how long I'll be in town."

"Yeah." He was in trouble, or something like it. Without thinking, my hand had strayed to my pocket. The outline of my knife, hard and deadly, reminded me of what my tough beau had once meant to me. Switchblades are illegal, but he'd taken this one off some street punk and given it to me. He'd done me a solid; that knife had come in handy. Maybe it was time to return the favor. Not that I'd meet him without the blade by my side.

◇◇◇

I gave him directions to Beauville's downtown. Since I'd grown up here, the area had actually grown to deserve the name. Before I'd left, it was two blocks long—a hardware store. The post office. A few shops. Sometime during my years away, a row of condos had extended the residential part of town almost down to the river, and the town had gotten itself together to cater to these new people. You could see it as you drove down Main Street. The barber shop had morphed into a hair salon; the toy store now sold cell phones. And the hardware store where my mother had bought a new set of locks and the tools to install them after my dad had taken off had been transformed into a bistro. With a city-trained chef and a menu focused on local produce, it seemed an unlikely addition; we were too far from Tanglewood to get that many tourists, and the condo folk were seasonal or retirees. But as long as it lasted, I'd go there—especially if someone else was paying. They did a good steak, and I was eating meat again.

Happy's, of course, still held down the end of our main drag. The dive bar where I'd learned to drink hadn't changed since my father's day. I thought of the smoky little room as I drove home. Tom would love it. Maybe he'd already found it. Our own new police headquarters was only two blocks away.

That thought, as much as anything else, cleared my head as I pulled into my own driveway. My day had started with a stiff and a scared cat. I didn't need to end it with something stupid and booze-driven. One cop per city was enough for any girl. Especially a girl with secrets.

Chapter Eight

Wallis had been noticeably absent as I sank into the tub. That didn't surprise me; she finds the idea of bathing uncivilized. But as the hot water did its work, I found myself missing my feline companion. I hadn't had a chance to tell her what the poodle had said, or what the Princess Achara had shown me. Creighton might be a good guy; still, there was no way I could share this new info with him. Besides, I wanted to talk to her about Tom. She and I hadn't been communicating back in the days of our city romance. At least, not that I'd been aware of. But she had to have been aware of him, and increasingly I trusted my tabby's take on people, often more than I trusted my own.

"Tom Knife? That Tom?" She appeared in the bathroom and jumped up onto the sink, smirking a bit as I started.

"Wallis—" I bit my tongue. I'd been wanting her to come by, and here she was. "Yes, 'Tom Knife,' from the city."

"Interesting." Her green eyes began to close, and I knew her well enough to recognize the look. This wasn't sleepiness; this was a cat considering the hunt. *"He was…lively."*

The hesitation made me aware of the gap between us. Wallis is good at translating, better than I'd probably ever be. But cats and people see things differently. "Polite" meant diffident, to a feline, because most cats find a direct gaze offensive. Lively?

"Oh, please, Pru. I lived there, too." She smiled. I got it.

"I don't know if I want that in my life right now." I wasn't being coy. There's no point in acting with your cat. "I mean, I've finally gotten a handle on everything. I've got some control."

"You mean with the tame ones you've got now?"

I was about to protest. Jim Creighton might be on the right side of the law. He was hardly tame. But whether it was a non-verbal nudge from Wallis, or my own conscience, I stopped myself. Jim and I hadn't seen each other socially for months. And Mack, the gambler who had left me alone at the bar, had been written off that night.

"And you know you're too young for—what's his name? Lewis?"

Llewelyn McMudge. The other man I'd danced with at the benefit. Donal's friend. I blocked that memory by conjuring up good ol' Lew. Unlike Don, he'd wanted more than one dance, and he knew how to have fun. He had the means, which helped. A car that purred like Wallis, and a country home over near Northampton. Probably a girl in every town, too, despite the gray at the temples and lines that hung in even when his hungry smile had faded. Still, sometimes it was nice to be taken out, especially by a tall, lean gallant who carried his years gracefully. I'd become rather used to steak dinners again.

"Llewelyn." Wallis flicked her tail in dismissal before jumping to the floor. *"Suit yourself, Pru. And happy hunting."*

Dinner. As I got dressed, I toyed again with the idea of taking Tom to Happy's. I'm human. It would be easy. But a little too much had happened that day. If I was going to reignite this particular old flame, I wanted to do so with a clear head. So Hardware it was.

Tom was waiting when I drove up, a square block of muscle lined up against the brick doorway, and in a rare moment of reticence I didn't voice the local witticism—that the owners had come up with the name only after rejecting Hammered and Screwed. He'd smiled the crooked smile anyway, as he held the door for me, and suddenly the place looked small town. Quaint, like it was trying a bit too hard.

"So what brings you to our one-horse town?" I'll admit, I was a little defensive. It wasn't that I felt much allegiance to Beauville, but what we did, we did right. I'd also made sure we'd put our drink order in before I turned on Tom. No point in giving him an excuse to run.

"Pru, Pru." He shook his head, that grin belied the dying fall of his voice. The scar twitched as he talked. "Since when did you become so suspicious. Can't we just enjoy the evening?"

I didn't even bother responding. We'd stopped seeing each other—broken up would have implied too much of a commitment—months before I left. After a moment, I remembered. He'd been the one to teach me about silence—about how keeping quiet gets the other person to talk. I needed to be direct.

"You said you were looking into something for someone." I watched his face. "Business or personal?"

The smile grew a little wider, thin lips revealing sharp teeth. I thought again about those rumors of wolves. "You jealous?"

"You're avoiding the question." I smiled back. We were on familiar ground now. Tag, he was it.

"You're right." We both paused as the waiter brought over our drinks and took our order. "It's business. For me, anyway."

My drink served as a useful prop. I sipped and waited.

"I'm not on the job anymore. I've got a little private consulting business now." He looked into his drink. "The money is much better."

I didn't believe it. Tom had never been interested in the money. He'd lived, like me, for the chase. The excitement. Then again, he could go a bit far in the pursuit of that excitement. The muscles, the appetite: they made things too easy for him. As he kept talking, I found I wasn't surprised. Tom Reynolds as a PI made some kind of sense.

"I'm just getting started, really. Getting some referrals. Looking into a couple of things. Anyway, one of my clients has asked me to follow up on something."

"Someone's spouse stepping out?" The mountain resorts weren't at their best during stick season. Then again, the odds of running into anyone you knew were small.

He shook his head. "No, more like a bad debt, but it's turned into something bigger."

"Blackmail?" This was getting interesting. Frankly, Tom was proving a better date than I'd expected. He'd aged some. Now that we were in the restaurant, I could see that he'd bulked up since I'd left the city, and not all in muscle. I might have showed the miles, too, though, and before long, we fell into our old familiar banter. I wanted to know more, and I knew how to talk to him: a little flirty, a little sharp. But as I was getting into it, our food arrived: two steaks, mine bloody rare. And when Tom changed the topic, I had all the work I could do to fend off his questions.

"Call me crazy, Pru. I don't see you as the caretaker type." We'd moved on to a good Brunello.

"It's not that." I was buzzed and I knew it. It had been a long day, and my eyes kept straying to his hands, thick fingers cradling the glass. I'd have to be careful, and the best way to lie convincingly is to mix in a little truth. "By the time she died, I'd kind of settled in here. I got her house and, well, it seemed like time to make a change." That should have worked. Tom knew I wasn't one for the long term.

He wasn't buying it. "Chicago, maybe. Even LA." He topped off my glass and then refilled his own. "You in the country? I don't see it."

"I grew up here." I was working too hard. "And it is a great house."

I regretted that one as soon as it was out of my mouth. I might invite him back at some point. Right now, too many alarm bells were going off. It hadn't escaped my notice that he was on a case. This wasn't purely a social evening.

To test my theory, I started yawning as soon as the check arrived and made noises about my early appointments. He didn't have to know they were with two miniature dogs. He didn't seem to mind, which piqued my curiosity further. So I kept quiet as he walked me to my car and waited. When he brought up business, I wasn't really shocked.

"I need help, Pru. That's why I looked you up. You were always good with people. I respect that." I could have smiled. People were never my forte. Respect wasn't his, either. "And you know everyone around here, I figure. You growing up here and everything." He was still talking, adding bits that he'd picked up over dinner. Still, I had the sense that he was reciting from a script. "I want you to introduce me to someone," he said. "Local guy. Big wig."

He wanted a job. A reference. Creighton's face flashed before me. There were similarities, but I couldn't see them working together. Maybe I didn't want to.

"He's wealthy. Maybe he can use someone discreet." Not Creighton then. But if he was thinking of Donal Franklin, he was out of luck.

"I'd like you to introduce me to one of your boyfriends, Pru. A hotshot named Llewellyn. Llewellyn McMudge."

I turned toward my car, hoping that the dark would hide my surprise. "Llewellyn?" I heard my voice crack and brought it down a notch. "I don't think I can do that. He and I, we don't have that kind of relationship." I pictured what we did have. A phone call every few weeks. A good dinner. A fun time. I turned down the presents he'd offered me. That necklace had looked too much like a collar, but I'd appreciated the attention. Beyond our dates, I didn't know anything about his personal life, and he didn't ask about mine.

"Pru, it's me. Tom." He leaned in, voice low and soft, and I remembered why I'd gone for him. "I know what you do to a man."

I like flattery. I smiled back, keeping my eye on his scar. "Really, Tom. It's occasional. Very occasional. And I don't even know what his business is."

"Really." I couldn't tell if Tom was surprised, or just acting. The tension was gone, though, and he sounded more like himself. "Well, why don't you take my card. Just give it to him, next time you see him. For old time's sake."

"For old time's sake," I parroted back. He leaned in and kissed me, a soft peck on the cheek. Leaving me standing there and wondering what the hell was going on.

Chapter Nine

"I don't know, Wallis." The tabby appeared to be sleeping, curled into a perfect disk on the sofa when I got home. The fact that she was downstairs, though, meant she was waiting. The way her ear flicked when I started talking confirmed it. "I don't know why Tom is interested in Llewellyn, or what he wants me to do."

Somehow, the suggestion that he wanted an introduction just didn't fly. Tom had no problem meeting anyone. No, he must have wanted info from me. Background. He'd been fishing, but I hadn't bit. Didn't mean I didn't wonder why, and I mulled over the possibilities. "It's not that I can't see Llewellyn sneaking out with someone's wife," I said to my silent cat. Despite his silver hair, age hadn't slowed Lew down where it counted. "I just don't see him bothering with anything complicated. And I know he's not the client, or Tom wouldn't need me to vouch for him."

I paused to consider my own words. "Unless Tom knows something and thinks Lew will hire him to investigate." As I hung up my coat, I tried to picture what that something could be. Like Donal, Llewellyn was the kind who always seemed to have money. The kind who knew other wealthy people, their habits and their tastes. I remembered him laughing about Donal. "Sometimes, I think Don is getting old," he'd said. "Wants to leave it all to good works." At the time, I'd laughed too. Now the comparison sat badly. I turned toward the couch, my own thoughts surprising me.

"Could be it's something personal with our guy Lew," I suggested to the supine cat. "Something he'd pay to know. Maybe there's a Mrs. Llewellyn McMudge."

"Stranger things have happened." She appeared to be waking, but I knew better. She'd been letting me sort out my thoughts before interceding.

I opened my mouth to protest. The man I'd partied with was not the marrying type. He was here today, gone tomorrow. Gallant after his fashion, he was...I stopped before the words could form. What did I really know about my sometime playmate, besides that he had money and taste and enjoyed good times? Very little. And I had never really bothered to find out more. Swallowing my half-formed answer, I looked down at my diminutive companion, waiting for the feline equivalent of "I told you so."

Whatever else she picked up, she must have gotten my confusion. Even, I'll admit, my dismay. *"I find that sometimes sleep is the best option."* I sensed rather than heard that thought as the weight of the day collapsed onto me. Before I could agree, she rose, stretching in a long yawn that reached from her front paws through her arched back. Then, with a look, she jumped down from her perch and led me, also yawning, up the stairs. My head was spinning as I collapsed onto the bed, and it wasn't just the wine. Three men. One dead. One...returned. It was too much to take in as I slipped into oblivion.

◇◇◇

Wallis joined me at some point during the night. The soft thud of her landing on the bed was comforting, waking me as it did from evil dreams in which fluttering papers were sinking slowly, soaked in blood. I was struggling against them, feeling myself weighted down by their heavy wetness when she woke me, and I felt a wave of warmth for my longtime feline companion. I rarely expressed how I felt toward her. Neither of us were the type, but I was grateful for her presence in our big old house. More grateful than I'd have been for any of the men who had recently shared my bed.

Donal Franklin's death had disturbed me, and the mystery of his Persian meant I wasn't going to be able to walk away from it anytime soon. Wallis and I would disagree about that, but even she had to understand that I had taken charge of the creature and that meant assuming responsibility for her life. I couldn't abandon her.

Besides, the puzzle aspect intrigued me. First Donal, then Llewellyn. Something was going on that I didn't understand— and I didn't think the cat was at the heart of it. If gossip was saying that the Franklin marriage was on the rocks, then the white Persian was more likely an innocent bystander than a perpetrator. I needed to talk to Llewellyn and the widow, maybe even to this Robin. More than anything, I needed the white Persian to tell me what she had seen.

Tomorrow morning, I would get to work. The presence of Tom had distracted me. Maybe all the more because of the questions Wallis had raised about Llewellyn. About us return-ing to the city and about my relative solitude out here. I'd get on it. Tomorrow.

◇◇◇

Wallis was gone when I awoke. She didn't show even as I cracked three eggs for breakfast. Maybe that was the point. I had to figure some things out by myself. But if she thought I'd be poring over my soul alone at the windowsill, she had another think coming. I had dogs to walk. After a few bites, I scooped the rest of the eggs into a saucer for her, and started on my day.

Besides, I had a few other cards up my sleeve. If they weren't aces, they could still score me points. Growler, my first client of the day, was one of them. It had taken some work, but Growler and I had a relationship. A self-possessed bichon frise who had little use for humans, I'd won his respect, if not his affection, partly by looking beyond that fuzzy-cute exterior and acknowledging the alpha dog within. We didn't talk much, but I listened to his requests. In return, he often gifted me with his acute observations—often gleaned from the scents around town. Today, I wanted to get on his good side. Ignoring his human—a chain-smoking busybody named Tracy Horlick—I let him ramble down to the school yard. There was a new dog in town, a purebred saluki, and Growler wanted to check him out. I gave him his head, let him set the pace. His person was a gossip of the worst sort—always ready to pass along the latest scandal. Growler wasn't necessarily kinder, but his information was better. If there was something funky with the Franklin marriage, he might have caught the scent. If nothing else, he might be able to fill in the blanks Lucy the poodle had left.

Growler talked on his own terms, though. I had to wait till he offered. We were heading toward the river, following the big dog's scent, when my cell rang. With an apology to the bichon, I answered.

"Pru?" The question in the voice as much as its low guilty timbre clued me in. Albert, our local animal control officer-slash-dog catcher.

"Yeah?" He wasn't a bad guy, not really. He's not Jim Beam, either.

"Um, Pru? I hate to ask. But could you come down here, like, now?"

My sigh should have carried all the way to the shelter. Growler had already turned, those button eyes telegraphing resentment. "I'm working, Albert."

"There's a lady here. She's freaking out on us. She says you stole something." Behind him, I could hear another voice. High pitched. Angry. "She says you've taken her cat."

Albert. Knowing him, this could be anything from a real accusation to some client's fit of pique. As much as he fancied himself a ladies' man, the flannel-clad animal control officer was as terrified of the gentler sex as the chipmunk who had just spotted Growler was of the dog. I wouldn't get anything useful out of him, and as I called to the bichon—who had caught the chipmunk's sent—I knew that avenue had been shut down as well.

"Sorry, little guy." I muttered under my breath. As always, I'm never sure how much verbal communication is necessary.

"Useless." I got that back, clear as day. *"Women. Can't put two and two together."*

"Speaking of," I drew a breath, unsure how to continue. "Lucy the poodle was asking after you." Silence. "I think she likes you."

"Stupid bitch."

I stopped short at that. He was a dog. He meant it in a technical sense, I was all but sure. Still, the little bichon had already let me know his sexual preferences, and his chain-smoking owner had left him with a strong aversion to anything female. Did he dislike the yappy toy—or was he warning me off trusting her? I wanted to ask, but I was already on shaky ground. Growler had started tugging at the leash and so without another word I let him lead me back to town.

Chapter Ten

Here's another reason I prefer animals to people: the lack of drama. An animal will kill you, rip your throat out if it feels threatened or you look like dinner. But it won't throw a tantrum. Given the choice, I'd take the teeth.

Right now, I didn't have the choice and vented by cursing out loud as I manhandled my car toward Albert's office. Returning Growler early hadn't helped the situation—either with the bichon or his person. With her unerring knack for picking up the whiff of gossip, Tracy Horlick had been waiting. I cut her off before she could say anything—but from the yelp of pain that escaped as I pulled the door shut behind me, I knew Growler was going to pay for it. No wonder that dog hated people. I figured I was bitching for us both as I went back to my car. Once I had run through my extensive repertoire, I started to wonder what had actually happened.

Taken? What did that mean? I hadn't *stolen* anything, much less a cat. I ran through my current clients: dogs, for the most part, except for her Highness, the Princess Achara, who never left her house. I'd brought the white Persian to the county shelter the day before. But that had been on police orders. Something was odd here, and I was going to get the worst of it.

It's not that I don't trust Albert. The man is a mess, dressed in flannel from Labor Day through the Fourth of July, and neither the plaid nor the stout body it covers are likely washed more than a dozen times during that interlude. As far as I could figure, his only qualification for the job was that he was someone's drinking buddy and, when he was kicked off the police force for sheer stupidity, somebody had pulled a string or two. Old Sheldon had retired by then, and while Albert had taken a crash course and knew words like "zoonotics" and "feral," he was not that much different from our old-time dogcatcher. He was also a coward, afraid of many things. Most notably, despite the occasional off-color joke, women. That there was some broad in his office screaming bloody murder, I believed. I had heard her shrill voice in the background. What she was actually going on about? That I'd have to find out for myself.

Albert did have one redeeming trait: his ferret, Frank. I made a mental note to watch my use of the possessive. Wallis would give me hell if she'd heard that. Old habits do die hard, however, and I doubted that the sleek little mustalid who cohabited with Albert did so out of choice. Frank—I'd recently gotten Albert out of calling him "Bandit"—was as sharp of eye and wit as his human was dull. If Frank were there, and I could have a moment alone with him, I'd get a better idea of what was really going on. I might even get some insight into the whole Franklin affair. Frank picked up on things. Actually, he frequently picked things up—a tendency to covet small, shiny items had gotten the small beast into trouble more than once—but those bright eyes saw even more.

As I pulled into the town office's parking lot, I realized that Albert's summons might have another benefit. Albert's office, which also housed our minuscule town shelter, was right next door to the police department. The two buildings had been constructed after I left, when the new money had started flowing in. Red brick, in a tribute to the town's old mill buildings, and fronted with the kind of modernistic glass entrance that did neither old nor new style a favor, they leaned up against each other. Cheek by jowl, as some wag had said. Which was which could be left to the onlooker. But if I lingered in that see-through alcove, I might manage to run into Jim Creighton.

Hell, I could corner him afterward anyway. He was a boy scout at heart, which meant a workhorse. And I still had questions that he could answer.

I didn't have far to go. As soon as I stepped through those double glass doors, I saw my sometime beau. He was leaning back on Albert's desk, listening to a distraught woman whose voice was broken by rasping breaths. He saw me, too, and nodded, and I came closer. The woman, up close, was a wreck. Red nose, those gasps clearly coming after a bout of sobbing. Plump, maybe a bit overripe for her knit suit, she was still pretty, or would have been if her face hadn't been swollen with grief. Maybe it was her smooth dark hair, drawn back into a tortoiseshell comb and neatly curled. Maybe it was the younger man—her son? a brother?—who stood next to her, gently stroking her back. Something about her reminded me of a cat. I immediately felt guilty.

"Hi, may I help you? I think there's been some confusion." Jim Creighton's eyebrows went up slightly. He's not used to hearing me sound contrite. He's still a cop, though, so when I caught his signal to be quiet I shut up.

"Mrs. Franklin? Louise?" He stood and gestured to the woman. "Would you like to sit down now, please? I believe we're about to clear this all up."

"Franklin?" I'd wanted to meet the widow. I hadn't thought I would today. "Mrs. Franklin?"

That did it. The plump brown tabby noticed me, turning to look at me with eyes of a startling light grey.

"You! After all I've been through—"

She nearly hissed, and I—accustomed to angry animals— took a step back. Something about those eyes, particularly against the dark hair, was uncanny. Striking, yes, but disturbing. I glanced away from their cold, direct gaze. Albert, I realized, had disappeared.

"Louise, please." Creighton was in calming mode. I noticed his voice, low and even, with professional respect, as well as the gentle downward motions he made with his hands. The man knew his job, and I relaxed, curious as to how this was going to play out. "I am sure there has been a misunderstanding."

He was smiling as he talked, but now he turned to me. "Pru Marlowe works with many of the animals we bring in. I have no doubt she has an explanation for the disappearance of your cat."

The Persian? I could have spit. "What happened? I brought her in to Doc Sharpe yesterday. After you called me." That last was aimed at Creighton.

"Ah, mystery solved. I'm afraid I'm to blame, Mrs. Franklin." He was using her name an awful lot. Was this part of his calming technique, or was something else going on here? "You see, when Ms. Marlowe helped us out yesterday, she must have thought the cat needed to be taken in for veterinary care."

"But—" The sputtering was back, albeit softer. Dark lashes fluttered over those striking eyes. A bit theatrical, if you asked me.

"And now, I'm sure your cat is in safe hands?" This last came with a look at me.

"Of course." I couldn't read this scene. "I was afraid the cat had been hurt. She was agitated. It made sense to take her to a vet." I wouldn't have brought any animal to our town pound. At least now I understood what was going on. "This is the Beauville shelter, and Albert's a trained animal control officer, but the county shelter is a fully functional animal hospital. Doc Sharpe runs it." I thought about the deafness, but decided to leave it. This woman had had enough to deal with today. "Your cat is fine."

"You authorized that?" She'd turned on Creighton now. "You could have told me. I was frantic."

"Now, now, Mrs. Franklin. Louise. I did tell you—"

"I didn't know. How could I?" She wasn't listening, instead rattling around in her bag. Creighton reached for a box of tissues, but she beat him to it, pulling out a lace-edged handkerchief to dab at her eyes. "You didn't say."

"We were talking about what I would have to take with me—only as a loan, of course—to submit as evidence. And I'd gotten up to your husband's collection." He was good at keeping calm, but I could hear the frustration in his voice.

"You were interrogating me, and all I could think was, 'Where's the cat?'"

"I'm sure I—"

"And there was a window open. Someone had left a window open. The cat was alone. Unsupervised and it has never been outdoors. There are woods out here. Wolves—"

"Your cat is safe, Mrs. Franklin." Even Creighton has his limits, and Louise Franklin was acting more like a fishwife than a new widow. "I'm sorry that I suggested coming down here. I wasn't thinking. But Ms. Marlowe is an animal expert, and she exercised sound judgment bringing the animal to Doctor Sharpe."

He looked up at me. This was my cue.

"We wanted to make sure the cat hadn't been hurt." Even as I said it, I winced. I'd been stupid. It wasn't fear of losing the cat that had this woman so panicked, but her actual bereavement. I may not be the most sensitive observer, but even I could have figured out that she was flailing. "Your pet is fine—will be fine."

"It's not that." The sniffles were fading. The widow was getting a little control back. "It's that the cat—Fluffy—was all alone. And it was a gift from my husband." Wrong thing to think about. Her eyes were welling up again. "A very expensive gift. It shouldn't have been left all alone."

"I'm sure you can go visit her at County." I thought of Fluffy, all fluffed up with fear, and wondered what the Persian really called herself, in cat terms. That's usually one of the first things I get. Well, maybe she'd be more willing to communicate once she'd seen the widow. Louise Franklin wasn't the kind of classy silver fox I'd imagined—and her escort was a little obvious—but maybe her cat loved her. "And she'll be released as soon as Doc Sharpe can do a thorough exam on her." No need to tell the grieving widow that the cat seemed to prefer to be alone. Hell, that animal wouldn't let anyone near her.

"I don't want that cat released. I want to get rid of it. It's a horrible animal!" More tears. Understandable, probably. But something was hitting me as wrong here. A moment ago, she had been panicked, afraid the cat had gotten lost or been stolen.

This wasn't the time to discuss it. "Why don't we give it a few days, Mrs. Franklin. Fluffy is in good hands, and you don't have to make any decisions right now."

"I want that cat gone." She was on a tear. Face buried in the lace, her shrill voice barely muffled. "Awful creature."

I swallowed my distaste. She'd been through hell. "If that's how you feel, Mrs. Franklin, I know of several reputable rescue groups." Someone would want a pedigreed Persian. Assuming the animal would settle down. "They can arrange an adoption."

"*Rescue?*" She looked up mid-dab. "Adoption? Are you crazy or just stupid?"

I wasn't going to answer that one. I wasn't the one who had named a cat "Fluffy."

"That cat is a valuable animal. Didn't you hear me? It was very expensive. A breeder will pay good money for that animal."

This woman wasn't being rational. Then again, her husband had just been killed. I'm not the most patient, still I tried to keep my voice calm. "The rescue groups are very reputable." Until we resolved the deafness issue, no breeder would touch her, even assuming the cat's papers were in order—and as good as the grieving widow seemed to believe. I had my doubts. "I'm sure that within a week or two, they can place her—"

"Are you deaf?" Her choice of words caught me up short. "Or just dumb?" The insult didn't. Before I could let loose, though, Creighton stepped in.

"Mrs. Franklin, I know this has been a horrible time for you." He actually had his hands out, ready to restrain whoever needed it. "Please, why don't we have your friend take you home? Let's let the animal professionals worry about this, okay?"

"Rescue." She sniffed once more. I don't think it was the tears. "Please."

People. There was a reason I was lived alone.

Chapter Eleven

As annoying as they are, people are a necessary part of my business. And so as the widow was being helped into a rather nice leather coat, I gave her the rundown on Doc Sharp and County.

"Doc Sharp will have given your cat a thorough examination by now. From what we could see, she may have gotten banged up a bit." What we could *see*. I'd let the good vet explain the rest.

The widow gave the kind of ladylike snort I'd expect from Princess Achara. Well, she had been recently—and violently—bereaved. Though come to think of it, she had seemed more upset by the fact that her cat had been taken without her express permission than that her husband had just been killed.

Creighton's no mind reader, but I could tell from the look he shot me—brows ever so slightly raised—that he knew what I was thinking. The look worked, and I kept my mouth closed. Grief. It did funny things to people.

She took off, finally, once everyone seemed to have fussed enough, her hunky escort in tow. I'd have liked to query him, at least find out what he was being paid, but I doubted I could afford his time. Instead, I hung around, hoping Frank would pop out of some hole in the desk. In the meantime, I queried Creighton.

"So?" The reappearance of Tom, my burly New Yorker, had me back on my game. Tom had been a cop, too, back in the day. He had taught me the silence trick. Next best thing, he always said: leave the question open. They'll fill in the blanks.

"So, what?" Creighton probably went through the same training.

I pulled up a chair to stall for time, leaning back to rest my feet on Albert's desk. "That's the widow? Excuse me, didn't her husband get killed yesterday? Shouldn't she be planning a funeral or something?"

"The funeral director is taking care of that, Pru. Her assistant is helping, too." He choked on that, but got it out. "She's all over the map emotionally. You should have seen her earlier. I did. That sometimes happens."

Creighton does a good deadpan. Good enough so I couldn't tell if he was using it now. His lack of response brought me back to something else that had come up. Eve Gensler had said something about the widow's health. She could have been talking mental health.

"All over the map, huh? Was that usual for her?" I tried to study his face, but he'd closed the cover. I thought of Mrs. Pinkerton's snippy aside. "And that boy toy?"

"Pru." It was a warning. Assistant indeed.

"So what *was* going on back there? I mean, before she started freaking out."

Another shrug. I should have known.

"Come on, Creighton. You were asking her about the gun, right? And she starts freaking out about her cat?" About a cat she didn't even want. Maybe the lady was sick, maybe not. The whole thing seemed odd to me.

"The window *was* open." He gave me that. "At first, we thought there had been an intruder, but there's no evidence of one. Nothing missing, as far as we could tell. We're waiting for an inventory from the insurance agency, but the victim had his wallet and his watch with him. Hell, some of those antiques were worth as much as—"

He looked around. The town splurged on this new building. It's still not much.

"And you checked outside?" The room had been on the ground floor.

"You going to tell me how to do my job now?" His mouth got tight. "Or maybe you think that out here in the boondocks, we don't understand big-city forensics."

A noise behind me stopped me from having to respond.

"Um, hello?" Albert was standing behind me. His blue parka, patched with duct tape on the sleeve, implied that he'd been outside, but I'd been keeping half an eye on the door and suspected that he'd been hiding in the back. "Everything okay?"

"Hey, Al." I avoided answering his question, but I did take my feet off his desk. He unzipped his jacket and took a seat. "Cleaning cages?"

"Checking supplies." I was right. He'd been hiding. "You want to help, Pru?"

"I came to visit Frank, actually." I smiled as I said it. This had become a running joke between the two of us, and Albert was good-natured enough to take it, even when I added my usual line. "I always seek out the company of the most intelligent male in the room."

Creighton made a sound that could have been a cough. Albert didn't say anything, but he reached into his jacket and brought out his slinky pet. The shiny black eyes blinked at the light, and I didn't try to hide my glee.

"Frank."

"She likes my ferret," Albert said, not so sotto voce. Creighton watched us both.

That was the problem. Unlike most of the folks in this one-track town, Creighton had a brain. We hadn't spent that much time together, but he'd picked up something. He knew there was something going on beyond what everyone else said about me being a single woman with a cat—or me just "getting along" well with animals. He had watched me with Doc Sharp, and with Pammie, the vet tech. They worked with animals, too. And he saw the difference.

On the prowl?

The voice sounded so clear in my head that I almost responded out loud. I caught myself in time and tried to reach

out to the ferret with my thoughts. Yes, I was on the prowl. For
answers, for truth. Trouble was, I wasn't sure what exactly was
bothering me.

"We're done here. Right?" Creighton was talking to Albert,
which confirmed my suspicion that the fat man had called for
help after the widow had descended.

"Ah, yup." Albert had the grace to look embarrassed, and
turned away to root through a desk drawer. "Thanks, Jim."

Juicy? Salty? Fresh? Frank, at least, had been distracted by the
movement. His sharp eyes now focused on Albert's hands. When
he came up with a peanut, the ferret leaped on it.

"Isn't he darling?" That was addressed to Creighton. It was
meant to throw him off track.

"You feeling okay, Pru?" He'd been heading toward the door.
Mentally, I kicked myself.

"It's been a rough twenty-four hours, Jim. That's all."

Another question seemed to form in his mind. "Look, I'll
take care of the widow. She's—she's had a shock. You can get
that cat back into shape, right?"

I could have sworn that wasn't what he had been meaning
to ask. I didn't want to answer any more questions, though.
"I'll work on it, Jim." What would happen to the Persian, that
was a question for a different day. "I'm kind of wiped. Okay?"
That did it. Creighton waved to us both and took off. Albert,
meanwhile, had found a few more nuts in his drawer cache, some
of which he shared with his pet. I needed to go see the Persian,
but the chance to confer with Frank—Albert's better half—was
too good to pass up.

"Something going on with you two?" For a moment, I was
confused. Albert was talking about Creighton, though. Not his
pet. Albert may not be bright, but even he couldn't miss all of the
signals we were giving off. "I mean, beside crime-scene stuff?" He
popped a peanut into his mouth, his eyes as eager as the ferret's.

"He's just jealous of all the time we spend together, Albert." I
leaned forward onto his desk, both to shut the big man up and

to make physical contact with Frank. It worked. I doubt Albert had been this close to a woman in years.

Frank, however, was more interested in the remaining peanuts. Had I discouraged him from communicating by ignoring him? How could I explain my all-too-human dilemma?

"Hey, little fellow." I reached out to the small animal, palm up and low. Still, he started back and I braced myself. Ferrets have sharp teeth.

Stop it, stop it, stop it. No, no, no. I won't! All of this hit me as the lithe creature gave a sharp squeal. *How could you?* He spun around, and dived into the open drawer, leaving me and Albert both staring.

"Guess your boyfriend doesn't like you anymore, Pru."

"Guess not." I was thinking as fast as I could. It wasn't me, it couldn't be. The little animal knew me too well and by training and instinct both, I'd approached him in a manner that should have signaled submission, if not friendship. Something had scared that poor creature out of its not inconsiderable wits.

Chapter Twelve

If I had been willing to explain the interruption in my day, the rest of it would have gone easier. Beauville gossip being what it was, I declined to blame my tardiness on either Creighton or the widow. Instead, I rushed through my next few appointments with a few muttered words about "an emergency." Lucy the poodle looked up at that, even if her person didn't.

"I am sorry, Mrs. Gensler." The woman looked like nobody ever apologized to her, and I didn't like being one more to take advantage.

"It's fine," she waved one hand in dismissal, exposing bitten nails. "My niece said she'd come by after her hair appointment."

"Oh?" Robin was certainly someone who could tell me more about the Franklins. "Should I wait for her?" Beside me, Lucy whimpered, and I silently apologized.

"No, no." Another wave of that battered hand. "She's so busy these days."

She said. I remembered what the toy dog had told me as I snapped on her leash and led her prancing out the door. I'd been warned, but I still wanted to talk with her. At the very least, she had to be more forthcoming than Louise Franklin.

"So, what do you say?" The poodle was trembling with excitement by the time we got to our first tree. I was getting images of every other dog in the neighborhood, and remembered that she had asked about Growler. Was the little dog going into heat?

"*Oh, please!*" A sharp bark stopped that thought. "*Just because I'm pretty...*" I got an image of dark hair, glossy as fur, and I wondered if the little dog had ever met the widow. But then we came across two squirrels, so caught up in their mating dance that the little dog almost had a chance. I gave her enough lead and watched as she stiffened with attention—almost at point—and began to stalk. The gray rodents raced up a tree in the nick of time, taking Lucy's focus with them. Once again, I couldn't help but notice the change in her behavior—from pampered toy to pure dog. Just as well. I had no desire to repeat Growler's response.

"*Mais oui.*" Once again, Lucy must have picked an image, if not the thought. "*If he wanted...*" Some thoughts are better left unfinished.

By the time we got done, it was past two. I needed to get over to the shelter, but I'd given Wallis my breakfast and the rumbling of my stomach was drowning out my conscience. Besides, if I swung by my house, I could consult with my tiger-striped housemate.

Twenty minutes later, she was sniffing at the sliced turkey I'd put on a plate for her. I'd cut it up, knowing from experience she'd drag it behind the sofa to eat it if I left it whole. She licked it delicately, her whiskers flexing as she took in its rich poultry aroma. When I recounted my interaction with Frank, however, she didn't even try to hide her glee. "*What do you expect? Little rat-like thing like that.*"

"Wallis..." As far as I knew, the two had never met. If they had, she might have found they had a lot in common. "He isn't a rat, you know that."

"*No, he's a weasel. That's worse. They think they're so smart.*"

That was it. My tabby was jealous. I'd come home to find her sitting in the window, letting the sun warm her mottled fur. I'd reached for her—old habits died hard—and she'd allowed me to stroke her thick, smooth coat. For a few seconds there, I had thought we were on good terms. Now I realized she was just using the contact to amplify her access to my thoughts.

"Well, he does, Pru." She sat up on the sill, which put us at eye level. I didn't respond, beyond a stare and within seconds she had turned away. I'd won that battle. I'm also smart enough to know when to make peace.

"He's been useful, Wallis." I came closer, but kept my face turned toward the window. Hints of green had begun to appear amid the greys and browns. A light, hopeful green. "I mean, he gets to see a lot of what goes on at the pound, and he's more reliable than Albert."

She chuffed, a feline laugh. *"The squirrels in the attic are more reliable than that loser."*

I was about to agree—it felt good to be back on a collegial footing—when it hit me. "Wallis, how do you know what Albert is like?"

"Fat guy? Flannel?" She was staring intently at something in the yard. I saw wind in the trees, nothing more. *"He came by a few times, last year."*

"Once." He had, early on. Everyone in town knew my mom, and when she'd passed most of them had stopped by. Some of it was idle curiosity, I knew. I'd not been very visible during my few months back. Either way, the casseroles had maintained us both for several weeks. I had an image of Wallis glaring at me from inside an empty cupboard. I'd not been taking very good care of myself. I'd only started to come back to life when the dragging routine of hospice had pulled me back under.

Wallis. In the cupboard. She hadn't liked all those people in the house. Strangers, and loud strangers, after the relative quiet of the preceding months. "Did you even meet him?"

Nobody likes being reminded of her weaknesses. Wallis' ears flipped back. *"Like I had to."* The voice in my head had a snarl in it. *"You think I can't learn all I need to from your puny mind? Your memories? Your smell?"*

"Sorry." Tabbies could be so sensitive. "But, wait—" Something Wallis had just said had sparked a memory for me. Something about smell. "Wallis?"

Too late. She had jumped down and was pointedly ignoring me as she marched off to another window. I'd made my choice, that silent walk said. I was beneath contempt.

I was also the one who put food on the table, and I had already angered one client this morning. Grabbing my car keys, I set out to see what I could salvage of the rest of my day. Maybe whatever I'd been thinking would come back, with the help of the various pets of Beauville. Even if it didn't, I wanted to get through my paying duties in time to go see that Persian. I didn't think she had been tuning me out willfully. Not like Wallis did, and I didn't want to ignore that one, small plea. *Help*, the cat had said. *I'm sorry.*

Maybe I was distracted: the rest of the day went over like a dead weight. Dr. Simpson's shih tzu was still using the bath mat for a litter box and wouldn't tell me why. The Fowler dog hadn't forgiven Mr. Fowler for anything. I felt more like an animal handler than a trained professional. Six years of school and I was walking dogs—barely. The Fowler dog, more hound than anything, hadn't even been willing to leave the block.

Maybe Wallis was right. Dinner with Tom had thrown me. The big guy and I didn't belong together, not anymore. Reflected in his eyes, I'd seen how small this town really was. How much I'd retreated. I mean, I didn't want Tom, a beat-up ex-cop, but—Llewellyn? Really?

In all fairness, it had been a few weeks since my latest playmate had called. That call had resulted in a weekend in Saratoga. Some kind of business trip for him, a few stops to justify a weekend's indulgence. Since then, nothing. Well, easy come, easy go. Our kind of fling had a built-in shelf life, I told myself as I switched on the radio. If Western Massachusetts has one thing, it's good college stations, and I let the mellow sounds of vintage Sonny Rollins smooth my bruised ego as I headed down the road.

I needed what cool I could summon, once I got to County. On a good day, the combination shelter-animal hospital was a little crazed. Animals are there because they're lost or they're hurt. And the people, who either come to give up a pet or in the hope of finding one, aren't much better. Doc Sharpe does what he can. Maybe that Yankee reserve made it all palatable somehow. Me? I just gritted my teeth.

"Hey, Pru." Pammy was chewing gum and twirling a loose strand of her strawberry blonde hair. I hadn't realized she had that much coordination. "Doc Sharpe wants to see you."

Good thing I'd come by then, I wanted to say and didn't. Because the person who was probably supposed to call and tell me was still sitting in front of me. "He in the back?" The less contact I had with her, the better.

"Hang on." With a deep sigh, she pulled herself to her feet. Following her bouncing ponytail, I remembered myself at her age. That gave me a little sympathy. At least she was gainfully employed. Meanwhile, she was wrestling a ring of keys off her belt loop. "Here you go."

"Thanks." I was wondering why the new security, but it would be easier to ask Doc Sharpe. He was in the dog room with a somnolent bitch. She'd just been spayed, I could tell from the stitches. All she was thinking about was a grassy knoll and one particular elm. The anesthesia had been good.

"Oh, Pru. There you are." The vet turned from the cage. "Just finishing up in here."

"Couldn't Pammy have handled that?" I know a conscientious vet wants to check on his patients after surgery, no matter how routine. But transferring a healthy dog to her cage?

"It's no bother. And we really should have someone out front." He was turned toward the hand sanitizer, mounted on the wall, so I couldn't see his face. Sometimes the limitations of my gift are very frustrating. "Now, about that cat."

Was he psychic? "Yeah, I was wondering." I followed him into the cat room. "That's why I came by."

"So Pammy didn't tell you?" I hadn't wanted to rat her out specifically. I shrugged. "Well, we've been busy. The owner called."

So that was it. I had a feeling if the wealthy widow had made her presence known, Doc Sharpe would want the shelter looking like a real business. And that meant someone sitting at the front desk—even if it left him short-handed. It probably also meant the end of my access to the Persian. "Let me guess. She wants to transfer the cat to some fancy place in Amherst or Boston."

"Not at all." Doc Sharpe looked at me over his glasses. "Not once I'd told her that you were the best."

"And she believed you?" I caught the look—and revised my words. "She wants me?"

He nodded, once. "She wants you to work with the animal. She puts the highest priority on it."

I shook my head. "Doing what? Is it the deafness that concerned her? As long as she keeps her a house cat—"

"That's the point." Doc Sharpe was standing in front of a cage. At first, it seemed empty. Then, squashed in the back, behind some torn-up newspaper, I saw white fur. For a big cat, she'd made herself as invisible as possible. "She says the cat was fine before the, uh—incident." He recovered quickly. "Says the cat has been in perfect health. But she doesn't want to keep it. She wants to sell it."

I shook my head. The woman hadn't seemed deranged, not in that way, and I'd hoped she'd have let go of that particular delusion.

Doc Sharpe was avoiding my eyes, but he'd seen that. "That's what she says. Says the cat has papers—in her name, so the, uh, title is clear. Says she's valuable." He was doing his best to be noncommittal. "There's a problem, though."

"You mean, besides the deafness?"

"I'm wondering if we missed something. She's stopped grooming—at least her midsection." He opened the cage and nodded for me to come forward. As soon as I did, the low growl started up. I heard that loud and clear—and nothing else. Maybe that was her message: this was one kitty who didn't want to be touched. Still, I leaned in, focusing on the white back, the pink-tinged ears that I could now make out flat against the head.

"You might want the gloves." Doc Sharpe was the master of understatement.

What I wanted was him gone. "It could be stress. This animal's been through a lot. Can't she take her home? Give her some time to settle down?"

I shifted to look at the vet. He might be a cold fish, but this bothered him too, I could see that. "I gather not." His mouth was tight. "At any rate, the animal has to be socialized—or resocialized—before she can show it."

"All right." I dragged out the words. I had wanted to spend some time with the cat. Now I had my excuse. Still, the situation was odd. I was going to have my work cut out for me. "She agreed to my rates?" Officially, I was freelance, working on a referral basis.

"She didn't ask." Doc Sharpe had closed the cage door and was fumbling in his pocket. That Yankee reticence again. What the hell, I probably charged less than her manicurist. I looked through the barred door as the white cat settled in. With the door closed, she was calmer, even though she clearly still smelled and heard us. As I said, strange.

"She gave me a contact number." He fished out a pink message sheet. "Not hers. She's busy with, well, with everything. You're to call as soon as you can. Here."

He handed me the sheet. No name, just a number, scrawled in his nearly indecipherable doctor's handwriting. I had to squint to make out the numbers. Once I did, I read them again. "This is her contact?"

"Friend or relative or something. Someone handling the business side of things for her." He looked over my shoulder. "I should have written down the name. Sorry."

It didn't matter. As soon as I'd seen the number, I'd known who it was. I'd seen it often enough on my own cell. Llewellyn McMudge. My missing beau. The widow's helper. And now a part-time dealer in cats.

Chapter Thirteen

I was grateful, then, for Doc Sharpe's reserve. If he saw anything on my face, he kept quiet. He probably thought it was about the cat.

Actually, he wouldn't have been that far off. The whole thing was hitting me as pretty strange. Your husband dies, you act odd. I get it. And, yeah, if your pet is somehow involved, maybe you lose whatever warm and fluffy feelings you had for that warm and fluffy animal. Much as I prefer the four-footed to the two, I could understand that too. But to make plans to *sell* an animal, just two days after your spouse has kicked? That was a first, even for me. And to use Llewellyn as a go-between? When Doc Sharpe had started talking, I'd thought of the widow's companion, the pretty boy who had escorted her to the town shelter. He was supposedly her assistant. Not my sometime playmate, no matter how much he liked to be of service to the ladies. Add in Tom's interest in Lew? I don't believe in coincidence, not when someone has just ended up dead.

If I couldn't question the cat, my next thought was that I needed to grill Tom. My burly ex might no longer be on the job, but he was on a case. He knew something. My musings as to what that might be were interrupted by the good Doc.

"If you have a moment," he'd said, clearing his throat. "There are some clients I'd like you to meet."

I'd been standing there so long, he probably thought I was Pammy. At least my mouth hadn't been hanging open. And so

I shelved my desire to dissect the former cop, and went out to the waiting area, where the good vet introduced me to a young family whose puppy had bitten their son. It was the perfect distraction. They were already looking bereft, sure that Spotty was going to have to go to that big farm in the sky. Spotty was a beagle mix, not a bad choice for a family. With those ears, he even looked like the boy, whose floppy brown bangs hid eyes that were probably big with tears. The parents, basically kids themselves, looked tired. I knew the type. Clueless. They'd undoubtedly left the boy and puppy alone, and the two young animals had ended up roughhousing. A little supervision, a little training on both sides, and things would work out. Would that all tragedies were so easily diverted.

I talked with the four of them and planned a home visit. That was mainly for the parents, of course. They were the ones with the training problem; the kids had just been kids. I did try to home in on the puppy, however. He was the one who would come out the worst if this didn't work. I don't believe in aversion training, not even using suggestion. Why terrify the poor pup? I did focus on gentle play, though. *Softly, softly,* I thought the words as I stroked his velvet head. *Bigger than you, but very young. Very tender. Protect him.* The Pru Marlowe advantage. It worked better with adult animals, the ones I could reason with. This puppy? Well, I wasn't getting much by way of an acknowledgment. Puppies, like kids, have pretty short attention spans. I repeated myself, focusing on what would fit with the puppy's instincts: *protect him!* It was worth a shot.

I left them with Pammy. She had a bunch of giveaways, chew toys and the like. The fun part. But the visit made me think. Home visits are always more successful, animals being almost as territorial as humans. If I were really going to rehabilitate the Persian, I needed to take her to her home. To the Franklin house. The scene of the crime. Maybe Lew could pull some strings, or even sneak me in. After all, I didn't know if Louise Franklin was staying there. I'm not a girly girl, and even I had a twinge at the idea—sleeping upstairs from where one's spouse was shot. It would be risky: going back to a house that must still reek of death would be difficult for a sensitive animal. I couldn't see an alternative.

That didn't mean there wasn't one. I needed to spend more time with the cat. Alone. At least figure out what her role was in all of this, and get a handle on her apparent deafness. I'd do that before I called anyone. Certainly before I called Lew McMudge.

"Pru?" A familiar male voice broke into my reverie, and my heart leaped a few inches. Mack Danton, my favorite broken-down gambler—and the date who had inadvertently introduced me to both Donal Franklin and Lew McMudge when he'd left me at that country club bar.

"Mack." Lew. Tom. A warning bell rang clear and strong in the back of my mind. Too many old beaus were showing up. I'm not *that* hot.

"Hey, darling." He'd seen my initial smile, damn him. His instincts were good that way. "Fancy meeting you here."

"I work here." Honesty caught up with me. "More or less. And you?"

He smiled, that slow easy smile that I'd found so damned attractive when I'd first met him. We'd had chemistry from the start, not the least because I recognized his type right away. Mack Danton wasn't the kind of man you could rely on. If anything, he was like my ex-cop Tom in that respect, only leaner and maybe even more disreputable than the big New Yorker. But that smile projected the kind of raw appetite that makes a girl feel she's wanted, at least for the moment. It hadn't lost much of its appeal, and my body responded before my head could kick in. I'm no fool, though. Like the smarter animals, I'm trainable, and I'd learned that sexy grin could mean something else, too. When he leaned back like that, hips forward, eyes half closed, something was going on. Mack smiled when he didn't want to talk.

"Mack? Over here." A woman's voice, high and insistent, and the smile faded. "Mack?"

"Sounds like your mistress is calling." I didn't even turn to look. I didn't mind, not really. Still, it was fun to yank his chain. "Have you slipped your leash?"

"Very funny, Marlowe." His voice had gone into its low growl mode. Whoever was calling him, she hadn't brought him to heel. "I'm doing a favor. For a friend."

"Mack?" The friend in question appeared, perfectly done with a deep red lipstick that played up the chestnut in her shoulder-length brown hair. She looked young—younger than me, anyway—and in a few years that slight pudginess would settle into fat, those big brown eyes sink into her face like raisins. For now, though, she was quite the little package, completed by a good leather bag that she held like it was her first ever and a voice that suggested she had a strap on my ex as well. "Did you find her?"

"Here she is." The growl was still there, downplayed a little. And the smile was back. "Robin, I don't believe you've met our local animal trainer."

He knew better, so I didn't respond. Instead, I held out my hand. "Pru, Pru Marlowe. I work with Doc Sharpe and the shelter here on a referral basis. Freelance." She carefully tucked her purse under her elbow and reached out to take my hand in hers. I couldn't help noticing the rock on it. Green, surrounded by little diamonds with enough sparkle to make me think they were real, it matched the bag in quality, if not style. She saw me looking and smiled. Someone had come into good fortune. When she didn't say anything, I figured I had to take the lead. "Are you having trouble with an animal?" It took all my strength not to look at Mack when I said that. He wasn't buying jewelry for anyone.

"You know my aunt, don't you?" Her rounded face opened up in a smile. "You walk her dog."

It all clicked. "You're Eve Gensler's niece." This was a small town.

She nodded eagerly, making her hair bounce. "Aunt Eve told me about you, and so when Don started asking for some help, I told him about you."

Don? The cast of characters was getting out of control, but just then she reached into that bag for a handkerchief and started dabbing at her eyes. "Donal Franklin?"

She started to smile and ended up blinking as she bit at her perfect lipstick. "His cat." She blinked again.

I assumed I was supposed to feel sympathy. I also assumed I was supposed to fill in the rest. "The white Persian? He wanted me to do something with her?" Maybe the behavioral problems predated Donal's death. Maybe he'd had a premonition that the cat would kill him.

Her hair bounced again. This was getting dull. Robin was better accessorized than old Mrs. Gensler, but I wasn't seeing anything more going on mentally.

"What did Donal Franklin want me to do with his cat?" His? Hadn't the widow referred to the Persian as a gift? "And how may I help you today?" I pasted on some kind of a smile to grease the wheels. Mack knew me well enough to stifle his own growing grin. Robin, however, only grew more flustered.

"Well, she'd given him the cat, you know. But it hated her. I don't know why. Neither of us did. Don loved that cat so much. And I—"

She sniffed and brought the handkerchief to her mouth. I relented. "I'm sorry. It's pretty horrible." Those dark eyes looked up at me, the tears making them even larger and more vulnerable. And here I was, about to make them overflow when it hit me.

"*She* gave *him* the cat?" Another sniff. "Well, that explains the papers, but I don't know what I can do for you." That sounded awful. I tried again. "Louise Franklin has already made arrangements for the cat. She gave me the number of a friend she wants me to call when the cat is ready to be released."

"But Don always says—" Rapid blinks drove the tears back. "Don *said* that his wife hated the cat. That's why he and I—that was why he was going to call you."

The tenses were tripping her up, and so I didn't pursue it. I'd heard enough: the antipathy wasn't recent. Still, this could have a silver lining. "I don't know the history, Robin." I felt we were on a first-name basis by this point. "But she might be willing to give up the Persian, if you want to adopt her."

It would take some work. The aunt had told me Louise Franklin had taken Robin in. The way this girl was talking, it sounded like Don had taken an interest too. At any rate, this pretty brunette seemed to miss the cat—and the man—more than the widow did.

"Maybe I could just take her now?" She looked so eager, if she'd had a tail, she'd have wagged it. "While everything gets straightened out?"

I shook my head. I wasn't getting involved in a custody case. "Sorry, no can do." The red lips quivered. "It's not just the question of ownership," I explained. "You see, once the Persian has a clean bill of health, I'll still have to do some behavioral work with her. She's been through a lot."

Then I dropped the bomb.

"And I think the best way to do that is to get the cat back into surroundings that feel comfortable for her." No response. "To take her back to the house. To the Franklin house. Do you think you might be able to help me with that?"

"What? No." The girl seemed taken aback by that. To do her credit, she seemed to be thinking about it. "No, that wouldn't be—wouldn't be a good idea." She suddenly got awfully busy stowing her handkerchief back into her bag. I waited, wondering what would come next.

Whatever it was, she'd stowed it with that hankie. When she looked up, her pretty face was blank. "You'll call me, though, won't you? Let me know?"

I felt the pull of those big dark eyes. "I'm sure this will work out." For the first time that day, I felt confident of a resolution. At least for the cat.

"Well, until then."

She turned toward Mack, that little bag tucked underneath her arm. "I think we're done here." One touch on his forearm, and he leaped forward to open the door. A friend? I knew Mack. He wasn't the type to do favors, even for a damsel in distress. He wasn't the domesticated type, either. Not that I cared.

Still, there was something a little doglike about the way he'd jumped. About the way he followed his mistress out.

"Well, that was interesting." I wasn't talking to anyone in particular. A soft cough behind me let me know that I wasn't alone. "Doc?"

"Didn't want to interrupt." He was staring off into the middle distance. We weren't that busy. "The Smalley family is in reception. Once you've finished with them, could we meet for a few minutes?"

"Sure, Doc." I tried to remember what he'd told me about the Smalleys. Something with allergies. Their little girl's nose matched her hair—both a startling red—and as I approached, she sneezed some more. I wasn't sure exactly what I was supposed to do. Even with my gift, I'm no miracle worker. But I was billing by the hour, so I went through everything I knew about grooming the long-haired dachshund the family had adopted for Christmas. I gave them the name of some doggie shampoos and dug up a few pamphlets about HEPA filters. Either the kid would outgrow the allergies or she wouldn't, but I left them with some free samples and a little hope. More than many of us had at the end of the day, and I went to look for Doc Sharpe.

I found him in the cat room. He'd managed to extract the white Persian from her cage and had her on the metal examining table. She was calm now, almost unnaturally so considering the noise and olfactory confusion of the shelter. As I closed the door behind me, I tried once again to reach out to her with my thoughts. This time, I added thoughts of Robin. Young, soft. Possibly more involved with the cat—and her owner—than the widow had been. Again, I got nothing—almost a solid nothing, as if the cat was intentionally keeping me out.

"How's she doing?" I walked up to the other side of the table, the better to assist if he needed me.

"Better, I think." He was looking at her teeth again, and she wasn't resisting. "She's still not grooming, but we can give that some time. And the deafness seems to be lessening. I'm not entirely sure, but I think she looked up as you opened the door."

I hadn't seen anything. Then again, if she was locking me out, that might have been intentional.

"It's this foreleg that's worrying me now." He reached for the right paw, and she pulled back. I started to reach for her, but something stopped me.

"Do you want to do an X-ray?" X-raying an animal meant giving it general anesthesia. Without a full medical workup, including blood tests, that was a risk. "Would Mrs. Franklin give her permission?"

"I don't want to bother her. Though you could ask her caretaker, when you talk to him." Lew. Hard to think of him as anyone's manservant, though Doc Sharpe could have been reminding me of my duty. He'd overheard at least some of my conversation with Robin, and he was too smart not to have the same suspicions. "For now, I'm going on the assumption that it's a bad bruise or some kind of a sprain."

"Kickback." The word came out. One of Tom's words.

"Excuse me?" Doc Sharpe looked up.

"From the gun." We were both silent at that, but Sharpe's hand must have moved, just a little, down the Persian's leg. He must have touched the tender area, the bruise. Because right then, the cat started to struggle.

"Pru?" I didn't need prompting. I reached for the animal's back with both hands, the better to hold her steady. *"You can trust me."* I did my best to send my thoughts to the cat as I reached for her. *"I can help."*

"No! Never again! No!" The cat went wild.

Chapter Fourteen

I'm usually pretty quick, but that sudden outburst had unnerved me. As a result, I got thwacked. Blood was running down my forearm as I maneuvered the white Persian back into her cage and locked the door behind her.

"Sorry to catch you like that." Doc Sharpe was behind me. For a moment, his words confused me.

"My fault," I rallied. I didn't want him to start hovering. "We knew that leg was sensitive."

I washed the parallel scratches, then he applied an antibiotic cream, patting my arm dry before unpeeling the butterfly bandage. That was kind, the cut was on my right forearm, where I'd have had trouble getting at it myself. As soon as he was done, however, I wished him gone. I needed to think about what had happened.

"You want to get out of here?" He was looking at me funny. Something showed.

"What? No." Did he think a cat scratch would deter me? Then again, he'd given me my out. "Though if you don't think you'll need me…" I flexed my hand. The scratches pulled. The white Persian had gotten me good.

"Go home, Pru."

I looked up at the vet, but I couldn't read his face. Another reason I prefer animals.

On the drive home, I thought about what to do next. "*Never again,*" the cat had said, and I was tempted to give in. It would be so easy to let the Persian go. She wasn't wanted by Louise Franklin, but I'd have an uphill battle getting the widow to relinquish her for free. Particularly, if my suspicions were correct, to Robin Gensler. What's sauce for the goose isn't always sauce for the gander, not in the goose's opinion. Besides, the cat was a mess. From what Robin had started to tell me, she'd had some kind of problems before, so it wasn't likely she'd be pet-friendly for the foreseeable future. The world is full of excess animals. Most of them don't make it.

Then again, this was the fault of human beings. If this was a pedigreed animal—nobody really calls cats "purebred," because most of the specialty breeds are crosses—then we made her. Any temperament problems were probably our fault. Short tempers, hypersensitivity—it all goes along with breathing problems and spinal dysfunction when you interbreed animals for their looks, for how we want them, rather than what's best for the beast. I couldn't let a healthy animal be euthanized, an animal who had asked me, however faintly, for help.

The memory made me woozy for a moment, causing the double line on the highway to merge and dance. It was lack of sleep. Had to be, and so without access to caffeine, I pulled over for some air and stepped out onto the verge. Four o'clock. March. Almost dark. Winter cold, with frost just a few degrees off, but I could smell spring in the dampness, in the hint of green and the mud. Leaning back on my car, I felt the warmth of the engine. Listened to it tick, like a live thing, and looked out over the bare woods that fell away from the road. Out there, life was stirring again, too. At this hour, I was hearing little of it. Some small bird was nesting, grateful for its down. Something else—a fox, perhaps—was stirring. Would these two adversaries come into contact tonight? Would one not live to see the morning? I took a deep breath. This was the way it should be, without my kind interfering with it all.

But we had. And so I pulled the piece of notepaper out of my pocket and dialed Lew's number. I wasn't sure exactly what I would say to my absent date and rehearsed some options as the phone rang. I'd make it clear that this was business. That we were on friendly terms. I wouldn't refer to that weekend in Saratoga. And I wouldn't ask how he had gotten involved with the merry widow.

Years of training have some residual benefits. As the call connected, I pitched my voice low. Calm as well as sexy would get me what I wanted.

"Lew? This is Pru Marlowe calling." I assumed he had caller ID, but I wanted to give him a moment to collect himself.

"Pru, what a surprise." The voice on the other end wasn't the one I had anticipated. Slightly higher, a lot younger. For a moment, I was disoriented. "Then again, I'd heard you two had been spending some time together."

"Creighton?" My own voice ratcheted up. Not what I wanted. "This is a business call, Officer. And I'd appreciate it if you would respect that and put Mr. McMudge on the phone."

I didn't know what I expected. The low laugh on the other end certainly wasn't it.

"I bet I can do you one better, Pru. In fact, I'd like to invite you to speak with him in person."

I waited.

"In fact, if you can tell us where he is, Pru, the department will be deeply indebted to you."

"Excuse me?"

"Llewellyn McMudge. *Your* Llewellyn McMudge has gone missing. Just when we really wanted to speak with him about his new interest in antique guns." There was quiet on the line. "Anything you know about this, Pru?"

I didn't, but I wasn't surprised. Lew and Don were friends. So they shared a hobby? Well, they were wealthy boys who could afford their toys. Had Robin been one of those pricey playthings? Had I? I banished the thought. Better stick to the literal truth.

"I'm calling about the Persian," I said. He'd been there when Louise Franklin said she wanted to sell it. He'd heard her outburst, and I told him how she'd now hired me to rehabilitate the beast to see if we could interest a breeder or some other buyer.

"Rich people, Creighton. They collect things. Cats, guns. And the widow gave Llewellyn's name to Doc Sharpe. Told him he should be my contact."

"Huh. He's awfully good at making himself useful, isn't he? The old family retainer?" He waited, but I didn't take the bait. "Ever wonder what he does for his money, Pru?"

"We didn't have that kind of relationship."

Quiet on the other end. I'd have bet my own scarce savings Creighton was wondering what kind of relationship we did have. "Let me know if you hear anything, Pru," he said finally. "And be careful. You know him. You don't know everyone he hangs out with."

I couldn't deny that. Meanwhile, I had a question of my own. "Speaking of rich people, don't you think it odd, first that the widow acts so concerned about getting rid of the cat and then she's so insistent that it not be given away?"

"Well, the cat reminds her of her husband." I'd told myself that, too. "Of what happened to him. I could see wanting it out of the house. Or maybe, I don't know. Maybe she never liked the cat."

Unbidden, Robin Gensler came to mind. If there had been something going on and Louise Franklin had been aware of it, the cat might be more pawn than pet. It wouldn't be the first time an animal had been injured out of spite. I opened my mouth to pose this theory to Jim—and caught myself in time. I didn't need to stir up trouble. Not till I had that cat placed in a good home, anyway.

"There are a lot of maybes in this, Pru." He sounded tired, this strange case weighing on him. "Look, why don't you come in tomorrow. We'll talk about it."

At another time, I would have joked. We knew each other well enough by now. I could take some liberties. There was something in his voice, though. Something beside fatigue. And he'd given me license to sleep on my suspicions. It wasn't like anything was going to happen tonight anyway. "Okay," I said. "I'll come in tomorrow."

If Creighton noticed my hesitation, he didn't let on. He was the wrong kind of animal, and I couldn't read him. Instead, I went home to my cat.

Chapter Fifteen

"Don't even think about it."

Wallis rarely laid down the law. Being a cat, she didn't have to. A few subtle hints. A lash of the tail. I get the message. This time, though, she was not taking any chances.

"Wallis, I wasn't."

"Yeah, right." I'd only walked in when I saw her, waiting for me. Now I turned to hang up my coat, and heard the ripping sound of her claws in my mother's old couch.

"Wallis!" I whipped around. She wasn't even pretending to stop. Instead, she pinned me with those cool green eyes and reached up an inch further. "Look, can we talk?"

The claws stayed where they were, far enough extended so that I could see the pink at their base. *"When you say 'talk,' what you mean is, 'Can you convince me.'"*

I shut up. She was right. "Look, Wallis, I wasn't intending to bring the white Persian here."

"Not consciously." She sheathed her talons and sat back down. *"You were wondering what to do with the cat. Why that cat was important."*

"To the widow. To Robin Gensler. Not to me." I was fudging a bit and hoped she wouldn't notice. "You have to admit, there's something strange going on here."

"Maybe." She settled down onto her belly, her tail wrapping around her legs. And I realized, she might be able to read my

thoughts, but she didn't have all the info. *"I have enough."* Her tail lashed.

"Look, let me tell you what I know." I needed to make peace. I lived here, too. Besides, Wallis was the only other creature I could trust to be straight with me.

"Damn right." She couldn't suppress the low purr that my unintentional compliment had prompted. I pretended to ignore it as I put my thoughts in order.

"To start with, the widow is off somehow. For one thing, she doesn't care about cats." Yes, I was playing on Wallis' vanity a little. It had worked for me before. "And, okay, maybe their marriage wasn't the greatest. They didn't seem like the best matched couple. But you'd think she'd be a little more visibly upset."

I pictured the pretty widow. She'd been angry, but she'd never lost control. "She only gets loud or upset when she wants others to react." Creighton's questions. The gun. "Or when she needs to control the situation. It's like she's trying to use aversion training on us."

"Oh, nasty." Wallis' ears went back. She hates loud noises.

"And the girl Robin. She's quieter, but there's something odd going on with her, too." An image of a mouse—gray and terrified—came to mind, courtesy of Wallis, most likely. It seemed at odds with the young woman I had met, toting Mack along like this month's prize, after the purse and the ring. I blocked that thought as quickly as I could, but Wallis' ears had already pricked back up. "No, I'm not doubting you. She is anxious, that's for sure. And I don't think she's a friend of the family." As I said it, I tried to figure out why. "She and Louise Franklin clearly hadn't spoken. Not about the cat, anyway. And, well, she seemed to be siding with the Persian against the widow."

"And there's something wrong with that?" I couldn't tell if Wallis was being serious or toying with me. She could be hard to read, too. I decided I had to take her question seriously.

"There's something off about it. About her."

"So negative." It had worked. Wallis was engaged again. *"You say you don't know what is happening, but really it's always the same story. Hunters hunt. Prey... "* She licked her chops.

"Are you saying Robin is prey? She's afraid? Of the widow?" I paused to consider this. If what I suspected was true, I could understand that, a little. "But wouldn't Donal Franklin's death have put an end to their rivalry?"

I was answered only by silence. At least in her mind, Wallis was on the prowl.

Chapter Sixteen

I woke with the birds. Now that spring was on its way, they had the potential to become seriously annoying. It wasn't the sound. It was the inanity. "*I'm here! I'm here! I'm here!*" Or "*You're back! You're back! You're back!*" All with the kind of vacuous intensity that explained the term "bird brained." Neither size nor relative cuteness, I'd learned, was proof of anything in terms of character. This morning, though, I managed to block out most of the content. It wasn't quite the usual tweets and twitters. Those days were long gone. But at least I wasn't caught up in some trivial domestic drama—whose down was softening what twig—or some puffed-up robin's territorial machismo.

Grateful for small blessings, I descended to the kitchen. Wallis was nowhere to be seen. Which could have been intentional; she likes keeping me in my place. Or it could have been the call of those birds. I don't like the idea of Wallis out hunting. I know she's not the biggest predator in these woods. But with our relationship on its current footing, I no longer felt comfortable insisting on my rules in the house.

I'd hoped to follow up on our conversation, though, and her absence left me hanging. Wallis had hinted that the widow was on the hunt herself. Looking for something. As I made my coffee, I tried out the possibilities. Creighton said the widow had an alibi. Her phone placed her miles away. She insisted that her husband had been alone in the house. And the evidence, supposedly, pointed toward the cat. Toward an accident. Even with the Persian's apology, I didn't buy that for a minute. Though it did make me grateful that I couldn't tell Creighton the little I had picked up from the white cat.

Of course, Wallis could have been talking about something else entirely. Hunting, hunters…The appearance of Tom and even Mack had gotten me thinking about some extracurricular fun of my own, the kind my warm-blooded companion would certainly pick up on. Even Lew seemed to be in play, somehow, though perhaps more on the widow's team, this time out.

It was all a little too much too fast, and I tried to ignore a niggle of unease as I drank my coffee and pondered the day. Growler to start with. I had told Jim Creighton I'd come by first thing, but I had a job to do. Besides, I'd not had a chance to really talk to the irascible bichon yesterday, and his nose had helped me out of a jam before. I also had some questions for Eve Gensler. Her poodle, Lucy, was too flirty to be trusted. But maybe her pale owner could fill me in. Now that I'd met the niece, what she'd said about the Franklin marriage had more credence. Robin was more than a gossip. She was a possible correspondent in what could have been a divorce case. Or at least a contender for the cat's affections. Whatever role Mack played I didn't know. Didn't want to know. But I'd be damned if I was heard asking any man about the girl who seemed to be his latest playmate.

If I was hoping for a tête à tête with Growler, however, I was to be disappointed. The clear early morning had clouded up by the time I got to the Horlick residence, and fat raindrops were marking the dirt on my windshield as I pulled up. I didn't care; I'd grabbed a slicker and an umbrella both on my way out. But when Tracy Horlick opened the door, she looked up at the sky as if it might be poisonous.

"Looks bad." The cigarettes had made her sound like something out of an old Western. "Real bad."

I stifled the urge to laugh. "Almost time for April showers, Mrs. Horlick." I peered past her, looking for the dog. Experience had taught me that the bichon was usually dying to get out of the smoke-filled house. "Is Growler—I mean, Bitsy—ready to go?"

Tracy Horlick trained one gimlet eye on me. I could have kicked myself.

"Oh, come on." I plastered a stupid grin on my face to make a joke out of my lapse. While I prefer to use an animal's chosen name out of respect, I couldn't forget who paid the bills. "Don't tell me you've never thought that such a tough little feller needs a tougher name?"

"Bitsy is a bichon frise." The way she said it, stressing the French pronunciation, made her lipstick crack. "Not some mutt."

"Gotcha." I nodded and reached for the lead. I didn't need her making comparisons to other animals in my care. Or to me, for that matter. "So where is Bitsy?"

"This weather." She gestured with her cigarette, oblivious to the ash that threatened to fall. "I don't like it. I'm not going to have him walked today."

A muffled yelp made its way to me. Indignant, to the point of being incoherent. I heard it as a cry for help. She'd locked him in the basement again.

"A little rain won't hurt him." I was on my best behavior now. "And he should have his exercise."

Too late. I'd pissed her off, and she was going to take it out on the dog. "And then I get to have a wet dog in the house? Do you know what that smells like?"

Yes, I did, though with her habit, I was surprised she could still smell anything. Still, I owed it to the dog to keep trying.

"Why don't we go for a short walk? I'll only charge you half for the day."

Wrong note. "He can use the yard. I don't have to pay for that at all. And you, with your fancy friends—you don't exactly need the money." With that, she closed the door fast enough so that I had to step backward to avoid getting hit. I didn't know what I had done to piss her off that much. Fancy friends? Did she mean Lew—or Louise Franklin?

Of course. Old lady Horlick was friends with Eve Gensler. If the widow was clamping down, exacting some kind of revenge on Robin, then the weird bridge-playing sisters of Beauville might well join forces against her. I thought of what Wallis had said. Tracy Horlick lived for gossip, the nastier the better. For her to shut me out meant she must no longer want my info. Or, I mused as I walked back to my car, she'd found a more compliant asset.

Replaying my history with her, I drove slowly to the Genslers. It was early for the poodle pit stop, but I wanted more time to think. Besides, if Eve Gensler could tell me anything about her niece, I might end up with something to bring to Creighton. When you want information, barter works best. And the dog wouldn't complain. Come to think of it, I wasn't sure if that little poodle would even notice the difference.

"Oh." Eve Gensler's round face looked at me blankly. She was wearing her housecoat. Then again, she always was. "You're early."

"I know." Again with the big fake smile. "Another client cancelled, and I thought Lucy might appreciate getting out a little earlier. I can even take her for a longer walk."

"Oh." That sounded noncommittal, but she shuffled off down the hall in worn slippers. The door was open, so I followed her. Rain is all very fine, but I don't mind coming indoors every now and then.

"I finally met your niece," I called, staying on the mat. I was fishing, but I also couldn't afford to lose all my clients. "She's quite lovely."

"Oh, thank you…" Eve's voice was soft under ordinary circumstances. From the other room, it was basically inaudible. She kept talking, however, and I waited, reminding myself that paying customers were allowed their ways.

"But she hasn't gotten snippy with it." She reappeared with the poodle already on her leash.

"Excuse me?" I squatted down to greet Lucy. She sniffed my hand silently, gathering up the details of my day. "I'm sorry, Mrs. Gensler, I didn't hear you."

"Hmm." She sniffed, and I wondered how much time she'd been spending with Tracy Horlick. "I was just saying, now that she's gotten herself all done up with her fancy friends and all."

She clearly wasn't talking about Mack, and I waited for her to continue.

"How nice for her, Mrs. Gensler." It was a prompt, but she didn't respond. "I'm glad she's meeting interesting people." Nothing.

I opened the door, ready to try my luck with the poodle. The sky had lightened a bit, but the air had gotten colder. I thought I could smell snow. "Come on, Lucy. Fancy a run?"

"Don't overdo it." Eve Gensler piped up again. "She's a delicate little thing."

"I understand." I didn't. This pale shadow of a woman had never tried to second-guess me on dog care before. Something was going on, but I'd sort it out later. Lucy barked once—a short, sharp yelp—and wagged her stiff tail. Jumping up on her hind feet, she bounced around in a circle, almost like a circus performer. It struck me as a little obvious, but Eve Gensler melted.

"Isn't she adorable?" She reached down to pet Lucy's fluffy head, and the little dog wagged her tail so hard her body shook. Then she looked up at me and barked once more. That was my cue, and we were gone.

"Where to, boss?" I was joking, but only slightly. I'd never managed to really break through with the little toy. Recently, I'd begun to wonder if it was me—if my preconceptions about the breed had encourage her standoffishness. Of course, she could just be stupid. Still, it was worth the try.

Stupid? And who picks up the waste here?

Her response took me off guard, and I stopped in my tracks. She responded by pulling on the leash. It's a bad habit, one that I'd learned to train dogs away from. In this case, however, I understood, and with a silent apology gave her some more of the lead and picked up the pace. This wasn't the first time that my stated job and my real motivation were at odds, but with time the dichotomy was becoming more obvious—at least to me. With a twinge of conscience, I thought of Growler. Tracy Horlick had said something last week about "nipping" and I'd said I'd look into it. Nipping—biting by any other name—was a really bad habit. If for no other reason, it could lead to an animal being surrendered, or even summarily euthanized if the bite went too deep. I'd tried to explain it away, telling the old bag about play aggression, about how her little neutered male needed to enact the gender roles dictated by his genes. She hadn't bought it, I could tell. Maybe because I was lying. I mean, what I was saying was true ninety-nine percent of the time. But in Growler's case, something else was going on. That little dog hated the person fate had stuck him with. I couldn't say I blamed him.

Lucy, though, seemed to be a happier dog. Eve Gensler might not be much of a person, but at least she wasn't actively aggressive—and she really seemed to care for the poodle. Whether Lucy reciprocated or just had the old woman's number, I couldn't tell. I'd picked up that she'd knew how to play her person, but the fact that she'd also accepted the name the little gray woman had given her was unusual. I used it now to try to break through.

"So, Lucy, what's up with the Gensler family?" I said the words out loud, much like I'd talk to Wallis. In my head, though, I tried to picture Eve Gensler and found myself focusing on the housedress, which must have once been pink. I'd meant to wait before asking about Robin, the niece, but as soon as I'd thought of her, her pretty, plump face sprang into my mind.

"*Huh!*" Lucy barked. I stopped and looked at her. She was standing tall, her stiff little tail wagging fiercely.

"What is it, Lucy?" She relaxed and kept walking "Are you trying to tell me that she's—what?" A dog's tail wag can mean a lot of things: friendly or excited or even dominant…

"*Belly up.*" The words came to me, along with an image of a sniffling muzzle reaching up to lick another. Combined with what I suspected about Robin, I saw it as suggestive. At the very least, flirtatious.

"*Huh!*" Another chuff from the poodle.

I raised an eyebrow. She tilted her head. "Isn't this what you recommend?"

"*Not for me.*"

Well, Lucy was spayed. I filed the hint for later. At times like this, I really missed Wallis. Not only could my cat and I actually converse, she occasionally offered to intervene—"boosting" my sensitivity to help me get the gist of what other animals were saying. Other cats, anyway. I couldn't imagine her translating for a dog.

"Lucy?"

Another bark interrupted me. Louder this time. This time, the message in it was clear as she pulled again on the leash. "*You, however, could learn a little something from that one,*" she had said. "*And tell Growler, if he wants—*"

Not that again.

"*If he wants, he can get along a lot easier.*"

"You want me to tell him how to train his person?" The idea made me smile, despite everything. With another huff of a bark, Lucy pulled me along the walk.

Chapter Seventeen

"Hey, Jim. Good to see you." I wasn't nervous, not really. The rest of the walk had been uneventful. Frustrating, really, and my inability to get any other reaction out of the small beast had been annoying. That last bit had sounded positively condescending, though it was possible she was repeating something she'd heard. Something meant to put someone off. Robin, Eve. Maybe even me. Still, by the time I got to the police station, I tried to banish any questions from my mind. Calm, that was key. Creighton might be more than a cop, but he was never less. By taking the lead, at least conversationally, I established the rules of the exchange up front. We were friends at least. I wanted our meeting to be cordial.

"Pru." He didn't. Great. "My office, please?"

I followed him down a short corridor that had quickly come to look older than the rest of the building. The bitter tang of stale coffee permeated the air. Maybe it was just a generic cop shop smell, but it brought me back to my teens, when I'd been hauled into the old headquarters once too often.

I wasn't a kid now, though, and I stood tall as I walked by Creighton through the door he held open for me. One desk, a little too neat for me to understand. A plastic chair, designed to be uncomfortable. I was suddenly aware of the morning's activity. I had washed my hands, but I'd been out in the rain. Well, too late to do anything about it now. Trying not to think about how I looked, I sat. And waited. One small window opened onto the alley behind the building. One tree, still bare, stood there alone. I made myself turn back toward the man who'd brought me here. At the very least, he could offer me some of that overcooked brew.

"Coffee?" He knew that much.

"Thanks." He turned away from me as he left. Only then did I realize that I'd been hoping to catch his eye. I turned back to the tree. Fewer expectations. By the time Creighton returned, mug in hand, I had my cool back. I waited while he placed the thick ceramic mug in front of me and took his seat. When he did look at me, his eyes were strangely flat.

"What's your relationship with Llewellyn McMudge?" The wind in that alley couldn't have been much colder.

"Is that what's going on?" It didn't feel right, but I forced a laugh. I'd never made Jim Creighton for the jealous type. Then again, he was a good boy. Traditional at heart. "What do you think my 'relationship'"—I made air quotes with my fingers—"with him is?"

"Just answer the question, please." The last word was tacked on. It didn't help my mood.

"Casual." Anything else he was going to have to work for. As it was, he nodded. I'd confirmed something, and I didn't like how that made me feel. "What, Jim. Jealous?" He wasn't going to make me feel cheap.

"When did you see him last?" He saw how I was sitting, lips tight, and continued. "This is official, Pru. I need to know."

"You need to know?" I put all the sarcasm I could into my voice. I've learned a few things from Wallis. "And dare I ask why?"

"Answer the question, Pru." I swear these new buildings had no insulation. I could feel the frost from the window. "When was your last contact?"

He was getting snooty. He was also a cop, so I thought back. "A few weeks ago." That had been our weekend in Saratoga. It had been fun, and I'd been a little surprised when he hadn't called. Then again, I hadn't called him. Either way, Creighton didn't need to know the details.

"A few weeks." He weighed it in his head. "So you last saw him in February, early March?"

"Yeah, first week of March. First weekend." This was getting weird. "Why?"

"Have you talked to him since then? Texted, emailed, whatever?" He paused, as if to consider me. "Please don't get legalistic with me, Pru. I need to know if you have had any contact with McMudge."

"No." Then it hit me. "And I only called last night because of the cat."

I was baiting him, just a little. He didn't respond. "And just because of the cat?"

"Yeah, and you picked up." The awkwardness of that call came back to me. I was not happy in the role of supplicant. "I was thinking of trying him again."

"Pru, is that the truth?" He leaned forward on his desk. I couldn't avoid his eyes now. Those lovely baby blues were latched onto mine, searching for something I couldn't name. "Please, I need to know."

That phrase again. He was a good cop. I'd spent enough time with Tom to know the difference. I looked at him, the questions forming in my mind. He could pull my phone records, if he had to. Trace my movements. He didn't need me to answer, not really. He wanted me to, I realized, with a shudder that I tried to quell before it showed. Caught in those spotlights, I didn't mind so much as I would have, a few months back. Instead, I swallowed and put on a smile before answering.

"Cross my heart and hope to die, Jim." My voice held, steady and low. "I haven't spoken to Llewellyn—or seen him—since the beginning of the month."

He smiled at that. Tried not to, but I caught the twitch at the corner of his mouth. I liked that. He had misinterpreted my comment. I'd have taken a call from Llewellyn, sure. What the hell. A girl likes to know that she's appreciated.

"Really glad to hear it, Pru."

I could have purred. He wasn't done, though.

"Because, you see, we're investigating everyone who has been in contact with Llewellyn McMudge. Everyone who he had on speed dial. Everyone he'd been close to."

"There were so many?" We had never made any pretense of monogamy. Still. With a slight sting, I realized that maybe Wallis had been right. I should be getting out more. I looked out at the gray day, ready to go.

Creighton didn't answer. But the onetime beau sitting across from me wasn't done yet.

"You see, Llewellyn never came home last night. That's what I was dealing with when we spoke, Pru."

So Lew hadn't come home. The cops had had been at his house. This was getting interesting. "Have you talked to the widow?" I had an image of a king-size bed in that grand old house—or maybe in one of the nicer resorts. "She's the one who used him as a man Friday, or whatever you call it."

"I'm talking to you, Pru."

I ignored him. "You know, I wondered about that whole scene the other day. Her fussing about the cat. What was it you said—that you'd been asking her about the guns?"

"About the collection. The dueling pistol was a new acquisition, and a pricey piece from all we've heard. Not just because of the silver engraving on it, either. That bulb on the outside, the 'scent bottle' that held the fulminate for the charge? That was only in use for a few years, until percussion caps came in, so that helps date it to 1800 or so. Also makes it more or a rarity. Funny thing is, we're not sure where it came from. There's no rider for it on the Franklin's insurance. No record of a purchase—cash or charge—in their accounts. And, well, let's just say, we're looking into its provenance. But she's been tied up with funeral arrangements, which is another reason we were trying to contact McMudge. We know he could make himself useful in a variety of ways. Facilitate things. Maybe you knew that, too."

"Now, now." We were back on our customary footing. A little flirtatious, a little adversarial. "I wasn't involved in his business dealings, whatever they were. But why the fuss? He'll surface." He was probably in the Bahamas. Or Tahiti. I looked out at the cold and wished I'd pushed for Tahiti.

"That's not the problem, Pru. He already has." Creighton waited a beat. It worked. I looked up. "Your good buddy, Llewellyn McMudge? Early this morning, his car was found down an incline just this side of the New York border. His body was inside. We're waiting for the report from the state police but the preliminary looks a little odd."

I gasped. Whatever I'd been about to say—something about his womanizing. Something about the widow. It all died in my throat. "Lew? Dead?"

"Several hours, by the time we found him."

I'm no wimp, but suddenly the extra coffee seemed like a very bad idea. Lew was no gentleman. He was never going to be the love of my life. But he had been fun, with a taste for pleasure, for adventure. "But he was so alive." It sounded inane. I knew it, and I said it anyway.

And when Creighton smiled, I couldn't help it. I stood up to smack him.

"Whoa, whoa." He held up his hands in defense. The bastard was almost laughing. "You—you've got it wrong."

"I don't know what kind of screwed up, jealous—"

"Pru, please. I'm just relieved."

That shut me up. I sat back down and waited.

"You're shocked. Hurt even. I'm glad."

I had enough of my self-possession back to glare at him. Wallis would have been proud.

"I mean, I'm glad that you were shocked. That you are... dismayed. It suggests that you didn't know about McMudge, about Llewellyn's death before now."

"Suggests?" I was growling.

"Look, Pru. A man is dead. A second man, and this accident looks a little less freakish and a little more intentional. You knew both. I have to investigate."

I bit back anything I would have said. He saw it.

"This is good. This gives me hope."

I didn't care how cold it was outside. I didn't care what anyone else said. I slammed back the chair and was heading down the hall before he could stop me. I hadn't cried in front of a cop when I was a seventeen-year-old caught joyriding. I wasn't going to start now.

Chapter Eighteen

Momentum carried me out the door, but the shock—and the nasty slap of the cold—stopped me short of my car. Llewellyn dead? It didn't seem possible. The man I'd known had been so alive. A little sleazy, sure. What had Creighton said, he'd "facilitated" things? I didn't know what he meant, exactly, though I'd bet Tom did; I couldn't say it surprised me. Hey, it showed initiative. Appetite. All the things I couldn't make jibe with the idea of him dead. With the image now filling my head of his friend Donal as I last saw him: still, cold. Already assuming that fake waxy look that sets in so fast.

I shook my head, wrapped my jacket a little tighter. I hadn't taken the time to zip it, and now my hands were shaking too much to even try. My mother had died almost a year before. That had been different. She'd been so sick, so out of it, that she was gone weeks before the end. Times like that, death really is a release.

Maybe it was that she had never been as alive as Llewellyn. How could she have been, once her husband had taken off, leaving her with a precocious kid who turned into a wild teen? When half the town knew about her husband's drinking and gambling, and the other half had partied with him? She'd laced herself up tight, early on, to deal with the twin faces of Beauville. The more I took after my dad, the rougher things got at home. When I left for the city, we were both glad to have seen the last of each other. By the time I came back, she was already fading. And then she was gone. But alive? No, I'd never seen her gorging on oysters. Stupid with champagne or sex. Laughing as she drove too fast with the top down. Lew had done all those things. He had been alive. Had been.

I swallowed and looked around the parking lot. My old house was on the outskirts of town, and even my GTO wouldn't get me home with blurry vision. I blinked, getting ready to try, and heard a voice. Albert, standing close behind me.

"Pru, are you all right?"

It was too late to run. Too late to hide. But not too late to do a little damage control. A big gulp of frigid air helped me find my usual snark, or something near. "Depends who you talk to, Al." I arranged my face before turning around. "What gives?"

"I saw you come out. You looked, I don't know." Head down, his scruffy beard only a few shades darker than his down vest, Albert resembled some shaggy forest creature. Only bears don't gossip at Happy's each night. I needed to change his impression—and fast.

"Cop shop. What do you expect?" I managed a smile. If it was off kilter, so what? For all the portly man in front of me knew, I'd been interrogated under the lights. At this point, that seemed like it would be better for my reputation than the truth.

"You in trouble?" From anyone else, it might have been sympathy. I could see the gleam in Albert's little beady eye. "Bad?"

"Nothing I can't handle." A sudden thought hit me. "Why do you ask?" If he had info, I wanted it.

"Well, I saw you run out and I had the strangest thought that I should go after you. Maybe it was Frank using mind control or something." He chuckled. I didn't. I knew the ferret was smarter than his human.

"You brought Frank in today?" It was tempting, but in my current state, I wasn't sure I wanted to risk it.

"Yeah, wanna come play with my ferret?" Albert kind of wagged his head, letting me know that he was joking. As if.

I gave him the dead-eye stare. It was useful to keep him in his place. Besides, I really didn't want to have Frank freak out on me again. Losing Lew was bad enough, I didn't need to be rejected by a ferret.

"Sorry," Albert mumbled, beard back into his down. He really wasn't worth much, even as an adversary. And then it hit me—Frank probably really had manipulated the fat man into coming after me. That meant he had something to tell me. At the very least, it would be distracting.

"I'm just giving you shit." I reached out to pat his arm and thought better of it. "Shall we?"

<><><>

Glass entranceways are not as bad as glass houses. As I walked into the foyer that led to the shelter, however, I couldn't avoid looking over at the cop shop. No Creighton in sight. Just to be sure, I swung open the inner door with assurance, shoulders back. Immediately, I felt better. An animal shelter isn't usually a happy place, but it was my place. Besides, between seasons the town shelter tended to be empty. No tourists to complain about raccoons. The pets abandoned last summer had already been adopted—or destroyed—and Albert's congenital laziness kept him from working too hard at trapping or community outreach. The building was quiet. At least until a small sharp voice started up, close inside my head.

"And what are you going to do about all of this?"

"Excuse me?" The moment's quiet had lulled me into a false peace. Now I started.

"Huh? Sorry." Albert covered his mouth. He must have belched.

"Nevermind." I was grateful for the cover. "So, Frank's here?" I made my way over to Albert's desk. Sure enough, the voice was louder there.

Albert scuffled over ahead of me and opened a drawer. A small masked face popped up, its black eyes shining bright.

"Took you long enough." I shrugged. Albert was his responsibility.

"And the snow cat is yours!" I couldn't help staring. Luckily, in addition to his psychic communication, the little creature was

chattering away. Albert turned too, oblivious to our conversation. *"Hurt, angry...sound familiar?"*

"What do you think's got into him?" Albert was still rummaging in his desk, and I wondered what else he kept in there.

"Maybe he doesn't like being locked in a drawer when you go out." I pulled up a chair and sat down, gingerly extending my hand to the lean animal. Just as gingerly, he reached out a black forepaw. We both braced. Whatever had passed between us last time had been painful. "Hey, little guy." I kept my voice soft. The words were meaningless, it was the tone that carried the import. Frank knew me. He trusted me. I was telling him, with my body and my voice, that I was safe for him. That he could risk it. Only just then, Albert slammed a drawer open, breaking the tentative connection.

"Tasty!" Frank hopped sideways, a sign of excitement. *"Juicy."* I got an image of a bird's nest as he must see it: the eggs tempting and a little too large, like cuckoo's eggs. I didn't know if he was thinking of some treasure stashed away in the desk or if he'd actually gotten out into the early-spring woods.

"Do you want a treat?" I tried to keep my wording innocuous and reached out once more.

"Shiny leaf!" He'd moved on. I got a flash, just for a moment of green and glitter. *"Want more!"*

"Frank?" Was it gum? A bag of candy? I murmured, hoping Albert wouldn't interrupt again. "What's shiny? What's 'shiny leaf'?"

"'Scuse me?" A hand went up to the beard, and I realized Albert had been shoving something in his mouth.

"Shut up, Albert." Whatever he'd been eating now powdered his beard with orange. "And you really shouldn't be feeding your ferret Doritos."

"I wasn't." He held up a bag of Cheetos and smiled. His teeth, where they weren't orange, were gray. I turned away in disgust. Maybe I moved too fast, because Frank recoiled, too.

"The terror..." It was happening again. He was closing off. Panicked. I needed to try a different tack.

"What did you feel last time? What happened?" I focused on the ferret's sleek fur, trying to will my thoughts into some kind of concrete form. I breathed in his scent, slightly musky but so much fresher than Albert's. *"Can you tell me? Give that to me?"*

I felt something, the beginning of a thought. Frank was trying to convey something, to let me sense what he had experienced.

"So, you involved with the killer kitty?" Albert had come around the desk. Belly in my face almost as I looked up, startled. Jeans hiked up, hands thrust into his pockets, he was not a pretty sight.

"Albert." It must have been my tone. He backed away, but whatever link I had with his smaller, cleaner housemate was broken. I looked over at Frank. He was still on his hind feet, forepaws close to his chest. Neat. Adorable, even. But mute, to me anyway. Whatever he had tried to say to me was gone.

"Well, are you?" Now that he had retreated to a safe distance, Albert was braver.

"The cat in question is not a killer." A wave of fatigue washed over me. Would my species ever get it? "There was an accident, some kind of horrible accident. That doesn't mean—"

I caught myself in mid-sentence. Terror. That's not what Frank felt. It was what he had picked up—a sense memory, some kind of smell, from my hand. Wallis had said as much, telling me about Albert through such secondhand clues. It was all coming clear now. Someone had been holding the white cat. Pressing her leather paw pads into the trigger guard. Forcing her, terrified, onto the trigger. *"Let go! No, stop!"*

It made a lot more sense than the accident theory, no matter what the widow had said about Donal being alone. Plus, it would explain the cat's reluctance to be touched, even more than some tenderness in the foreleg. That tenderness might prove useful, though. I couldn't tell anyone what I heard—what I suspected. But if I could prove that the cat had been injured in a struggle...

"What? I'm sorry, okay?" Albert was standing there, looking confused. Not unusual for him, but not what I needed right now. I must have been staring. "I was just teasing because, you know, you have a history with animals."

"It's fine." I waved him away. I didn't need him to explain or to apologize. What I needed was a moment to think. The man had been alone, or so Creighton believed. Well, that didn't figure—not with what I suspected. He'd been on the phone. With his wife, Louise. Maybe she had heard something. And if she had, and hadn't come forward, maybe that meant she was involved.

I didn't relish the idea of broaching the widow. There was something strange about her. Something beyond the usual neediness of grief. There was that boy toy on her arm when I'd first met her. Her assistant. An odd accessory for the newly bereaved. Plus, she had been involved with Llewellyn. Perhaps she had even superseded me in his affections, such as they were. It stung, I'll admit it. But that wasn't what mattered now.

Could I win the white Persian's trust? Get her to talk to me? I had a sinking feeling about that one. Whether because of the shooting—I could no longer think of it as an accident—or the trauma, I had failed to make any sort of connection with the longhaired survivor. But I wasn't doing much better with Frank today either. I'd had a restful winter. Lots of sleep, some fun. Could it be that the strange ability was fading, leaving me alone in the world of humans?

"Uh, Pru? You okay? I really didn't mean anything." Albert was rocking back on his heels now. I considered summoning up a smile for him, but knew that would throw him worse than anything. So I scowled.

"I've got a lot on my plate, Al. Do you mind?"

In response, he slunk back around to his chair. "Fine." He sounded a little hurt and started muttering to himself as he reached for the ferret. "If you don't wanna talk..."

He never finished. Fast as a cobra striking, the ferret turned and bit him. Two drops of blood appeared in the soft pad of his palm as he pushed his chair back to the wall. "Jesus!" He waved his hand in the air, then decided to suck on it. Frank and I watched him, both fascinated and appalled.

"Guess you startled him." It was the best I could do. The ferret and I had been on the brink of something before Albert had interrupted. We'd both felt it. "You probably want to wash that. Put some kind of bandage on it." I didn't need Albert risking an infection and possibly taking it out on his pet. Besides, I wanted him out of the room.

"Yeah, I guess." He got up. Good. "Doesn't know which side his bread is buttered on."

We had a minute. Maybe two. I couldn't count on Albert's sense of hygiene keeping him any longer. Leaning forward, I focused on the ferret once more. Locking onto his shiny black eyes, I let the question form in my mind. *"What happened? What did you see?"* Only a few minutes before, we'd been close to a breakthrough. *"What did you feel?"*

Frank stared back, clasping his little paws tight in concentration. I strained to hear. Water running in the other room. Albert, still grumbling as he washed. And I felt my resentment growing. Albert, Beauville…humans in general. Go back to the city? Hell, I needed to get farther away.

A bead of sweat trickled down my back. Albert had started humming. Otherwise, the room was still. No familiar tickle in the back of my mind. No smart little voice. No Frank.

Then the bathroom door slammed open, and Albert was back, settling into his chair like an aggravated beanbag. "We're out of Band-aids," he said.

From Frank, I got nothing. I had to face the truth. My gift had started to fail.

Chapter Nineteen

"Sometimes there's just no talking to you." Wallis' voice dripped with sarcasm. I didn't care. I could have scooped her up in my arms and hugged her. That's how grateful I was to get home and to hear her—to really hear and understand—the cantankerous tabby's voice.

"Don't." Her tail underscored each word with a lash. *"Even. Try. It."*

"Okay, Wallis. I won't." I was ridiculously teary, more of a mess than I'd been since, well, since I'd fled the city.

"If you're losing it again, I'm not hanging around." She looked up at me. The difference in our size in no way diminished her authority. *"Got it?"*

"Got it." I knew that I had broken into a big, stupid grin. I couldn't help it. When I'd left the shelter, desperately trying to hang onto my cool in front of Albert, I'd been in a panic, or as close as I'd come in nearly a year. The birds. The Persian. Frank. The silences weren't aberrations; they were the norm. I was losing my gift, and the idea of being cut off—of not being able to eavesdrop on the non-human conversations around me—seemed horrible. Like suddenly going deaf.

"Be careful what you wish for, huh?" Wallis' tone brought me back to the here and now. I'd gotten myself home and she'd been waiting. Sitting on the kitchen table and eying me with that cool tabby look. For a moment, she'd sat in silence, then she'd said

it for the first time—"*Be careful what you wish for*"—and that's
when I had lost it. Sobbing and grinning like a fool.

"*Like a human.*" Wallis had settled onto her belly now, white
paws tucked neatly under her snowy breast. She looked resigned,
if not relaxed. That was a load off.

"So I can still do it." The horror hadn't worn off. "At least
with you."

Wallis' apple head tilted up, green eyes appraising. "*Do you
even hear yourself?*"

I did. I'm not the needy type. Never have been. You could
blame my father for taking off, or my mother for strong-arming
her way into survival. You could blame my temper. Lots of
folks—usually men—had. All I knew was that relying on others
has never been part of my makeup. Right now, though, I felt as
limp as an eviscerated mouse, and I looked to my cat for approval.

"*A mouse would be more interesting.*" She had turned away. "*A
mouse you can play with.*"

"Come on, Wallis." I took a deep breath. I had to get some
control back. "It was a shock. A big one."

"*As big as the first time? When you ran screaming out of the
house and into a hospital?*"

"That's not fair." She looked up at me, but I held her icy gaze.
Yes, when I had first heard her speak—first heard all the animals
around me speaking—it had been rough. Yes, I had fled. Packed
my old car up and run away. But I'd taken Wallis, taken good
care of us both. Hadn't I?

She didn't answer. Didn't even look at me. Didn't have to,
really. I knew as well as she what she'd say. Now that I had calmed
down, it hit me. For the past year, give or take a month, I'd
been cursing this so-called gift every day. It had come in handy.
Certainly helped me in my work. But it had driven me from the
city I'd loved, and made me feel even more of an outcast than
usual. Now, if it was gone, shouldn't I be happy?

"It's not that simple, Wallis." I was talking to myself as much
as to her. She flicked one velvet ear, the black tip accentuating the
movement. "It's not just that I've gotten used to it." I struggled

to put my feelings into words. "I mean, knowing what various animals are thinking makes helping them easier."

I thought of Growler, whose animosity toward his owner had led to a number of small rebellions. I didn't know if he could play her, like the poodle did her person. I couldn't help him, not without getting him away from his owner, Tracy Horlick. And she was the one who paid my bills. For a moment, I wondered if the thought of the little bichon had been my own, or if Wallis had tossed it to me as a rebuttal.

"I don't have to stoop to that." The other ear twitched. *"To… dog tricks."*

"I know. Sorry." It had been my own guilty conscience. Though I could counter with the case of the puppy at the shelter. If I had made myself understood then the chances of the young dog finding a permanent and happy home were greater. Weren't they?

Silence. I was fooling myself. I had become used to hearing what the animals around me said. In truth, I found it more interesting than most of the human conversation in this town.

"Of course." A low purr was starting deep in Wallis' chest. The echo of it rumbled through her voice. *"We're the most intelligent creatures here."*

"Then why couldn't I hear Frank today?" The panic began to creep back, closing up my throat even as I formed the words. "I could, and then I couldn't. It was like we were disconnected. And he was trying, I could see that."

"Weasel. She wants to talk to a weasel." Wallis was getting sleepy. That was always a hazard when I needed to talk. As obligate carnivores, cats slept seventy to eighty percent of the time, anyway. Now in her thirteenth year, Wallis had made an art of the nap.

"And what about the Persian? I'd been assuming that she didn't want to talk to me. But maybe she's trying, and I can't hear her."

Wallis shuffled a little, making herself more comfortable as she drifted off. "If it's me, Wallis, what do I do?"

She snorted ever so slightly. Another thought struck me. "Could it have to do with her hearing? Maybe if she can't hear, she can't speak?"

"Cats talk. All cats can." I was losing her. Already her voice was faint, the rhythmic sway of the purr lulling her into sleep. *"And you can hear them, if you get your mind straight, Pru. You know you can. But Pru?"* She was fading now, almost gone. *"Cats can't shoot."*

Chapter Twenty

I woke with a dry mouth and a sense of dread I couldn't place at first. I was in my bed, warm and safe. Wallis had her back toward me, but there was nothing unusual in that. Then it all came rushing back. Two men, both of whom I'd liked—one of whom I'd been close to, after my fashion—had died within the last three days. The second death, not twenty-four hours ago, was already being considered suspicious. The first, as I well knew, was not what it had seemed, either. Three days...

"I've got to talk to that Persian." I sat up, determination doing the job that caffeine usually would. "I've got to make her see, make her open up to me."

"And you're going to do that...how?" Wallis didn't even turn. I got the thought as she ran one white-mittened paw over her ear. Suddenly, my tongue felt even furrier, and I slumped back.

"I wish you wouldn't do that." Nobody brings you back to earth like your cat.

"What? Multitask?" Wallis looked over her shoulder at me, round eyes innocent and wide. *"Or keep myself looking sleek and sexy?"*

"Wallis!" I was in no mood. "You're spayed."

"And your goal is always to reproduce?"

I pulled myself out of bed. "I'm not having this conversation." As I headed toward the shower, I was sure I heard her chuckle.

The Persian. She was the key, and Wallis had said that I could get through to her—if I wanted to. If she wanted was more like it. The more I thought about it, the more I became convinced that the white cat had been deliberately blocking me. The question was: how?

The hot water helped, and coffee finished the process, letting me think rather than simply react. Fluffy, if that really was her name, knew more than she was telling, but I couldn't keep throwing myself at her. I had to find a way in. With Frank, it might have been easy. Something shiny. Something to eat. This cat, though. I didn't think she wanted anything. From me, anyway. From her former owner? From his widow? It was worth a shot. Somehow, I had to let her know that I was on her side. One of the good guys.

For that matter, I had to make sure Creighton knew it too. My brief show of grief might have won me some time, but he was too astute an investigator to let go until he followed up on the loose ends. One person who had known both victims? Hey, even I'd be curious.

Creighton had mentioned a funeral, and I'd been too out of it to push for more. No matter. Opening my laptop, I typed in a few commands. A few clicks, and I had what I needed: Donal Franklin's death notice. Devoted husband, loyal friend. There wasn't much about his past, how he'd come into his money. But then, he'd been fifty-six, too young by any means to be in this particular column. A faithful supporter of the Olde Tyndale Country Club and regular at the Tynedale Classic. Those of us not in the club were obviously out of luck: the little item also said that services would be private.

I dressed and poured the rest of the coffee into my travel mug. Halfway out the door, the other connection hit me. Mack. He'd known Lew. I recalled them greeting each other at the club that night, before he'd gone off after larger—or more gullible—prey. Had he known Donal? I didn't recall them talking, but it seemed likely. Mack had had some scheme. He always had some scheme. He'd been trolling for backers among the crowd that night, and Donal was a big fish. At any rate, he sure seemed to know pretty little Robin Gensler fairly well. That might be work, or it might be pleasure. For Mack, the lines sometimes crossed. Either could be motive if he'd gotten in over his head. Money, however, that would be what sealed the deal.

"Oh, Mack." As I drove, I thought of my former beau. Now that I knew him better, I could see that he was fraying on the edges. He'd not had a good break in a while, not since his old buddy and business partner—the computer whiz Charles Harris—had cut him off, and then sealed the deal by dying. The strain was showing around Mack's eyes, his lean body already a little thinner. If Lew had been mixed up in something, Mack might be, too. Could Mack have—? No, I didn't see him as a killer. That didn't mean he wasn't involved. Deeply involved. Mack was desperate. How far he would go for a score I didn't dare guess.

Propping the mug between my knees, I reached for my phone. One eye on the road, I started to key in Mack's number when a flash and then a shadow caused me to swerve.

"Damn!" That coffee held its heat, and I slammed on the brakes as steaming liquid seared my thighs. Cursing my old car and its inadequate cup holders, I dropped the phone and groped instead for the fast-food napkins I knew I'd left in the backseat. What had startled me? A quick scan of the sky didn't show anything out of the ordinary. No wheeling raptors, nothing larger than a lost and lonely gull, doubtless searching for the town dump. Then I saw him: a young male redtail hawk, regal and stern. He'd grabbed something gray—mourning dove, most likely—and now perched on a lone streetlight. His rounded head turned as I stared up at him. I was no threat. Maybe he wanted to see if I was potential prey. Then he dipped his curved beak to the mass of gray feathers and pulled. His beak came up red, the flesh already opened by those merciless talons. This was a hunter, and as I watched him begin to take his prey apart, I realized what had stopped me. Despite my brief attempt to set the tone with Creighton, I'd been played all along—jerked around between Tom and Mack and, yes, even Jim. It was time for me to focus. I had skills they didn't know about. And not all of them involved talking to animals.

Chapter Twenty-one

"Mack? It's me. Call me back." I'd be damned if I'd be cowed by our past—or by my former fling's new alliance. It was early, too early for him to be awake, but I didn't care. Something about the day was already off, and I wanted to find out what was up. Besides, the man still owed me for leaving me at that dance. Mack always had a problem paying his debts, however. So it was with great surprise that I heard my cell ring not five minutes later. The ring sounded particularly shrill and I swerved slightly before catching myself. That wasn't like me, and I cursed as I reached for the phone. The sun, that had to be it. I'd just turned east onto Route 2 and the sun was in my eyes.

"Mack?"

A chuckle on the other end of the line pointed out my mistake.

"Tom." A beginner's error.

"So, who's this Mack who you're waiting for?"

"A source." I could almost hear his scarred grin getting wider. "Are you still trolling for clients?"

"Not anymore." I waited. I could outwait Tom. The road sped by, empty and lifeless. "I never did get to talk to your friend Llewellyn."

So he'd heard. But it wasn't my place to give him any more information.

"You could have warned me, you know." He sounded peevish.

"Oh?" This was just too good, and for a moment I found myself enjoying the note of discomfort in his voice.

"Your local boy scout wants to speak to me. Seems he has some idea that I had business dealings with the late Mr. McMudge."

"And, you didn't?" A slight shadow, another redtail, crossed the road. The bright sun was giving me a headache, but I couldn't hold the old phone and reach for my sunshade at the same time. "Isn't that what you had asked me about, Tom?"

"I'd wanted an introduction, Pru. I've got no use for a stiff."

I winced. The sun. Tom. I was dying to know more—to find out what Lew had been mixed up in, and why Tom was tracking him. I couldn't ask outright. Not Tom. "You never said why you were looking for him, Tom. Not really." Wrong tack: he could hold a silence as long as I could. The pain had started throbbing, a small hammer and anvil behind my left ear. Holding the steering wheel with my knee, I pulled the shade down. "Look. Can we meet again?"

Another chuckle. "Sure, Pru. Let's say tonight? What's that bar called—Happy's?" Someone had been telling him about our little town. Telling him or showing him.

I didn't care which. I just needed to get off the phone and off the road. "Sure, Tom. See you there." I hung up. If he needed directions or wanted more of a date, he could call back. Then it hit me. He had called me, but I'd been the one who'd asked all the questions. All he had done was make that one comment about Llewellyn. He had wanted to find out what I knew. Whether I knew that Lew was dead. I didn't get how Tom was involved, but I'd known him well enough at one point to understand what had just happened. He was on a case, official or not. And I was in his sites.

Chapter Twenty-two

My headache didn't improve, despite a refill of high-octane truck-stop joe, so I'd chased it with a ninety-nine cent pack of aspirin, the tablets crumbled in the plastic packet. That didn't help my mood, nor did the slow once over I got from the counter's only customer—a grizzled cowboy type with hair a little too long for the times. A year ago, I'd have considered him. Endorphins can do wonders for pain relief. But I had responsibilities now. Which didn't help my mood either.

I was on my way to get some answers, by stealth if I had to. Which was why I was dressed in more or less formal clothes—black jeans, a black shift under my parka—as I cruised down the road back toward the Franklin house. I'd already decided that I'd blame Creighton if the widow threw a nutty on me. He'd been the one to hand the cat over to me, and with Lew out of the picture, it seemed reasonable that I'd go straight to the source with any questions. I didn't imagine the widow would want to speak with me. She'd made her dislike for me—as well for the white cat her husband appeared to have cherished—clear. Still, I needed info. I needed at least to find a way into the sleek feline's fur-lined skull. Louse Franklin was my best bet.

I'm not a total fool. On the seat beside me was a crumb cake, courtesy of Beauville's best bakery. There'd been nothing at the truck stop that would've passed muster. Between the cake and my attire, I intended to look like someone making a sympathy call. Cover can be useful when you're on the prowl.

I didn't see any cars parked in the long semi-circular drive as I pulled up to the big house. I rang the doorbell anyway. Behind the throbbing of my headache was the fear that the widow would have fled—gone to Boca to recover. Or Brazil. Still, when showing up unannounced, it makes sense to ring the bell before breaking in.

"Oh, good morning." I'd expected the handsome young escort from the shelter to answer the door. A maid, a relative. Anyone but Louise Franklin herself, looking a lot softer than the harpy I'd met the day before. Dressed in wool pants and a silver-gray sweater that matched her eyes, the new widow appeared younger than I remembered. I swallowed the knot of guilt that rose up in my throat.

"I'm sorry to come by so early." I started talking before she could close the door. Seeing her like this, my suspicions felt out of place. Even cruel. "I wanted to apologize for the way I must have sounded. And, well, to bring you something in your time of mourning." I held out the crumb cake and she looked down at the white bakery box as if it were an alien. Or a cat. "I'm an early riser. Maybe I misjudged the time."

It was a lie, but the smile I added must have made it fly. Louise Franklin looked up as if seeing me for the first time, and I was struck again by the unexpected lightness of her eyes. "I'm sorry. Please, come in. We were—I was having tea."

She turned and I followed her down a hall. We passed a closed door, her husband's study, and she gestured me into a sitting room, all done in pale green. "Please, have a seat."

I took a few steps into the room, but stayed standing as she walked away. *We*, she had said. Had she given the butler the day off? Was there another guest—perhaps one who had stayed overnight? Or was she simply talking from force of habit?

"May I help with anything?" I called down the hall.

"No, no. Make yourself comfortable," the voice came back. I did just that, turning over cards on the chinoiserie end table until I found what I wanted: a note from the funeral director. The services were scheduled for tomorrow: Saturday. Someone from the club had agreed to give the eulogy. I made note of the time and the place—graveside services at the Tynedale Memorial Park, of course—and managed to make it to the window as my hostess came back in with a pretty little cup on its saucer and a matching plate that held several slices of the cake.

"Do you take cream?" She didn't seem to find it odd that I was admiring her view, and poured from a pot that must have been steeping a while. I shook my head, trying to rally my thoughts. A private graveside service. Well, I'd be there, somehow, if just to see who else showed up. But I was having misgivings. The woman who handed a plate to me seemed as refined and gentle as, well, a housecat. "People have been so kind."

That did it. I needed to be about my business—or leave this woman in peace. "Mrs. Franklin, Louise?" She sipped at her tea, which looked to contain more milk than tea. "I assume you've heard about Llewellyn?"

A slight wince. Had Llewellyn been more than a friend? He did like the ladies. I couldn't see a way to ask, so I stuck with my plan.

"Well, I was wondering because, you know, you had told me I should go through him in regards to your cat." What had she called the Persian? "In regards to Fluffy."

She looked up. Blinked, her eyes growing larger and more liquid.

"Yes, I did. He was good at—" She bit her lip. I wondered what I would do if she started crying. "He had been a great help as I settle things."

A cat wasn't a thing, I wanted to tell her. I stopped myself. Took a breath. I needed information, and lecturing her wasn't the way to get it.

"I know you said that you wanted to put the cat on the market. But I need to clear things up." Her fingers grew white where they gripped the teacup. I was onto something. "First of all, the papers. They're in your name." I didn't mention what Robin had said. "Not your husband's." Nothing. "You bought that cat."

"Of course, did I say otherwise?" She put the teacup down. "That day—those first few days. Yes, the cat was a gift for my husband. He loved animals."

"My wife wants me to try new things." Donal's voice echoed in my mind. I was missing something. "You don't?"

A little sniff as she turned to refill her pot. "Would you expect me too? After…" By the time she lifted her cup again, she had regained her poise.

I needed to rattle it. "Robin Gensler seems to like the cat."

"Robin Gensler—" she bit down on the name before it could bite back. "Robin is a very capable young woman who helped me with my affairs. That was all."

I hadn't said anything to the contrary. This was getting interesting. "Are you sure?"

It was risky. Crossing a line, and I waited for the explosion.

"Of course, I'm sure." It didn't come. "Robin Gensler is a young woman of exemplary character."

"But you wouldn't consider releasing the cat to her?" I didn't know what was going on here. I didn't get a chance to find out.

"No, definitely not." The widow shook her head and reached for the teacup. "I want that cat sold. Haven't I made that clear?"

"Yeah, you said," I retreated, "I would have to do some work with her."

"That's fine." That testiness had traveled to her voice now, matching a new tightness around her lips.

"There's a question of how to proceed." An alarm bell began ringing somewhere behind the low throb. "I'd like to bring the cat back here, at least temporarily."

"Out of the question." She cut me off, slashing the air with her hands. I couldn't really say I blamed her. "I will *not* have that animal in my house. It or—or—that gun."

I nodded. I figured the pistol would still be in police custody, but at some point…"Had your husband been a collector?" I wanted to know. I also wanted to give her a chance to cool off.

It didn't work. "No, never." Her mouth was set now, showing her age. "He was interested, sure. He liked pretty things. Pretty *rare* things. But I wouldn't—not in my house."

No question about the pronoun now. No question of exploring new interests, either, for that matter. I was getting a sense of this woman. She wasn't ill, no matter what Mrs. Gensler had been told. Not unless being spoiled and rich was a communicable disease. But no matter what she'd encouraged her husband to try when he was alive, now she was scared—scared and trying to cover it up—and her frightened outburst had given me an opening.

"So, did Mr. McMudge find it for him?" I was doing my damnedest to avoid the word "procure."

That was what the widow heard though. "He may have," she said, her voice as tight as if she had bitten into a lemon. "It was one of his…contacts. All I know is it was a gift. I was spending the week. I always get ready for spring at Canyon Ridge. When I came back, it was here. He said it was a *gift.*"

She might as well have called it a curse. Considering what happened, I could see why. "From Mr. McMudge?"

She shook her head once, but didn't speak. Robin, I thought. A princely present in exchange for the ring? Or had the young woman come into money of her own somehow and wanted to be generous? I remembered what Mrs. Gensler had told me about Louise taking the young woman in and wondered how far her generosity had extended.

I'd need more leverage before I could pursue that avenue. "I should let you be, Mrs. Franklin. And I should get back to your—to Fluffy." I looked around. The room was elegantly appointed, but spare. "It would help if I could have something that would be familiar to her. A toy, maybe. Or a blanket she slept on."

She looked away. In profile, I expected to see her tears. Instead, I saw the muscles work in her jaw. "There's nothing. I threw it all away. That *animal.* " She said it like it was a bad thing. "I want it groomed to sell. That's why I asked Mr. McMudge to deal with it."

"I'm sure he would have." I was trying to be sympathetic, really I was. But that tone…"He was very good at being useful. Especially to women."

"Are you implying—?" The tears were gone now. "How dare you? Mr. McMudge was not a *friend*. He was a valued associate of my husband's, and in polite society—"

I didn't need the rest of it. Maybe I'd been projecting. Maybe I'd read the whole Robin situation wrong. What I did know was that I had to backtrack now, and fast. "I'm sorry, Mrs. Franklin. I simply meant that he might have gone the extra yard to help out Fluffy. Maybe he had something that belonged to the cat? A cushion or a blanket?" I tried to picture what had been in that study. All I could see was an ornate gun, the silverwork scrolling up the barrel. "Maybe something of your husband's?"

"For the cat?" The anger was cooling to something nastier, and the way she put her cup down made me worry about the delicate china. "Can't you just give it some drugs or something?"

"It's not the same, Mrs. Franklin."

"You're the expert." She was gathering herself together, her voice once again composed. "I'm sure you'll find a way."

It was futile. Any shot I'd had, I'd blown with that comment about Llewellyn, and I was being dismissed. She stood, and I followed her as she walked, much more briskly this time, down the hall. I managed to murmur something that was intended as condolences. I doubt she heard me. When she closed the door, she didn't quite slam it. She was too well bred for that. However, she had given me an idea. A Persian needed to be groomed, and an expensive pet usually had at least a few toys. If she had really thrown everything away, I bet I could find something in the trash. Something that would remind the cat of its home—and maybe unlock some memories.

I was in luck. The early morning sun cast enough shadows for me to feel inconspicuous as I made my way around the side of the house. This far out of town, residents either hauled their own trash or hired a private contractor. While I didn't imagine either of the Franklins at the county dump, I was pretty sure they'd have a regular pickup, and the way things had been going for me, I half expected to be skunked. If I'd been more lucky, the oversized Rubbermaids I found behind an old carriage house wouldn't have contained the remains of last night's dinner: two nice-sized T-bones, potato skins, and something that smelled like rum cake. Of course, that could have been the two bottles of Burgundy scenting the remains. Didn't this woman know anything about recycling?

The amount of food, more than the wine, gave me pause. Louise Franklin didn't look like a meat and potatoes type, and that kind of spread was awfully fancy for drop-in guests. Still, unless I took bite prints off those bones I didn't see what I could do with the information. Maybe she'd ordered up her husband's favorite to make herself feel better. Maybe Thursday night was steak night. The rich are different from you and me.

I thought of two dogs I knew who would have made quick work of the cold meat, congealed fat and all. It was the waste, as well as the slick feel of that cold fat that turned my stomach. And this was a woman who didn't want to give a cat away to a good home. I abandoned that bag with disgust, wiping my hands on the damp ground.

As soon as I opened the next one, I realized my mistake. My headache must have distracted me from the obvious. Nothing from the study would have been put with the kitchen trash. Not in a house that big. Papers. An ashtray—crystal, by the look of it—the corner broken off. I wiped my hands on my jeans and pulled the bag out of the barrel. That chipped crystal looked dangerous, and I decided to empty the bag onto the ground. I'd clean up after myself. Maybe.

And maybe I was fated to be disappointed. The papers were blank, except for some smudges, like someone had been blotting a pen. The ashtray could have been knocked to the floor. I was still squatting, surveying the mess I'd made when I heard the footsteps.

"Well, well, well." I whirled around, trying to think of some reason for the mess around me. I didn't have to: it was Mack.

"Well yourself." I stood and faced him as he stepped out of the morning shadows. "What brings you to this neck of the woods?"

"An errand for a lady." He held out his hand. In it, he held a wide wire brush, the kind used on longhair cats.

I reached for it, but he drew his hand back. "Not so fast." His lean face split open in a grin. "But thanks for confirming its value."

"What do you mean? It's a grooming brush." A little late for nonchalance, and we both knew it. He looked at the ground, where trash was spread around me. He didn't have to say anything. "So, I wanted it. I'm working with the cat, remember? And if Mrs. Franklin won't let me bring the animal back into the house…"

"You wanted to bring it something that smelled like home?"

"Something like that." He nodded, the smile growing wider, and I thought of Robin. Her hand on his arm, and the way he'd jumped to get the door for her. "You were sent to get the cat's toys, too, right?" Another nod. He could afford to be generous, he had the brush. "So she thinks she's going to get the cat after all?"

He shrugged. "I don't try to figure them out. I just do what I'm told or I don't get paid."

I considered him coolly. As hard up as he might be, I didn't make Mack for a gigolo. In truth, he was a little long in the tooth and definitely an acquired taste.

"Wait, you don't think—" He started laughing. "I'm doing errands for her, Pru. Errands."

"Ah ha." The thought of Mack as a hired hand made me a little sad. Not enough to quench my curiosity, though. "And she has you dumpster diving?"

"My current employer has had a bit of a falling out with the recently bereaved. If I can facilitate things—"

I didn't want to hear it. I could see how this domestic drama had played out, and I was in no mood to replay this little triangle. "Mack, I need that brush. I'll give it back."

He looked doubtful.

"I could pay for it, too." I looked around. This was not a place to linger.

"I don't want your money, Pru. Not that you have much anyway. Of course, if you want to barter..."

"Mack." I liked his dirty mind. I did. Right now, however, my head was throbbing and I needed to be on my way. "Come on. If she really wants the cat, this will help us both. She's not going to get even a chance at her until Doc Sharpe releases her. And he's not going to release her while she's freaked and aggressive. Besides," I was playing my last card, "if I can get the cat calmed down, I'll recommend Robin as her caretaker. At least to foster her, get her socialized again. Then, maybe when the widow Franklin comes to her senses, she'll be in the best position to adopt."

He mulled this over. If Robin had been Donal Franklin's lover, especially if Robin had given him the gun that killed him, I didn't see Louise Franklin ever giving her the time of day. Still, the widow seemed determined to be polite to the younger woman. Was that all an act? I didn't know—and Mack didn't either, and so I watched him, looking for something that didn't fit. Something that would tell me he was lying.

I didn't see it. "Fair enough, Pru." He handed the brush over. "But you owe me. And I'm going to collect."

"You like steak dinners?" It was a stab in the dark, but he turned with a start. "With mashed potatoes and a good Burgundy?"

"Is that an invite?" The smile was back, wolfish and hungry, but I laughed. He'd been taken by surprise by my words. I spared a glance back at the kitchen trash, but he was watching me too closely. I had to get out of there. Instead, I knelt to shovel the loose papers back into their bag. He reached for the broken ashtray, hefting it in his hand before placing it in the opened sack. I'd felt the weight of it and from the look on his face I knew he'd had the same thought. If Donal Franklin had died of anything other than a freak gunshot, we'd both have been tampering with evidence.

Chapter Twenty-three

I needed to maintain my cool, and the headache didn't help as I walked up to Tracy Horlick's door about twenty minutes later. I'd wanted to go straight to the shelter, to see how the Persian reacted to her old brush. But I was late for Growler's appointment, and the old shrew was exactly the type to take notice of such things.

"Someone got up on the wrong side of the bed." She was waiting at the door, and exhaled a cloud of smoke, stale in the morning air. "Someone must have been out late last night."

"I'm sure someone was, Mrs. Horlick." I forced the sides of my mouth up in what I hoped looked like a grin. "Not me. I'm sorry for the delay." I don't like to apologize—gives people an edge—but I'd seen the look in her eye and decided to give her a small victory. "I had an emergency situation." It was close enough to the truth.

"That cat?" She wasn't prescient. She couldn't be. "Let me guess. Someone left another loaded gun around."

My face was getting stiff. "Not quite. Is Grow—I mean, Bitsy ready for his walk?"

Her eyes narrowed, more from suspicion than smoke, I guessed. I had to watch it. But the hostility of the other day was gone. Sacrificed, I assumed, to old Horlick's overwhelming hunger for gossip. "Pru Marlowe, you're up to something," she said. I was right. "Is it that widow—?"

Her speculations were interrupted, first by a short yelp and then a howl that sounded too large for such a little creature. I didn't get any intent from it, not directly. I didn't need to. Growler—Bitsy—was sick of waiting, and as his person turned— that howl was disconcerting—I saw my opportunity and grabbed the little dog's leash from its hook.

"Someone's got to go!" Trying to keep my smile in place, I leaned past the ashy harridan. "Come on, Bitsy. Bitsy?"

A low whine and the scraping of claws against wood let me know why the bichon hadn't already come bounding. With an audible sigh, Tracy Horlick turned and reached for a door. Growler came barreling out like a fluffy white cannonball, and I was grateful enough to follow him down the path.

"Hey, Growler, wait up." I caught up to the powderpuff as he stopped to sniff a curbside oak. He didn't respond as I snapped the lead onto his collar. Knowing what kind of person he lived with, I didn't blame him.

We walked a bit, and I let him set the pace. I confess, I was feeling a bit iffy about trying anything. My recent failures had left me more disheartened than I'd wanted to admit, even after my talk with Wallis. But once we'd gone two blocks and Growler had finished marking the usual spots, I realized I might as well make use of the little fellow's sensitive nose.

"Growler, would you do something for me?"

He was sniffing the trunk of a maple. Usually, I'd be getting images of what he smelled—particular dogs, even some memories of other animals in action. Now, my mind was blank. I told myself it was because the tree was a dead end, but the little dog's interest put the lie to that.

"Growler?" He looked up and just for a second, I got a flash of fur. Golden, black. A German shepherd.

"Rolf." It didn't sound like the bichon's bark, so I assumed he was naming the object of his interest.

"Rolf." I squatted and waited, unwilling to break the fragile connection. The little nose worked furiously and I remembered the steak bone. I held out my hand, hoping it still held some tang of grease. When he came up to sniff, I reached back and into my bag.

"Growler, I need help." I had no idea what my words sounded like, or if the idea of a plea translated. Still it only seemed sensible to be polite. "If you could, please, would you sniff this and tell me what you get from it?"

I pulled out the brush, and the little dog started back. Damn, Tracy Horlick. I should have moved more slowly, perhaps even introduced the brush by trying to picture it in my mind. That move, though—she'd hit this dog and more than once.

"I'm sorry, Growler. Truly." He held still, not retreating but not coming forward either. "Please?"

I laid the brush on the ground and he advanced two tentative steps, sidling up to it with a wary eye. For a moment I doubted the wisdom of my actions. I'd thought the little dog had been drained dry, but if he lifted his leg on it, no other animal would be able to get any other sent. Wallis certainly wouldn't try.

It was caution, rather than distaste that governed the little dog's approach. Once he'd seen that it was still—and that no human hand was reaching for it, he sniffed quickly. *"Cat!"*

If a thought could express distaste, this one did. I got a flash of something large and mean, stupid but all too fast. The word "cat" had come into my mind, but Growler's image of the feline ideal and mine were worlds apart.

He looked up at me as if I'd pulled a dirty trick on him.

"Yes, I know." I paused, unsure how to proceed. "I'm sorry. But—humans? People? Anything else?"

The bichon wrinkled the white fur above his button nose. For just a moment, he resembled his owner, albeit a much more attractive version. But then he leaned in again and that black button nose wiggled as it did its work.

"Nasty female." I could have laughed, but didn't want to break the little dog's train of thought. Besides, I had startled him.

"Nasty bites." He'd picked up on my thought and was correcting me. Maybe he had caught the scent of the poodle from my hand. I paused and let my last encounter with Lucy play

through my head: from her little dance to her final words for her canine colleague. I tried to keep my thoughts out of it—I'm no good at kissing up to bullies. Then again, nobody's tried to put a collar on me.

Growler seemed to take it in, stopping to sit and scratch one ear in what seemed an unusually contemplative manner. "Think it might work?" I said, finally.

"*Huh,*" he chuffed. The bichon might look like a toy, but he was a proud little animal, and I silently apologized. Better to move on to the matter at hand, I decided, and mentally pictured the cat. Nasty…bites…I could well believe that Growler would view the cat's fear-induced aggression as hostility. I had the wounds to prove it.

"*No!*" The retort sounded as loud and sharp as the bichon's bark. "*No!*"

I looked up. Those button eyes were staring into mine, but whatever they were trying to say, I couldn't get it.

"The cat isn't bad? The cat doesn't bite? What, Growler?" I was lobbing too many questions at the dog. I knew that. This kind of communication is simpler—it's all about the image. A question, a confirmation. Growler wasn't Wallis, and in my frustration, I was asking too much. I tried to calm down. "Sorry, Growler. What do you mean?"

Nothing.

"What is 'no'?" I pictured the cat again, asleep in her cage. Nothing. I tried to remember when she had slashed at me: angry cat could be an entirely different concept than sleeping cat to the little dog. Still nothing. So I let my mind wander, trying to visualize the white Persian in the arms of Donal Franklin. His hands, as I recalled, were large and calloused for a rich man. Working hands, he'd called them apologetically, when he'd taken mine to lead me to the dance floor. The thought made me choke up, just a little, and I sat back on the ground, remembering our one dance. He'd been a kind man. No wonder his women were fighting over him. Over the one creature he must have loved without reserve, without complications. Over his cat.

"*Stupid bitch.*" I heard Growler clearly enough, but he had turned from me. "*Females. Always in heat.*" And no matter how I asked, he refused to say anything more.

Chapter Twenty-four

I was a little concerned that Growler's scent would linger on the brush. Still, it had seemed a worthwhile experiment, and I tried to put it out of my mind as I made my way over to the shelter. Something had to get through to that Persian, and grooming was such a basic, intimate experience that I was hopeful.

I took out the brush. It may as well have been a stick of dynamite.

"Yow-ow-ow." The caterwaul brought Doc Sharpe running from down the hall. "Yow!" Even Pammy stuck her head in. I had knocked the brush off the examining table by then, and was using both hands to restrain the flailing, spitting cat. "Ow-wow!"

"Pru?" Doc Sharpe was nothing if not reserved.

"Cage, please?" He stepped in front of me to open the mesh door. I hefted the solid little animal and hurried her into the enclosure. High on the sterile white wall, a clock ticked. Not ten minutes had passed since I'd first come in with such high hopes. The howling diminished by a few decibels.

"Thanks." I leaned back against the metal table, taking a moment to catch my breath. Sharpe looked at me. He deserved an explanation, but I was still trying to figure out what had gone wrong. It was midafternoon by the time I'd gotten to the shelter. I'd made my normal rounds, but that was it. No rabid raccoons. No wildcats had left their scent on me. And I'd kept the brush in my car, isolated and, I figured, clean. "That was—I didn't expect that."

He waited. Behind me, leaning against the door frame, Pammy popped her gum.

"We need to resocialize this animal." I pushed my hair back from my forehead and realized I'd been sweating. "So I brought in her brush."

This was standard procedure. I was lucky. Everything I'd done today could have fallen under classic behavior modification. Everything except looting through the widow's trash, that is. I started talking more quickly, before Doc Sharpe would begin to wonder where I'd gotten the brush.

"The theory," I turned toward Pammy as if to explain, "is that an animal forgets its training, forgets how to interact with humans, after it has had a shock. And that Persian, well, she certainly has been through the mill. So I got her brush, which should smell familiar and started to groom her." I had also tried to connect with her, conjuring up images of the big, old house and the well-groomed woman I'd had tea with only hours before. I'd avoided thinking of her anger, or how I had provoked it. At least, I'd thought I had. The resulting chaos had caught me by surprise, and I rubbed a sore spot on my forearm—the cat had knocked the brush back so hard it was going to leave a bruise.

"In this case," I finished my tutorial, "the cat may not yet be ready to be reintroduced into the family."

"Or the animal may be traumatized beyond recovery." Sharpe had seen me rub my arm. "Sometimes an animal cannot be salvaged."

Pammy made a small noise. I was silent, but aghast. "Doc, it hasn't been that long."

He looked at me, his face set, and then up at the clock. "We are not a boarding service, and the original owner does not want this animal back in this condition."

"But this could have been my fault." I'd pushed too hard. Clearly, the house was the sore point—that's where the animal had been traumatized by noise. By shock. By the death of a beloved owner. I should have eased into it, begun by placing the brush on a nearby table or in another cage.

"You tried to groom the animal. That's as basic as it gets." He turned from me—and from the Persian's cage—and started to walk from the room. I needed to stop him, to intercede, but I didn't know how. As far as he was concerned, I had gone by the book.

"Her foreleg." I was scrambling. "I think I may have put pressure on the sore leg." As if in sympathy, I found myself touching my own arm. Already, the spot felt warm and I could feel the injured flesh beginning to swell. Doc Sharpe saw it, too, and narrowed his eyes in thought.

"That was careless of you." I could see him weigh my words. I knew he doubted me. "If you really did that." I held my breath. Even Pammy, for once, was silent. The clock on the wall ticked, and the Persian whined, low and insistent.

"Doc." I had nothing else to say. "Please."

He shook his head. "It's not like you to be sentimental, Pru. Sometimes we have to be professional." He looked up at the clock again, as if measuring the hours. I knew he could notify Louise Franklin that afternoon. Tell her the cat was unsalvageable, and that meant that he wouldn't even consider putting her up for adoption. Assuming the widow didn't make other arrangements, the cat could be euthanized in forty-eight hours. I thought of her words. Of how she considered her late husband's pet only for its commercial value. Once that was gone, there would be no hope for the poor creature.

"It's Friday," he said finally. "Let's give it till Monday. That should give everyone a chance to settle down." Give me a chance to get used to it, he meant. I nodded. I needed to do something and fast. "Pammy?"

He ushered her from the room, leaving me alone with the scared animal. "Kitty, don't you know time is running out? You've got to work with me here."

A low growl, that was all I got. Mentally, as I tried to reach out, all was black. This cat was not going to help herself, and I couldn't. Was there anyone else?

Robin Gensler—she wanted the cat. I didn't know what her involvement was, or how she figured into the Franklin marriage. At this point, I didn't care. I dialed her number.

"Robin? It's Pru Marlowe. Would you give me a call? It's urgent." I hung up, unsatisfied with my message, and bent to retrieve the brush. It had slid under the supply cabinet and reaching for it, I noticed how much dust had built up. Pammy had been letting things slide. I managed to snag the brush and stood, knocking the dust off its wire bristles. A good brush. I had one like it, back in the days when Wallis would let me groom her. But the hair that I pulled from it, long and almost as dark as my own, didn't belong to the white Persian. In fact, it probably wasn't feline at all. And it hit me: maybe it hadn't been the brushing that had set the white cat off. Maybe it hadn't been the memories of the house, or what had happened there. The brush had to be associated with a person, and that long, dark hair no more belonged to Donal Franklin than it did to Jim Creighton.

"Kitty?" I knew I was pushing it. The cat was no longer growling, but she wasn't going to consider me fondly no matter what. That clock, though, that was the enemy, and so I set the brush aside on the supply shelf near the cage. Not too close, but where the Persian could see and smell it. Then, moving slowly, I rolled up the hair and presented it to the front of the Persian's enclosure. Long and glossy: it could have come from Robin Gensler. If so, that almost confirmed what I suspected—Robin must have been a regular visitor in the house, at least a regular visitor to the late Donal. Or it could have been from Louise's glossy 'do. In which case, why was she now so set against the poor animal?

"Fluffy, or whatever your name is? Would you look at this? Is this from your person?"

Two blue eyes blinked up at me, and I felt a stray thought, almost like a tickle in my mind. For a moment, I dared hope.

"Not a friend." There it was. *"I didn't know."* Just a flash, barely there. The cold surge of anger I had experienced the day before was back, though it was weaker, as if the cat were giving up. *"Go away."* And the eyes closed once more.

"Pru?" It was Doc Sharpe. He had the door open, and from the look on his face I knew he wasn't happy to see me still there. "Don't you think we should let that cat be now?"

"I wanted to try one more thing." I'd gotten through, briefly but I had.

"Pru." It wasn't a request. He might not be my employer, but he was the source of the majority of my paying gigs. Plus, he held this cat's life in his hands. I looked into the cage, hoping for something. The Persian turned from me and curled up as if to sleep. "It's time for you to go," said Doc Sharpe. At least, it was his mouth that was moving.

Chapter Twenty-five

Sometimes you just want to go back home, crawl under the covers, and go back to sleep. You'd think a cat would be sympathetic to that. But, no, when I stumbled through the front door, cursing my blindness and sheer stupidity, Wallis was waiting. The look on her face stopped me cold.

"What?"

Her tail lashed once before curling around her feet. I looked down at my own attire, much less neat. Of course, I smelled of old meat, dog, and another cat.

"It's work, Wallis. You know that." Something about the way she twitched her ear let me know I wasn't getting off that easy. "And, yeah, I screwed up. Big time."

I passed her on my way to the kitchen. The situation with the Persian had not only left me with an aching arm but also aggravated my headache, which now pounded like the construction on Route 2. Throwing three aspirin into the back of my mouth, I scooped up a handful of tap water to wash them back and swallowed hard. I could feel, rather than hear, her tail lash, just once, waiting. "I don't know what you can pick up, Wallis. I don't even want to go over it again."

Silence. "Look, I messed up. It's the woman—one of the women—but I don't know how or why." Was the Persian reacting to the widow's clear dislike? Was the cat somehow disturbed by her person's attachment to the younger brunette? Or was there a whole other option that I wasn't considering? Whatever, I only had the weekend to figure it out.

Wallis wasn't helping. "What?" I asked her again.

"Clueless." Her muttered voice reached me as she walked into the kitchen. *"Clueless as a kitten."* She started to wash. I waited. One long white stocking later, she looked up. *"Don't you see? You're on the verge of making the same mistake."*

"Yes?" I knew she wanted me to do something, but I was missing what.

With the little shake that's the feline equivalent of rolling her eyes, Wallis went on. *"You're thinking of scent the wrong way. Do you remember the weasel?"*

"Frank? Yeah, sure." I wasn't going to correct her. Not now.

"Do you remember when he started? Got scared. Whatever?" I did, all too vividly. Frank recoiling in horror. That was the first time my gift seemed to fail me.

This time she did roll her eyes. She must have picked it up from me, because on a cat it looked downright silly. I squelched my laugh, however. I needed to hear what she had to say.

"The damned weasel wasn't horrified by you.*"* Her voice, even in my head, had taken on a peevish tone. *"He wasn't even scared, probably. Stupid rat doesn't have the sense to be scared."*

I bit my lip. She started on her other foot. "Wallis?"

"You're so literal," she said finally. *"When we smell something, we don't simply react to that smell. We get an entire picture. What happened that produced that scent. The history, if you will."*

"So Frank wasn't horrified—he was smelling someone else's fear?" I struggled to remember what had led up to that strange interaction. "Was Frank picking up what happened to the Persian?"

Again, that feline shrug. *"Or what the Persian witnessed or how the Persian had felt at some point in the past. Your sense of order, of how things happen, it's strange to us."*

I nodded. I'd often heard that cats in particular live in a dream state. An eternal present. Our linear sense of time wouldn't fit well with that. What I didn't understand was how this played into what I had just experienced.

"So, the brush just now—are you saying that the Persian wasn't terrified of the brush, or of whichever brunette had used it?"

It was Wallis' turn to stare.

"Okay, I'm being simplistic, but what am I missing here? Are you trying to tell me that perhaps the Persian was picking up on someone else's fear?" I tried to imagine either of the women, perhaps in the act of brushing the cat, suddenly startled. Suddenly confronted with a horrible scene.

Had someone been in the room when Donal Franklin was murdered? I made myself picture the scene. The man on the floor. The scattered papers. The open window...Jim Creighton had implied that they'd checked for prints. Something wasn't making sense, however.

The widow. She had been on the phone with her husband when it had happened. That was her alibi, and the horror of her situation. And if she'd been chatting with her husband, presumably she would have known if there had been someone else in the room. Wouldn't she?

Unless her husband had been keeping something from her. Suddenly, my need to talk to Robin Gensler was becoming more immediate. Except...

"Wallis, Robin is the one person who seems to care about the cat. She may be the key to saving her life, too."

That feline shrug, again. And then she turned and left the room.

I should have followed her. I know Wallis, that was what she wanted. But the greasy jeans were getting to me. Besides, I needed something for my aching head. I reached for the comfort of faded sweats. Sitting on the bed to pull on the soft, baggy pants, it occurred to me that the headache might be from my disrupted sleep. Maybe if I took a short nap. Curled up...

"Wallis?" I opened my eyes. The tabby was nowhere to be seen. It was a silly thought, anyway, the one that had flashed through my mind. I'd been half asleep. I mean, what would a cat know about preserving evidence?

Chapter Twenty-six

The doorbell woke me, and I sat up with a start. The room didn't seem appreciably darker, and as I ran my fingers through my hair, I tried to remember what other appointments I had today.

"One of your men." Wallis had curled on the bed beside me. That's right, I'd told Tom I'd see him again. But that was to be at Happy's. The doorbell rang again, and Wallis tilted her head in the direction of the door. *"You don't expect me to answer it, do you?"*

"Sorry, Wallis." I had to be coming down with something. This headache, the strange silence. I wondered if my sinuses were somehow involved in my sensitivity. Could congestion be keeping all the voices quiet?

"Didn't wake you, did I?" It was Jim Creighton, looking none the worse for wear if you didn't count the slightly sour expression on his face.

"Sorry, I've not been feeling well." His blue eyes took in my tousled hair and the baggy sweats. Once, during a February snowstorm, we'd spent the weekend together. It had been nice, until the sun came out. Two days of pretending I was normal. That he was a possibility. I'd raced home to Wallis as soon as the roads were plowed, but I'd not returned the sweats, and I could see that they brought up the same memory for him. For a moment, I thought he'd soften. I was wrong.

"We need to talk, Pru. Seriously." I stepped back to let him in. He knew me well enough to follow me into the kitchen. I needed to tell him about the cat, though how I'd explain the brush—or the Persian's reaction was beyond me. Something was niggling at the back of my brain. The brush…More coffee. That's what I needed.

"Hang on." I knew him, too, and I wasn't going to tackle whatever he'd brought over until I felt more awake. He wasn't sitting down though. Wasn't even leaning on the counter. So I downed some more aspirin with a handful of water from the sink and turned to face his questions.

"Tom Reynolds." This wasn't what I'd expected.

"What about him?" Wrong answer. Creighton looked pissed.

"Don't play, Pru. What's his story? Why is he in Beauville, and what's his connection with Llewellyn McMudge?"

I paused for just long enough to annoy him. "Pru…"

"Give a girl a minute, Jim." I tried a smile. "Just woke up and all. So, how did you know Tom was in town?"

"That's not an answer, Pru." As he said it, I realized: He had Lew's phone records. Tom was trying to reach Lew. And any one of a dozen good citizens could have seen me having dinner with a big stranger last night at Hardware.

"Honestly? I don't know, Jim." Always a mistake to start with "honestly." It makes you sound like you're lying. I had to offer him something. "He called me out of the blue. We had dinner. Turns out he wanted an introduction to Llewellyn McMudge." He nodded. He'd known this much. "But I don't know why. He didn't say."

It had been some kind of business deal. That thought came into my mind the moment the words were spoken, and as I poured the hot water over the grounds, I tried to remember if he'd shared any details, but my thoughts kept straying, distracted by something I'd forgotten. What was it—the shelter? Doc Sharpe? Whatever it was, I needed to put it aside and focus. What did I know about Tom's latest project? Had Tom told me that he wanted Lew as a client, or had I assumed that?

"So you didn't call Llewellyn McMudge because of Louise Franklin's cat." I filled a mug for Creighton. He ignored it.

"Wait a minute. That's not true. I did call him about the cat. I don't know if I'd have said anything about Tom. Tom's, well, he can get mixed up in things."

"So I gather." Creighton had leaned back against the counter by this point, but the way he'd crossed his arms didn't make him look particularly relaxed. I sipped my own coffee and waited. "I've got some feelers out, but NYPD takes care of its own."

"He's not on the force anymore." He had all my attention now. Almost all.

"Doesn't matter. Not when it comes to anything that could make the force look bad." He caught my look. "Come on, Pru. Tell me you didn't know."

I raised my mug in what I hoped was an eloquent gesture. I needed to end this conversation. "I knew he cut some corners sometimes. So when I'd heard he'd left…"

Creighton waited a moment. When it was clear I wasn't going to say any more, he filled in the blanks. "And you never heard anything about him going to work for a private consortium? A group looking to recover a missing item?"

That was it: the brush. I'd been so preoccupied with the Persian, that I'd left the brush at the shelter. I was losing more than my gift, I was losing my edge too. Silently cursing my stupidity, I took a breath. Tried to regroup. Creighton was watching me. He'd been looking for a reaction. "You ever hear anything about a stolen gun," he asked now. "An antique dueling pistol?"

"Tom? No." I put my mug down. "Wait—a dueling pistol? Like the one…"

He nodded, watching me.

"Shit." I'd known something was hinky about Donal Franklin's death. I didn't expect this. "*That* gun?"

"Possibly."

I wanted to turn away. I didn't want to hear about this. Not now. I'd known something was off, but I was following my own leads—trying to find out what had happened to the Persian. To do that, I needed to get that brush back. I also needed to get

Creighton off this track. If he started poking around, I didn't know what he'd stir up.

"Tom's not a thief. He maybe cuts some corners. But he wouldn't steal." Even as I said it, I wondered. I hadn't seen him in quite a while. He hadn't looked like the past few years had been kind.

"He knows people, though. As a cop, he'd have to." Creighton was saying what we both knew. Still, it didn't add up. "If he wanted to cross the line. Maybe if he felt he was being forced out. Getting a raw deal…"

"No." That wasn't Tom. I could see him blackmailing a thief, maybe. Putting a little too much pressure on a fence. But taking over?

"Pru, I believe you." He didn't look like he did, but he kept talking. "And I'm not looking for a thief, not really. Your friend, though, he may be mixed up in something that you shouldn't go near."

"Is this you being chivalrous, Jim?" I topped off my mug, all the while keeping my eyes on his face.

"It's me being a cop." He looked down at his own cup. I didn't think he was considering the merits of my dark roast. "It's the pistol, Pru. I've had some people look at it, and it turns out that the gun has a rather strange provenance."

I started to smile at the ten-dollar word. "It's not a joke, Pru. That pistol is more than a pretty toy. It's a two-hundred-year-old hot potato. It's British, but it had been presented to Napoleon at some point. It was part of a set then, but over the years, the other was lost. Some think it went down on the Titanic, but that's probably crap. Whatever its history, this one ended up in a museum—gift of an anonymous donor. And then it went missing, too. For some reason, nobody was looking too hard, and when the Feds heard where it had turned up, we understood why."

He gave me a stony look. I shook my head. This wasn't making sense.

"Someone applied some pressure and got the museum to deaccession the gun. It was legal, but barely. Over the winter, the new owner decided to turn it into cash. The museum tried to buy it back, but they were told there was another buyer. A private buyer. And then, beginning of March, the gun disappears."

"Lew? But he wouldn't have..." Suddenly, my coffee didn't taste so good. I didn't know what Lew would do. For a client. For a friend. On a dare, even. "But, say he *was* the private buyer..."

Creighton's eyes had never looked so cold.

"Something went wrong with the deal, didn't it?" I scanned his face. "Somebody reneged or—" I was out of ideas.

Creighton wasn't offering any. "We're looking into it, Pru." He pushed the mug back and stared at me. "And I want you out of it."

"They wanted the gun back?" I thought of Lew, dead by the roadside.

"The gun or the money. Though, at this point, it might be more about honor."

I nodded. The weekend in Saratoga. We'd made some stops. I realized Creighton was watching me. "Louise Franklin. She was away that week, she said."

"At Canyon Ridge." He finished my thought. "Doing Pilates or power yoga or whatever they do out there. Yeah, we checked. That place keeps track of every minute. The Feds—" He stopped himself. "Look, I've already said too much, Pru. Just—will you back off? Tom's involved in this somehow, and I need to know you're safe."

"You need..." I wanted to throw his words back at him. I'm not the type to be kept.

"Strange, isn't it?" I looked down. Wallis was twining around my ankles, looking for all the world like just another pet. *"Here's your new cop boyfriend, in your kitchen, asking questions about your old cop boyfriend and your—"* She opened her mouth, baring her teeth as if smelling something foul. *"Your Lew."*

I nodded, remembering just in time not to respond out loud. At least the interruption had given me a moment to rein in my temper—and served to remind me of my own questions. "I don't know what to tell you, Jim. I've got some questions of my own I need to answer."

"Oh?"

I was winging it. What else could I do? Confess that I'd mislaid a stolen cat brush? In light of what we'd been discussing, it seemed laughable. "That Persian, Jim. She's not getting any better. Not even with my 'magic touch.'" I could see the relief on his face. He was about to dismiss my concerns; I could sense it. I didn't want to be interrupted. "There's something going on with that animal, Jim. Something odd. I think it's all somehow connected."

I paused. This was the hard part. *Translate.* The word came to me, like a command. "I think the cat witnessed something."

"Pru, really—"

He was done. He'd delivered his message, and he was ready to leave. At any other time, I'd have been grateful. Jim Creighton was a little too smart for my comfort level. Right now, however, I needed him to listen.

"No, really, Jim. If it had just been an accident—even a loud, horrible accident—the cat should be getting over it. Instead, what I'm seeing is more like the reaction to abuse." That was it, the key to explaining the behavior. "Like someone had been cruel to the animal."

"Are there physical signs?" He was trying to muster some concern. I had to give him that.

I thought of the injured foreleg. "No, not really. Nothing that isn't consistent with the accident," I was forced to admit. "It's more behavioral. And you've seen how odd the widow is about the cat."

"She doesn't have any reason to love that cat." He seemed to be thinking about it. "She may never have. I told her I still need to examine it, once anyone can, and she got all flustered. But I don't really see—"

"That's just it, Jim. How clear are you on her alibi?"

"Wait!" He started to laugh, and caught himself. "Are you suggesting that because the widow may have been mean to her husband's cat, you suspect her of killing her husband?"

That was exactly what I suspected. And there was no way in
hell I could explain it. "You just told me the gun was stolen or,
well, taken from someone dangerous. The gun that killed Donal
Franklin. And you think Llewellyn was involved. Admit it."

He didn't deny it, which was the same thing.

"Look, Jim, I know Lew—knew Lew. He was perfectly
capable of giving someone an expensive gift. Even"—I thought
back on our time together—"an illicit gift. But not for a male
friend. Not Lew. If he made a present of something, it was for
a woman. And Louise Franklin used him to run her errands."

"I admit…" He stopped himself. "Louise Franklin was in
Northampton when her husband was killed."

"Her phone was." I wasn't letting go.

"She was. And she was adamant that her husband was
alone. She's made a point of that, and there is no evidence of
an intruder." He leaned back on the counter and sighed. I knew
that sigh. He was going to give me something. "Look, Pru, I
know what you're getting at, but you're wrong. Two shopkeepers
confirmed that a dark-haired woman with a fur hat came into
their stores."

"There are a lot of dark-haired women." Not all of them were
seeing her husband.

"She bought a scarf using her credit card. Some crazy expensive silk scarf. That's why she was calling her husband, to tell
him about it. The shopkeeper heard it all." He paused. I waited.
"I've also heard the 9-1-1 call. It was her, Pru."

"The widow inherits?" I wasn't giving up.

"You know I can't tell you that." He paused. "Look, there
are some irregularities, but if you're looking for a motive, the
will isn't it."

"But there was a pre-nup, right? A tight one, I bet." I didn't
know what Creighton wasn't telling me. I did know there was
something. His silence confirmed it.

"Is there something going on here, Pru?" He said finally.
"Something personal?"

"No, Jim. Not—like that. It's all about the cat."

His baby blues could have pinned me to the wall. I could tell I was blushing. I could also tell he was reading it wrong. I wanted to tell him, then, about the cat being a gift—about the widow changing her story. About Robin loving the animal. I didn't get the chance.

"Look, Pru. I don't know about your past, and I don't need to know what you do on your own time." I opened my mouth, and he raised one hand to silence me. "It's none of my business. But this is. It's serious, and there are dangerous people taking an interest. I care about you, and I know you're not telling me everything. That's fine, Pru. I can live with that. But I'd hate to see it take you down."

Chapter Twenty-seven

Creighton was right about some things. There was no way I could tell him about the brush—or what I'd gotten from it. I was pretty sure he'd find out I'd visited the widow, though, and that meant he'd be back, asking questions. And as much as I'd enjoyed his company in the past, that wasn't a conversation I was looking forward to. No, I needed to get a move on. My window of opportunity—and the Persian's, I recalled with a twinge of guilt—was closing fast. I checked the clock. Doc Sharpe would have left soon after me, locking the shelter behind him. I'd have to wait till tomorrow to get that brush. I didn't like feeling helpless.

"Robin? This is Pru Marlowe. I really need you to call me. It's about the cat." I had to figure she'd respond to the Persian, even if she didn't have much use for me. I tried Mack, too, just out of curiosity. When I got his voicemail, I hung up. The sun had set; as Wallis would put it, the hour of the hunt had arrived.

There's a reason I like bad boys, and it's not just that they are routinely more fun. Spend time with a man like Tom and when it's over, it's over. The break is clean. No hangover, no regrets.

I was muttering to myself as I got dressed, and I knew it. Wallis, on the bed, watched me without comment. "Okay, sometimes there's a hangover," I admitted out loud. Wallis lashed her tail in acknowledgment.

Creighton? I didn't know. Like Tom—or the Tom I'd first been drawn to—he was a cop. He had that control, a touch of menace that made getting anywhere a challenge. Creighton was in better shape than Tom—no scars, and none of that heaviness of muscle turning to fat—a trait I'd put down to the difference between Beauville and New York City, if not age and assorted other vices. The rest of it, I wasn't clearheaded enough to judge. Was it better to be warned—or was he just playing me? And why throw feelings into it?

A thud alerted me that Wallis had jumped off the bed. "What?" I called after her retreating tail. "It's not like you've specialized in long-term monogamous relationships, Wallis."

By the time I'd followed her into the kitchen, I'd changed my blouse three times, finally settling on a slim sweater with the right amount of cling. I wasn't sure what I wanted from Tom, but I'd be damned if I'd be corralled by Jim Creighton's higher expectations. Besides, Tom liked to look at me. And if he was looking at me, I had a better chance of getting the information I needed.

"I'm heading out." I announced to the empty kitchen. "The hunter of the household is going out to seek some fresh meat." I meant it as a joke, hoping to get at least the usual sarcastic comment from my tabby. Instead, I got silence. I wasn't sure if I had pissed her off or if the strange silence was finally descending over our household too. At least between my nap, the coffee, and the most recent fistful of aspirin, the headache had dulled to a muffled thud. "I don't know if you're playing with me, Wallis," I called into the silent living room. "But don't forget there are two of us in this house. And one of us has opposable thumbs."

It wasn't designed to win her over, but it made me feel better just the same.

Chapter Twenty-eight

With one thing and another, I had a good head of steam by the time I hit Happy's. Tom had said something to Creighton, of that I was certain. Between his insinuations and Creighton's possessiveness, I was going to be carved up like an Easter ham, if I wasn't careful. The point of different men is to keep your options open. Once they start acting like they own you, it's time to cut them loose.

Trouble was, I couldn't. Not in either case. Tom was history, or had been until he showed up. But he was involved in something and had dragged me in, too. I would kick him to the curb as soon as I figured out what—and how to clear my name. For now, I had to use whatever hold I had. And Creighton? Well, his recent actions were quickly burying whatever future plans I might have toyed with, back when I hadn't realized the connection between his Boy Scout good looks and his straight-edge mind. He was the law in this town, though. And, I paused and took a breath, he had called me about the white Persian. With everything else going on, I couldn't let myself get distracted. That poor cat. So closed off, so scared. The clock ticking.

Thoughts of the white Persian as I'd last seen her, huddled as far back in her cage as she could, focused me. I could make quick work of Tom. I was sure that however he had implicated me in all of this, Creighton was smart enough to see through it eventually. That cat, however. She needed help. And I was the only one who could do it. It should have been simple: get her to tell me what had happened. Get her to come out of herself, to be a house cat again, while she still had time. Get her okay'd for adoption. Maybe even get her into Robin's care. If only.

I reached for the twisted iron that served as Happy's door knob, only to have it open in front of me, spilling out smoke and two bodies, laughing and hanging onto each other.

"Hey, Pru!" It was Mack. He looked different at night. Looser. Maybe that was because of his drinking buddy. She was blonde and not dressed for the weather. "Haven't seen you here in a while."

"I've been moving in some classier circles." So much for our steak dinner. So much for Robin.

"Dumpster diving?" He nuzzled the blonde. She giggled.

"Dancing at the Beauville Country Club." That was where Mack had played his last chance with me. Played and lost. If he wasn't going to play any nicer now, I wouldn't either.

He just laughed. "You still sore about that, Pru? Ancient history. We both came out okay." The blonde blinked at me, but the thoughts were too well doused. Mine, on the other hand, were piqued.

"Yeah, if you weren't Donal Franklin." I'd been a fool. Mack had been at the widow's place. He'd been working with Robin. The question was only: what was his angle? I took a risk. "Then again, he must have left somebody a tidy sum."

"Hey, you should know. You've been screwing his lawyer." Mack was still chuckling. The look on my face sobered him up fast. "What, you didn't know?"

"Lew?" I felt like I'd received a shot to the head. Lew—the facilitator. Taking care of the widow's assets. Creighton had called him the "old family retainer," but I hadn't taken him literally. I'd seen Lew as the best friend and drinking buddy, and he'd been that, too. The rich are different than the rest of us. And I'd never bothered to ask. "Llewellyn McMudge?"

"Yeah, McMudge." Mack was looking at me strangely. "We were doing some business. Then he stopped taking my calls."

It was my turn to deliver the news. "He's not taking anyone's calls, Mack." I eyed him, waiting for the reaction. "Didn't you hear?"

"What? No." He stood up straight, almost losing the blonde. "Mackey," she whined, and tried to pull him down into a kiss. He pushed her away. "He's—I swear to God, Pru. I don't know anything. What happened?"

I told him.

"Shit." He seemed to be taking it in. His next question threw me. "Do you know what he was working on?"

"Besides errands for the widow? No." I couldn't resist. "Weren't you and Robin working on something?"

"That was nothing, Pru. Nothing with those guys, anyway. She wanted an escort." He almost choked on the word.

I smiled. "An escort." A cold smile.

"Not that way. Just, you know, company. A driver. She's not a bad kid, Pru. She grew up here, too, and she didn't have it easy. I mean, the clothes, the hair—that's all new. Besides, it's over. She was going to help me out with something. Kept saying the money was coming, but…" He shrugged. So much for chivalry.

"Maybe you couldn't give her what she wanted anymore." It was a mean thing to say. "The services weren't as advertised."

My jab hit home. Mack's jaw hung slack, his age showing. Not that the blonde cared. I stepped past them, into the bar, and thought about what I'd just learned. Mack wasn't with Robin anymore. She'd hired him, whether for a beard or for protection, I didn't know, but it hadn't worked out. That was information, and I could use it. I looked around for the next ex on my list.

◇◇◇

My eyes took a moment to adjust. The smoke, as well as the lighting, gave everyone a slightly sallow look. Tom was a big guy, however, and he'd have been easy to pick out at the bar or at any of the booths that lined the back wall. I didn't. Thank God for small favors. Tom still had a cop's instinct for connections, and I really hadn't wanted him grilling me on Mack. So it was with something like pleasure that I settled onto a stool by the bar.

The barman took one look at me and reached for the bourbon, but I shook my head.

"PBR." Beer would leave my head clearer. I could always amp up later.

He opened the can and pushed it over to me. I didn't rate a glass, but then he didn't even rate a name. Although the bar had been christened after its original owner, long dead of emphysema, each successive barman ended up with the same handle. The current Happy couldn't have been less likely, but I hardly remembered the original, who'd held court in my father's time. Knowing this town, I suspected the name had been sarcastic even then. At least that guy had chosen it, though. Now it came with the place, along with regulars like Mack and, okay, me. Who else, I didn't know. I'd been thinking of asking the barman about the widow. It seemed like a long shot, but with her taste for younger men, it couldn't be excluded. Only just then Albert sidled up to me in what I could only assume was supposed to be a subtle approach.

"Hi, Al." He looked up as if surprised to see me. I was the only person at this end of the bar. The only woman in the room.

"Pru! What a surprise." He wiped his hands on the front of his shirt, making me wonder where they'd been. "You know, you just missed—

"Yeah, I saw him on his way out." I stared across the bar. The mirror, grimy as Albert's plaid flannel, didn't show any expression, but I wasn't taking any chances.

"I was only wondering because—"

I was saved from Albert's badly camouflaged curiosity by the opening of the front door. Tom made a quick survey of the room and allowed his face to light up as he found me. I nodded, holding back my own smile. I had to work with Albert, more or less.

"Hey, stranger." Tom's voice oozed sex. Albert looked up, curious. I sighed.

"Tom, this is Albert. He's the Beauville animal control officer. Albert, Tom. Tom's a private investigator from the city."

"You're here about the shooting, aren't you?" I didn't think Albert knew anything. He just couldn't resist. Tom's muscle might be going to flab, but he was still a big guy. And with that scar? A man's idea of a man. "Did the widow call you?"

"Shooting?" Tom's face was blank. His voice bland. This was a technique I recognized. He knew it all. I'd have put good money on that. He simply wanted to find out what my portly colleague knew.

"Yeah, didn't Pru tell you?" Albert's hands had moved from his shirtfront to his beard. He was nervous. "She was at the scene. There was a cat."

The lines around Tom's mouth tightened as he tried not to laugh. "It's my job, Tom. The animal was in distress."

"Let me guess, the cat shot someone."

I never thought I'd have much in common with Albert. For a moment, though, I think we both had the same look on our faces. This time, Tom didn't hold back.

"Oh, that's priceless. Next you'll tell me that the cat shot someone with an antique gun."

"How did you know that?" I wouldn't have asked, but I didn't mind that Albert had.

Tom only smiled, and it hit me. "He used to be a cop, Al. It's like the priesthood." Somehow, the idea of Jim Creighton and Tom gossiping over beers didn't appeal to me. "They all talk to each other."

Tom, however, had stopped laughing. "You're shitting me, right?" His voice had sunk. Low and cold, it was a voice I remembered well. His work voice. "An antique gun?"

"A dueling pistol." I gave him that, and I watched him. But his mouth was closed, and he sat back on his stool, staring at some point across the bar. I wanted to see that point. "Spill, Tom. Why are you in town, really?"

My hand on his forearm drew him back, at least for the moment. His voice, when he started to talk again, was softer. A little less sure. "I needed to talk to some rich old dude. I told you that, Pru. Some guy you know. You knew."

"What about, Tom?" Nothing. "Why did you need to talk to Lew?" Albert was getting an eyeful, going back and forth. I couldn't help that. I needed to know.

"I'm freelance now, Pru. I thought, maybe, an introduction for old time's sake..."

I wasn't buying it. "Tom."

"It's a financial issue, okay? Someone owes a little something from a private transaction."

Two men were dead. Collection agencies don't kill people. "Who hired you, Tom?"

He shook his head. "I don't know."

"Tom." Albert's mouth was open. I didn't care.

"Honest, Pru. It was all through email. My fee came by wire transfer. Some insurance company."

"So how'd you know I knew Llewellyn?"

"I didn't. I had a name and a description, and I knew you were here." The smile was back. A flash of the old Tom. I could've kicked him. And myself. "You always were easy to read, Pru."

I had no answer to that. Still, there was more to learn. "Is it over, now?" Lew wasn't going to be paying anyone back.

Tom shook his head. He was beginning to get jowls. "I don't know. I don't think so. But I swear, Pru. I didn't have anything to do with that."

I nodded. Tom could rough someone up. I didn't think he could kill. Not for money. Still, this was a new Tom. Older, maybe more desperate.

"Besides," he looked nervous. "They had his name already. They knew about him."

"They?"

His mouth shut tight. The scar white against his cheek.

"So, tell me about the gun."

"I don't know much, Pru. Just that its pricey. Very pricey. And something went wrong."

I nodded. It was odd seeing Tom like this: off balance, a little nervous. I didn't want to think too hard about it. "And Llewellyn?"

"He was on the fringes of that group, from what I hear. And he was heard asking about something special. A gift for a friend…"

"So you're looking for the friend?"

He stared over the bar. I wondered what he was seeing in the mirror. "What?" I answered his unspoken question. "It's not me, Tom. And the cops have the gun now." I tried to read his face. How deep in this was he?

He shrugged. "Doesn't matter. Like I said, something went wrong. Someone's got to pay."

Seemed to me, someone already had. Before I could push for more, another voice chimed in.

"How did you get involved in all this?" Albert was waking from his stupor.

"The cop connection, Al." Looking at Tom, now, it was hard to recall. "His buddies would have access to phone records, the dealer, you name it."

"No, not him, Pru." I turned slightly. Albert was still staring, his mouth still slightly open. But his broad face was drawn. Behind his beard, I'd have sworn he looked concerned. "I mean, you. How did you know these two men, Pru?"

I sputtered. I really didn't want to explain my life to Albert.

"It was purely social, Al. Social and—casual." Tom raised an eyebrow at that, and for a moment, I saw the old Tom. I could feel the flush rising.

But for once, Albert wasn't interested in the salacious side. For once, he was looking at my face, rather than my breasts. His eyes were wide and sad. "Two men, Pru. Both of them dead. And only one of them had a cat."

Chapter Twenty-nine

Tom's motive, I now knew for sure, was more than social. My ex saw me as a means to an end, and it was with some difficulty that I convinced him otherwise. Yes, I might know two men, recently deceased. But my knowledge of their habits was slim.

"You really didn't know he was a fixer?" Tom had managed to shoo Albert off by then, and I'd graduated to whiskey at a booth in back, headache be damned. Tom was telling me about Llewellyn's habits, about his role as a go-between for wealthy clients.

"He was one of those all-purpose attorneys, from what I hear," he told me. "Protected by privilege—and by money. Working for Franklin, as he was calling himself, didn't hurt either. I gather he was one of those guys who likes to pretend he's wild. Likes playing in the dirt." He paused, a note something like concern creeping into his voice. "You didn't take him too serious, did you, Pru?"

"We had fun. That was it." I heard the defensiveness edging into my own.

"Just as well. He was also the type to suffer from cold feet, from what I hear." He looked around. "Your little friend, at least he had the balls to face me." He turned toward the bar, where Albert was trying to converse with Happy. "Or maybe, he just doesn't have the brains. Is he one of your animal pals? A chipmunk or something?"

"Chipmunks don't have beards." I didn't know if I was defending Albert exactly, but something about Tom's manner was getting to me.

"I don't know." He strained to look. "Think of it as fur."

Something he'd said. "What did you mean about Donal?"

"Huh?" He didn't even look at me.

"Franklin, 'as he was calling himself.' What did you mean?"

"Oh, Pru, didn't you know?" He turned toward me now. We'd never been close, not really. "Donal Franklin?"

I shook my head.

"He was connected. Way back, real old school. I heard he got out. Got married, went straight. I heard he wanted to make things right, but…" His voice trailed off, as I just stared. Donal. Tom. Maybe they weren't that different from Lew. Maybe no man was.

Except Creighton, the thought of the clean-cut cop came to mind. But Donal? He had seemed honorable. Maybe that was "old school." I didn't know what to believe. I didn't know if it mattered now.

The difference with Tom was in our shared past. We had had something in common, then. Now all I saw was a beefy guy, a scarred face with more lines than his years justified. I saw the toll of his job. Of the city life I'd left behind.

"You're getting soft out here." As if he'd read my mind, he turned my thoughts back onto me. I held his look, but I kept my mouth shut. "Which might be good for you, all things considered."

I tilted my head and waited.

"I know a little of what's going on, Pru." He stared down at his glass. "Enough, anyway. The folks who hired me, they don't just want the gun back. They don't even want the money. They want to send a message."

"You think they killed Lew?" The second the words were out, I regretted them. Despite what Albert had let slip, Tom had no confirmation that Llewellyn had died of anything but natural causes. "I mean, there's no evidence that it was anything but an accident."

"Accidents seem to pile up around here." Tom raised his glass, eyeing me over the rim. "Around you, Pru. And I think some people are going to have to start asking why."

Chapter Thirty

Maybe I was losing my head for drink. Maybe it was Tom. For the first time in ages, I overslept. Woke up groggy and a little sick, and thought about rolling back into sleep. It was Saturday, which meant I didn't have to walk Growler. Tracy Horlick might be lazy, but the five bucks more I charged on weekends had set her off in a huff when we first discussed pricing. She'd handle weekends, she'd told me, which probably meant the dog had the run of the yard for a few minutes. I doubted she was any more busy during the week than Saturday or Sunday, but she'd already agreed to weekdays so I let her fiction stand.

I had mixed feelings about my other regular canine client. Lucy was an odd one, with her little dance steps and her faux French. Despite my initial reservations, I'd begun to think there was more going on in her little poodle brain than I'd originally thought. Not that I necessarily liked her way of manipulating the world. Nor the implication that I could learn from her. Maybe it was just as well I wouldn't see her till Monday. That meant I could sleep in today, if I wanted.

Except I couldn't. Sitting up with a start, I remembered three things. One, the Persian had two more days. Two, I'd left that brush at the shelter. Maybe it didn't mean anything. Maybe it was evidence. Either way, the Persian had reacted to the brush—or the hair I had retrieved from it—and if I wanted to save that cat from the big sleep, it was my best chance of finding out how.

The third thought, as I peered out on a cloudy morning, was that today was Donal Franklin's funeral. I would be about as welcome there as his cat, but I had to check it out. Even if it was just to guilt the widow into giving up her late husband's pet before the Persian would be euthanized, I needed to be there. I needed to try.

I'd never gotten around to quizzing the barman about Louise, I realized as I showered and dressed. That was probably moot. She was playing in a different league. But thinking of the Franklins and their potential playmates made me realize I still hadn't heard from Robin. She was a crucial part of my plan, and while I assumed she'd still be eager to take the poor cat, I didn't want any surprises—for either of us. I thought about her as I dressed, digging out my black suede pumps for the occasion. My mother wouldn't have been proud. She'd have been surprised. If nobody knew who I was, I'd fit right in.

Creighton. I couldn't tell what he thought about Donal Franklin's death. If it really was ruled an accident, he'd have no reason to be there. The town wasn't that small. Only he had instincts like I did, and I suspected that he wasn't letting things go quite so easily. That could make things tricky for me. I wanted to poke about without raising any more questions. If he did show up, well, he already suspected me of more involvement than I'd admitted to. I'd wing it. I'd have to.

Lipstick. A glance at the clock. If I was going to be unobtrusive, I had to get moving, which meant delaying my trip to the shelter. I cursed Jim Creighton under my breath, and threw in Mack and Tom for good measure. The men in my life were becoming a liability, and the less interaction I had with any of them the better. The evening with Tom had gone downhill fast. He was drinking too much—the extra weight should have clued me in—and he was scared. At least that had freed me from the temptation of taking him home. But I'd tossed and turned so much that Wallis had abandoned the bed before dawn, grumbling under her breath about uneasy consciences, and how someone should just get herself fixed and be done with it.

Before I headed out, I did another little bit of Internet sleuthing. Llewellyn McMudge's interment plans were a bit harder to find, though, and I found myself calling around funeral homes like some kind of kinky death junkie. I found him at the third, where the receptionist's slight accent was probably supposed to make me think of Masterpiece Theater. Yes, they were receiving the McMudge family today. Yes, mourners outside the immediate family were welcome. I checked the time and took down directions. It was going to be close. At least I wouldn't have to change my outfit between one event and the next.

"I do not understand your species' fascination with the dead." Wallis had emerged as I was wrestling with my hair. Unrestrained, it curls, long and glossy. Men always want to run their hands through it, and I like having that kind of power. For a funeral, though—two funerals—I was trying for something a little less conspicuous. My mother had been an expert at this, restraining her own hair in such a tight bun that I had trouble picturing her with it loose.

"It's not the dead themselves," I tried to explain as I clipped my side curls back. "It's how they got that way."

"Who benefits, you mean?" She settled on the bed. The sight of me smoothing my hair back seemed to amuse her. *"You've missed a bit."*

"Thanks." I gave up and reached for my usual hair tie. So it wouldn't be fancy. "And, yes, who benefits. But also who shows up and how they act. I'll be looking for something wrong. Something off."

"You're trying to flush out prey." I heard a purr of satisfaction in her voice. Maybe I wasn't as clueless as she feared.

"Something like that." I grabbed my bag, and took off.

First stop, the Greater Beauville Memorial Park. My mother had bought a plot here, back when I was still in school. She'd always been one to plan ahead, and so I was somewhat familiar with this private cemetery just outside town. A sprawling lot— someone's idea of a no-fail business—it stretched from the flat valley bottom up into the beginning of the hills. My mother's grave was on the flat. Row E9 or some such, as if she were stored in condiments. But just as the spices may be one row over from the baked goods, the memorial park was adjacent to Tyndale Memorial. Officially, a small lane divided the two. Unofficially, the quality—and size—of the gravestones and statuary made the distinction clear. Still, there were within walking distance. If questioned, I had the best excuse in the world.

By pushing my GTO, I made it to the cemetery in good time. It was a pretty place, actually, if you ignored its purpose. Even this early in the season, some groundskeeper had been at work, potted plants lining the major walkways. Deeper in the grounds, I heard the rumblings of chipmunks and birds. One stodgy groundhog was waking, hungry and ready for spring. This was their season, before the hedge clippers and lawnmowers came out, and their self-involved murmurings made me smile despite myself.

I didn't have time to eavesdrop, however. Instead, I headed uphill to scope out the surroundings. Two turns and I found what had to be Donal's grave. A mound of earth, covered by an unrealistically green rug, stood beside an open hole. This early, not even the staff were about. I could have climbed in and waited if I'd wanted.

I didn't, and so for lack of anything better to do, I strolled back down, across the divider to E9. At least down here I had a good view of the road. There'd be a cortege, at least one limo, I figured. As they drove slowly by, I could turn and follow—a fellow mourner, come to pay her respects.

My mother would appreciate that, at least. A practical woman, she'd never mind her grave being used as a scouting point. Probably wouldn't mind it being used as a vegetable garden, for that matter. Growing up, I'd thought her humorless. Too strict, with no taste for pleasure. I guess my dad had the fun for both of them, and leaving her with a precocious brat and a drafty old house didn't improve her frame of reference. She never hit me. Not that she wouldn't have. Only by the time my sins merited it, I was too big. She clearly wanted the evil out of me, though, and was sure enough that I'd inherited my father's taste for whiskey, sex, and trouble that she never seemed to relax around me.

I bent now and brushed the dirt off her simple grave marker. She'd probably be shocked to see me here, though she wouldn't be surprised that I hadn't splurged for a proper headstone yet. Well, I had time, didn't I? Memory is funny that way: just about one year, and already I was feeling more filial than I had for the last decade of her life. She'd known something was up, when I'd come back home. She couldn't put it together anymore—the words and the thoughts just didn't hold still long enough. I could tell, though, by the way she looked at me. I didn't belong in Beauville. She didn't trust my motives.

Maybe she had a point. My thighs were beginning to ache, so I stood up and looked around. A pair of mourning doves were going through their inane rituals. Enough, I wanted to tell them. Get it on already. Build a nest. I couldn't afford to get distracted, though, and did my best to tune them out until a startled squawk alerted me to movement. Sure enough, a hearse had begun its slow ascent up the winding hill road, followed by a few town cars and the kind of sedans that spoke of leather seats and high-end stereo.

Just as well I'd left my ride in the lot. On foot, I looked respectable, as well as I could. I'd even found a little hat in the attic: my mother's, maybe, or something from one of her aunts. Either way, I silently thanked the squirrel whose foraging had been so rudely disturbed and made my way up toward that open grave.

I was lucky. By the time I got there, the service was just starting. About a dozen people were standing, although up front, I could see that a line of chairs had been unfolded. I circled the crowd, staying far enough back so as not to be noticed. Halfway around, I could have been a mourner, or simply curious. Either way, I had a good view of the minister, silver-haired with a low rumbling voice that carried the indistinct murmur of plush comfort. In front of the grave sat Louise Franklin, the handsome younger man behind her in attendance. To her right, a white-haired little thing sat ramrod straight: a matriarch of the old New

England type. I remembered the rumors about Donal. That he wasn't from around here, that he wasn't old money. The old lady could be Louise's mother, I thought. Or the rumors could be just that. I was about to dismiss them when a movement caught my eye. A man, toward the back. I couldn't make out a face, just a good suit. Something about the way he moved though—the way he avoided my line of sight—made me wonder.

The rest of the crowd stood then, and I lost him. From the similarity in age and the quality of the outerwear, I made most of them for friends or colleagues. Maybe even business associates. Not that I would know: I tried to imagine Llewellyn here, among the cashmere coats and the resort tans. It didn't work. Lew might have been Donal's attorney, but he'd played the role of his bad-boy buddy. If he were here, he'd be dressed a little brighter than these somber folks. His jacket would have a slightly slimmer cut. Not flashy, not exactly. But with an edge to it—an attitude that liked to one-up his straightforward peers. I remembered his words, how he'd cut Donal down ever so slightly: "He wants to put it all in good works," he'd said, with a sneer in his voice. Playing gangster? Yeah, maybe, only maybe he'd gone too far. Was that what had gotten him killed? Had he dragged Donal into something? *Back* into something?

I didn't know. I hadn't even paid attention, except to my own pleasure. Llewellyn had been my type. Not that different from Tom, now that I thought about it. Maybe that was what I'd been drawn to, all those months before.

The matriarch would have made mincemeat of either of them, from what I could see. Most of the women here could. Righteous, although that wasn't what Lew had been inferring with his snide jibe. He meant that Donal didn't have the sense to enjoy himself—to spend his money on *fun*. Women, horses, whatever. Though that analysis sure didn't fit with the rock I'd seen on Robin's hand. An emerald, or a damned good copy. Whatever else he might have scrimped on, I didn't see Donal Franklin buying anything less than the best.

◇◇◇

Robin. No, she couldn't be here, could she? Though if the girl had had any spunk, she might have found a way to say farewell to the man who most likely had been her lover. Hell, she could have stolen my play and hid out behind a tree. The statuary in this section of the cemetery could have shielded a marching band from inquiring eyes. But maybe she didn't want to remember him like this. Maybe she was afraid of the widow.

Maybe she had reason to be. I couldn't eavesdrop, not as much as I wanted, but I caught a few words. "Sorry," came up often, but one of the suits was talking more. I caught something about "the estate," and saw the look she shot at him. He made nice after that, and I sunk back, afraid of being obvious. I needed to find out about the will—about what would go where. A disappointed lover had just as much reason to kill as a betrayed wife. I'd thought it a little odd that Donal had chosen a woman who looked so much like his lawful wedded spouse. Maybe he had tired of the newer model as well. It happened. And left Robin with a pricey bauble and an attachment to the Persian? The token who reminded her of better days? Could there be a bequest that went with the cat—a Leona Helmsley deal for Fluffy's continued care and comfort?

I shook my head. If there were money attached to the Persian, Louise wouldn't be so eager to get rid of it. Robin was that cat's one hope, and I had an obligation to help the poor animal—whatever her involvement. But I found myself wondering about Robin's role in Donal Franklin's death as I watched the funeral cortege pull out of the cemetery. Where had she been, I wondered, while the widow was out shopping—and the Persian was watching her person take his last breaths? As soon as this day's grim duties were over, I would have to find out for myself.

Chapter Thirty-one

Llewellyn McMudge may have been in the same class as Donal Franklin in life, but his funeral was lacking. Maybe it was true what people say about lawyers. Maybe there was a reason he'd kept his profession from me.

As it was, only about a dozen mourners were gathered in the nondenominational chapel. Two women, who looked like sisters, sat up front. A third, dressed in expensive tweed, came in later and greeted them with a nod. Ex-wife, I placed a mental bet: the way she greeted the sisters made me think of shared suffering and hatchets long buried. Other than that, a few black wool overcoats spoke of the city. When I moved forward, I heard talk about clients—and about the unresolved cases Llewellyn had left behind—and my ears pricked up. But the gathering was too small for me to get in too close. There were no thronging crowds. No sharkskin suits. No tears, either.

I hadn't heard about a viewing. The McMudges were probably too refined for a wake. On a whim, I checked the visitor's book anyway. A half a dozen signatures—several of them with McMudge in the name. And there, from earlier in the day, was one I hadn't expected: Robin Gensler, in a girlish script that almost had me expecting a little smiley face above the "i." Well, this was a small town—and if Lew and Donal were buddies as well as business associates, there was no reason Robin should not have known Lew, too. But well enough to pay her respects? When she didn't—perhaps didn't dare—show up at the funeral of the man she seemed to actually have a relationship with? I shrugged as I added my own name to the list. Maybe she had liked Lew, too. Maybe Lew had been helping her out legally. Maybe she and Lew—no, I didn't want to go there.

Robin was cute, in a pre-packaged way. That picture-perfect hair and makeup weren't what I imagined Lew going for, but, hey, his moneyed friends would probably have been taken aback by my jeans and leather, if they'd ever met me. Clearly, he was a man of catholic tastes. It wasn't that I was jealous. Far from it. But my ego was getting a post-mortem bashing from Mr. McMudge, one that I had no recourse to set right.

It rankled, and I knew I'd hear about it from Wallis. It also came suspiciously close to what Creighton had said, which didn't endear Jim to me so much as make me wonder just how much he saw. That man was dangerous, and I'd do well to remember it.

I didn't have time to chew over my romantic life right now, however. There was movement in the room, and I looked up in time to see a latecomer arrive. It was the man in the back, the man from Donal's gravesite. Here, he stood out like a hawk in an aviary. It wasn't his clothes. Now that I was closer, I could see his coat: black wool, soft and fine, it probably cost as much as my car. The face above it was a different story. A chin like a jackhammer, and eyes that said he'd use it. As if aware of my gaze, they turned toward me, grey and cold, and I suppressed a shudder. No animal could make me feel this way. Then again, I'd never tried to talk to a shark. With an effort, I pulled away, and that's when I saw him. The guest next to the shark, also in a city coat though not one so fine. Tom.

I sidled over, not caring too much who noticed me. I hadn't expected to see Tom again, and I wanted to put him on the spot.

"Who's your friend?" I resisted the urge to elbow him in the ribs. I didn't pull the barbs from my voice. In response, he turned to the evil-faced man, and I realized Tom was unsure of himself. It didn't make me any happier, but it was interesting.

"This is Pru," Tom said to the stranger. He nodded as if he'd heard of me.

"Call me Bill." He held out a long white hand that seemed much too elegant for his face.

"Bill." I nodded. It would do for now. "Friend of Lew's?"

Tom winced, but Bill smiled. It wasn't a nice smile. He didn't answer.

"Because I was wondering what brought you here," I continued. "First at Donal's burial and now at Lew's. I haven't seen you around, and I know for a fact that Tom never got to meet the deceased. So, I was wondering if perhaps you knew him. Maybe you were an old friend of Donal's?" Nothing. "No, of course not." I looked him up and down. "You're the reason Tom was looking for Lew?" I was pretty sure that was the connection here. If I could shake these two up, maybe I'd learn something.

Bill, or whatever his name was, only smiled more. "And why would I be here if I had hired Tom?"

I shrugged. That part I hadn't figured out. "Maybe you want to check up on him. Maybe you want to make sure he's doing his job."

"Now, wait a minute—" Tom had kept silent till now. I knew he didn't like being talked about.

"Tom, if you won't talk to me, maybe Bill here will."

Tom wanted to say something, I could tell. But those long fingers reached out and touched his sleeve. Tom was bigger, by far, but he shut up. "What would the lady like to know?"

"More than you can imagine." I was stalling, thinking as quickly as I could. "For example, I'm hearing a lot about guns—antique guns—and I'm wondering if you are also a collector. Or maybe a dealer." The way I emphasized the last word should have made my intent clear.

"I have various business interests, and I'm always happy to give a lady credit." He showed big yellow teeth again, as friendly as a shark.

"No thanks," I smiled back, taking my cue. "Not my type of toy. But from what I hear, Lew was also involved with these pretty guns. Now he's dead too."

"And you think that maybe I or one or my colleagues were involved?" The hand restrained Tom again, making me think of a leashed dog. I shrugged. "Maybe I wanted the recently deceased gone for some reason?"

I shrugged again. It was all I could think of, though I couldn't fit the details together. It was the wrong response. The smile was replaced by a look of disgust.

"Mr. McMudge was a butterfly. A socialite. A playboy. But—" he raised one hand, palm up, in an eloquent gesture—"we knew each other. And you get to an age when funerals matter."

"What about Donal Franklin?"

"Donal Franklin was a man of honor." The sudden change in his tone made me want to know more.

"Wait a minute, the other stiff?" Tom was barking out of turn. Bill gave him a sharp look.

"You didn't sell him a gun?" I had Bill's attention now. "A dueling pistol with a silver-filigree grip? What about his wife, Louise Franklin?" I knew what Creighton had said. I didn't care. "The widow? Older woman. Good looking? Dark hair?"

He opened his mouth. He was about to say something, when Tom interrupted. Damn him. "Pru, I don't know what you think you're doing."

"I'm trying to figure out what's going on here, Tom." I could have kicked him. Or shot him, if I'd had that pretty toy. "Bill, you were about to say something."

"Duelling pistols are becoming quite popular these days. Even among the ladies." He had his cool back. "If you were truly curious, you could probably do a search. Might be interesting to see who is collecting."

"It just might." He wasn't scared, that's for sure. I didn't know what he was getting at. "Then again, maybe that's why you hired Tom."

"I didn't hire our friend Tom here to do anything." The smile was back, greasy and relaxed. I'd missed something. I'd lost him. "He and I simply met up to pay our respects. Same as Lew's other friends."

He leered, and I knew that I'd been placed. Well, maybe he really did know Lew. And just maybe, I didn't.

Chapter Thirty-two

I'm not good with anger. That was probably the other thing I got from my mother, along with the old house. And Bill with his insinuations and his leer had me seeing red as I made my excuses and turned away, desperately searching for something more to say beside the muttered "asshole" that only made him smile more broadly as I stalked off.

That nasty yellow grin seemed to hover, Cheshire-like, in front of me as I walked into what was becoming a cold and cloudy afternoon. It was the statue that saved me, a massive stone figure that loomed up like a stone stop sign, ending my mindless ramble. Those wings identified it as an angel. Some kind of guardian spirit. To me it looked monstrous, large and gray, but at least it served to rouse me from my funk. It also pointed out that I'd stalked off in the wrong direction. The small crowd had moved outside too, and I could see Tom and his slick buddy hovering by the fringe, deep in conversation as the rest of the small assembly made off to their cars. I watched, hoping they would leave too, but they were in no rush. I would have to pass by to return to the GTO.

"Great." I growled out loud, startling a chipmunk who'd been in the middle of something. Shelter, warmth…I got an image of little ones to come. "Sorry."

It wasn't just the tiny rodent. Now that I was aware of my surroundings again, I felt the chill in the air, the touch of moisture and frost that presages snow. I considered my outfit, particularly my lack of down or a sensible hat, and cursed under my breath.

That headache had lingered; I was coming down with something that I didn't have time for. Maybe if I walked quickly, cutting over the hill, I could get back to the car before the first flakes began to fall.

Muttering apologies to those concerned, I left the path and walked over a plot. Up the hill, the wind was stronger, piling the clouds up against the rim of the hills. I'd made a mistake in trusting March. It doesn't care what the calendar says; in New England this is still winter. The dirt, pitted and crumbling from repeated freezes, gave way as I climbed, and I stumbled, grabbing a thin birch as I crested the hill. Then I gasped.

Maybe it was the memory of that hawk. Maybe, for a moment, I was seeing from his eyes. Maybe it was simply that I'd never been in a cemetery and looked up. Now I did, and the view was incredible. There, off to the right, was Beauville, nestled down by the river that flashed and rippled through the still bare trees. Up ahead were the Berkshires, more hill than mountain, but still impressive with their dirty snow caps and evergreen mantles.

And there, just downhill through a stand of paper birches and only a little way off the path, was Robin Gensler. I couldn't hear her, not this far away, but she was glancing back toward the funeral site. To where Tom and his new buddy Bill still stood deep in conversation. They weren't the only ones. Even as Robin kept turning, looking nervously over her shoulder, I could see that she was talking to someone close by. It wasn't a casual chat, if the movement of her hands was any indication. And I didn't think she was trying to keep warm. At any rate, I wasn't going to miss an opportunity to talk to the one woman who might be able to help me save the Persian.

I waved, but the pretty brunette didn't see me, so I clambered ungracefully toward her, determined to catch her before she left. Only when I stumbled in the loose dirt, did I catch myself. That's when I realized who she was arguing with. Louise Franklin. Widow and chief mourner of the man who had been buried less than an hour earlier and about five hundred yards away.

I didn't know if I wanted to step into this. What had happened was clear as day: the younger brunette might have showed good sense in staying away from Donal's funeral. But she had gone to Lew's, at least to the visitation, and the temptation to visit her friend's—hell, her lover's grave must have been too great. Of course, I could be wrong. She could be here to meet Tom— or Tom's creepy friend—and used the services as a convenient excuse. Or she could have been shopping for a plot, though I wouldn't have put money on it. Whatever the reason, Robin didn't look happy. Running into Louise couldn't have helped.

I edged closer. I didn't want to step into a cat fight. I did want to help a cat. And if I could find out just who had been scratching what itch…

"I can't!" Louise's voice carried, and I allowed myself to slip forward. "'Cause only," I thought she said, her diction giving way under pressure.

Robin was moving, too: down the hill toward the parking lot. Louise had turned toward her, away from me, and the rest of her words were lost in the gathering gloom. It didn't matter, really. I could too easily imagine what they were shouting about. A love token, the love itself. Maybe it didn't matter. What did was that Louise was finally talking. Open. Hurt. Maybe I could get her to talk to me.

But the drama in front of me was unfolding too fast.

"You have—" Robin had turned to shout back her rebuttal. Whether that was it, or just the beginning, however, I wouldn't get to find out. She had seen me. Now she stood, white faced against the black of the trees. For a moment, we both froze, staring at each other. Then Louise turned toward me, too, and for a moment I had the strange impression that I was seeing double. This far back, Louise's striking eyes didn't register. Only that stare, and Robin didn't look any friendlier than the widow who had kicked me out of her house only the day before. Caught, I did the obvious thing.

"Hey!" I waved, plastering a big smile across my face. "So glad to see you. I think I got a little lost up here."

Robin spun on her heel and took off, as I stumbled down the hill. Louise stood her ground, watching me. As I approached, she blinked, her long, dark lashes turning those gray eyes as cold and closed as a metal security gate. If I'd thought I'd catch the grieving widow in a moment of vulnerability, I'd been crazy.

"Miss Marlowe." Was it my imagination, or had she emphasized the "Miss"?

"Pru, please." I slid and scrambled down to her. "Again, I'm so sorry for your loss."

She didn't respond. "And what brings you here?"

I toyed with the truth, or at least part of it. If I mentioned Llewellyn, maybe I'd get something from her. But Bill's comments had rankled, and I could easily see this woman, as sleek as a pampered cat, taking the same view. Lew must have had a reputation among his set.

"My mother is buried here," I said instead. It was worth it just to see her wince.

"I'm sorry." For a moment, I thought she'd stutter. Maybe I would have my entrée, but she turned away and, as I reached out for her, took a step and then another toward the lot. "Today has been," she paused. I waited to hear how she would explain the scene I'd just witnessed. "Wearing," she settled on finally. "Goodbye."

I watched her retreat, unable to come up with a good reason to make her stay. And I realized that by accident, I had stumbled upon one interesting fact: she hadn't been at Lew's graveside, hadn't even been close. If she had, she would have realized that I was there, though I'd missed her during my discussions with Tom and Bill. So what had kept her here, after her husband's burial, after the long, slow procession of exiting cars? And how had the face-off with Robin come about? At the base of the hill, she paused and pulled something small from her bag: a cell, a Blackberry. Grief may have slowed her down, but I had the strongest feeling that Louise Franklin wouldn't miss a social beat. I didn't know what I expected from a grieving widow. Sadness. Silence. A desire to avoid the world. Whatever it was, Louise Franklin wasn't it.

Not for the first time, I kicked myself for letting things go on as they had. If only I'd gotten a little more involved in Llewellyn's life, then maybe I'd have some clue about the relationships between these people. If only he'd taken me out among them, instead of to our hideaway weekends, our secret escapes. I shook my head. That bastard Bill had made me feel cheap, something I thought I'd long grown out of. Lew and I had had the relationship we'd wanted, and it was too late to do anything about it now.

I couldn't chase after Louise. She clearly wasn't going to talk. If she needed to, she could sic Creighton on me. Going after Robin Gensler seemed like the obvious next step. Maybe if I got her alone, I could find out why she'd shown up at the cemetery. Maybe I could use the fight I'd witnessed, rustle some feathers. The mood I was in, that would be fine, too.

I took out my own phone only to find that I was in a dead zone. I had to walk back to the lot before a signal registered. Even then, I could hear the call breaking up as I listened to Robin's voice mail for what seemed the hundredth time. The rich truly are different than you or I. They get better service.

"Robin? This is Pru. I'm sorry if I startled you just now. As you know, I've been trying to reach you. It's about the Persian. I'm going to the shelter to see her now. Call me, okay?" If that didn't get her, nothing would. For once, I smiled as I slipped the phone back into my pocket, I was even telling the truth.

Chapter Thirty-three

The weather echoed my mood as I drove to the shelter: dark and stormy. I'd broken a heel on the way to the car, and with snow threatening I suspected my one good pair of pumps were going to face more damage before the day was out. It had also occurred to me that since the hostilities had become open, I had less chance than ever of getting Louise Franklin to relinquish the Persian to Robin. That Persian would probably stand a better chance in the oncoming snow.

As if on cue, the first flakes started down. The spots on my windshield looked innocent enough, but I'd grown up in the area. I cursed myself for not throwing some boots in the back seat, and, while I was at it, for coming back to Beauville at all. Wallis had a point. We had a life in the city, where an ancient Italian would have tut-tutted over the condition of my soles and then worked his magic, reattaching the heel and smoothing the suede till my old pumps looked as good as new. Snow in the city was never as pretty as out here, but with the subway a block from my apartment, I didn't care. I didn't really have to deal.

I switched on the wipers and let their rhythm calm me down, turning off the highway to make my way on back roads. I was facing a problem. I needed to think, not deal with other drivers, and I welcomed the quiet as my tires left black trails on the newly frosted pavement.

The Persian had until Monday. Doc Sharpe might seem like a softie. That's what the families who came to find a puppy thought, and he cultivated the image for the good of the shelter. Underneath, he was pure Yankee granite. If he felt the cat could not be socialized, he was going to reclaim her enclosure for the next animal that came in off the street.

Of course, knowing the options, it might be possible to get Louise Franklin to relinquish the cat. She'd have to let go of her ridiculous notion of selling it, though. I briefly toyed with the idea of getting Doc Sharpe to make that call. She seemed like the type who would listen to a man. The problem would be to get him to side with releasing that cat to anyone. I could kind of understand his argument: plenty of pet-ready felines get destroyed each year, and the ones who longed for human contact deserved their shot at it. Only I knew some of what that cat had been through. And I knew that I had helped make her behavior worse.

My route didn't take much longer than the highway, and I had my argument ready as I turned into the shelter lot. Despite the weather, I had some trouble finding a spot and ended up waiting while a blue pickup loaded in three children and a cardboard carrier. Of course, it was Saturday. The busiest day of the week here at the shelter. At least some small animal had found a new home.

The scene inside confirmed my impressions. Snow or no snow, every family within forty miles had come out. I felt a fleeting moment of anxiety. March—that would be when those Christmas puppies and kittens were beginning to become less adorable, their messes bigger. But, hey, that could mean more work for me. Besides, the general tone of the din was joyous. Lots of barking and excited squeals, and few of the tearful wails that usually signal a goodbye.

Even the animals, from what I could hear, were happy, too. The voices were too jumbled for me to make out much. Maybe I'd finally mastered the art of tuning out. Wallis had said even the youngest kittens get the hang of it before long. But if so, it wasn't entirely voluntary, and after that brief spell of silence—my animal deafness, if you will—I was far from comfortable with any kind of dimming. And so even though it could mean bringing down an avalanche, I made myself open up. For so long, I had hated this gift. Now I wanted to hear everything—and I did.

Some of it was simple release: life in a cage isn't fun for any animal. Some of it was hopeful. That Lab knew the word "walkies" and was barely restraining himself. Even the more peaceful strains betrayed happiness. Over in the corner, an aging marmalade cat was gently kneading the lap of the woman who held her. She remembered being held, but that was oh so long ago.

The only discordant note was coming from the corner. Soft and so low, it was almost drowned out in the general cacophony—a higher pitch, strained almost to panic. A small animal was nearby, and he was in distress.

"Hello?" Half blind from the noise, I made my way toward the sound. It wasn't a cry. More like a low mumble, fretful and anxious. "Can I help you?" I tried to project my offer as I pushed by a kneeling pre-teen. I didn't need any special sensitivity to pick up on the look her mother shot at me. I didn't care. The kid had someone to look after her.

"Pru! It's you." I looked up, momentarily disoriented. The dark hair registered as fur. The dark eyes—then it hit me.

"Robin. I need to talk to you." I looked around. The small voice was still there, almost buried in the din. Not a ferret, I'd have known. A kitten? No. I followed it a step further, toward the cage rooms. "Would you mind?"

"I know. I got your message. I couldn't talk—back there." She reached for my arm just as I got the image of a twitching nose, dark eyes, and long, soft ears. A rabbit! A bunny who wasn't so much scared as anxious. Something wasn't as it should be, but Robin's hand pressed on my arm and I lost it. The small voice was gone. With less than charitable thoughts, I turned toward the plump brunette.

"I've been trying to reach you." I wanted to know what had happened—and why she hadn't called me back. But the small voice—a bunny had needed me.

For a moment, I recognized its face in hers. "I'm sorry." She stepped back, releasing her hold on me and bringing one, bare hand up to her mouth. "It's been awkward. Mrs. Franklin…" She colored, the pink in her cheeks making her look even younger.

"No, it's my fault." I shook my head to clear it. One problem at a time. "I've been looking for you to talk about Donal Franklin's Persian."

"I gathered." Her delicate brows raised in concern. At least she'd toned down the jewelry. "Is Fluffy all right?"

"Fluffy is essentially fine," I went into professional calming mode. "For now. But her behavioral problems are not getting better and, well, Doc Sharpe is beginning to look into other alternatives."

"Oh!" Maybe she *was* the bunny. "Well, that's good, right? Maybe I can take her?"

"No," I shook my head. I wasn't being clear. "Doc Sharpe is thinking that the cat can't be resocialized. And if Louise Franklin doesn't want her—"

"She'll be put up for adoption?" A tentative smile.

"She'll be euthanized." With the unerring timing of bad news, my bombshell fell in a moment of relative calm. Shocked faces looked up at me. A small child started to cry. "I mean, that's one possibility." I replied in my jauntiest tone. Children, like animals, respond as much to tone as to your actual words. "Let's talk."

Robin seemed as stunned by my words as that small child, and so I grabbed her by the arm and led her forcefully out of the waiting room, back into the building entry, the only semi-quiet place around.

"How—how can that be?" She was stuttering. "That's a perfectly fine cat."

"She's a lovely animal." I wasn't going to show her my scratched arm. I certainly wasn't going to explain my role in aggravating the poor beast. "But Louise Franklin has this idea that she can sell the cat to a breeder. Only no breeder is going to want an animal that is less than docile. And legally, Louise is the only one who can give her away. She can give her up, however, to the shelter. That makes it Doc Sharpe's call."

"Oh. Mrs. Franklin..." A woman of few words, she looked down. Blinked. I found myself worrying that she would start crying and then kicked myself. Since when was Robin Gensler my concern? Still, she must have picked up something. "And here I was, hoping I could still..." She looked up at me then. "I was thinking, maybe I could learn from you. That is, if you were willing to take me on as a kind of student or apprentice or something?"

Those big brown eyes. I could see why Donal Franklin could have fallen for her. It was with sadness that I shook my head. "I don't do apprentices. But, Robin, I did have some questions— questions that might help that Persian," I added in a rush.

She nodded.

"I know you care for the cat. That you had some previous experience with her." I paused, unsure how to present my questions. "Robin, is there something going on with you and a PI named Tom? Or his buddy, Bill?"

She shook her head. "No. I don't know who you're talking about."

She looked so blank I believed her. "Okay, then. What about with Donal Franklin?"

"It was..." She looked at the wall for answers. I did, too. The heartworm poster didn't help. "There was a moment. He said I reminded him of his wife when they first met."

I felt a cold surge of disappointment. Good ol' Don hadn't been so gallant after all.

She must have seen something on my face. "It wasn't like that at all." Of course not. "I was helping him with his collection. That was all."

"And that's why Louise Franklin is so friendly toward you?"

She swallowed. "She wasn't always like this. She helped me, at first. My hair...the clothes...But now, well, I'm kind of in a bad place. So, I thought—"

I shook my head. "I've had years of training, Robin. And, to be honest, there's barely enough work for me in this town."

She digested that in silence, and I found myself thawing a bit. I didn't believe in her innocence, but she had my sympathy.

Whoever had brought her into the house, she'd been used and discarded: the servant girl kicked out without a reference.

"Come on." I motioned back to the shelter lobby. "Let's go see that Persian. Maybe she'll take to you." Maybe we'd get world peace, too.

It might have been my imagination, but the lobby seemed to quiet as we stepped back in. It could have been the weather. More people seemed to be donning their coats with an eye toward getting home. Pammy was busy at the front desk, families crowding around to fill out forms. I looked for Doc Sharpe, but he was nowhere in sight. In one of the examining rooms, I figured. Or bouncing between all three, trying to handle all the walk-ins before their patience gave out. I already knew his take on the Persian anyway, and reached behind Pammy for the button that unlocked the door.

"It's open." She didn't even look up. She must have felt my eyes on her, though, because her tone had turned peevish as she added. "I'm just too swamped to handle everything."

"Fine." I led Robin Gensler over to the shelter door, and as I reached for it, I heard that voice again. Small, quiet. *Oh dear, oh dear, oh dear…* "Robin, can you hang on for a moment?"

I stepped back into the lobby. To my left, Pammy's ponytail bounced up and down, visible through the throng. To my right, the plastic chairs now held an assortment of coats, as parents suited up their offspring for the storm. "Hello?" I kept my voice soft, turning my head slowly to pick up that faint strain.

"Oh dear."

I looked around. There was no animal in sight, while behind me, I heard a voice.

"Pru? Is this okay? Maybe I should leave you alone?"

Robin. "No, it's fine. I thought I heard something." That much was true, and it was with a sigh of resignation that I pulled open the door to the cage area and motioned her in. The fact that I then almost walked into her I blamed on my own preoccupation. The cage room hits people like that. Floor to ceiling cages, stacked wall to wall: this first room was filled with dogs

"Excuse me?" Robin Gensler was standing by Fluffy's empty cage, looking through the soft towel rags that lined it as if they would offer up a full-grown feline. "And you are?"

She looked up, mouth open, and I jumped in to explain. "This is Robin Gensler. She knew the Persian, and I brought her by in the hope that she could help—" I didn't get to finish the sentence.

"And left her in the cage room." His eyebrows lowered as he glowered. I had broken one of the shelter's firm rules.

"I brought her in, and when we found the cat missing, I thought it best to look for you. I didn't know what you'd be doing…" I let the sentence hang. He could fill in the details for himself. He did, with a harrumph, but I wasn't getting off that easy.

"A cat that you care for goes missing. And you're the one who has been breaking the rules, Pru."

"I didn't take the Persian." Would I have raised the alarm if I did?

"Even to save it from euthanasia?" *Watch out*, the Siamese had been telling me. Had she been warning me about Doc Sharpe?

A gasp broke into our conversation. Robin was staring at the vet. "You were the one? You were going to kill Fluffy?"

I shot Doc Sharpe a look. He glowered back.

I glanced over at Robin. She was holding the rags up to her chest like a shield. "I'm confident we can avoid that."

"Maybe you already have." Doc Sharpe's voice had a testiness I didn't recognize.

"Anyone could have come in, Doc. Pammy left the door unlocked." Hey, I knew I hadn't taken the cat. Doc Sharpe didn't seem to be listening. "Shall we go ask her?"

He ushered Robin out, still clutching the cage cloths, and I led the way. The crowd around Pammy's desk had been winnowed down to one hunky teen. Too young for the junior college student, but she seemed to be enjoying the attention.

"Excuse us, please." Doc Sharpe nearly swatted the young man away. "Pamela. Did you let anybody back into the cage area without proper authorization?"

It was the wrong question, put the wrong way. Pammy swallowed and looked from her boss to me. In that moment, I knew we weren't going to get anything.

"Only that dark-haired woman. She said she was with Pru. She said it was okay."

Chapter Thirty-five

Doc Sharpe gave Robin a once over and then ushered Robin out, still clutching the rags that had lined the Persian's cage. I followed, promising to let her know the moment we found anything. Then I returned to deal with the good doctor.

"I did not authorize anonymous visitors." He had to know that. He had to know Pammy was trying to save her own job. "I only left Robin because I needed to find you, and I didn't know if you were doing surgery or with a client."

"I know, Pru." The eyebrows had lowered, showing frustration rather than anger. "I know. But this is…highly irregular."

His word choice almost made me smile. "That's one way to put it. Look, the door was unlatched before I got here. Let me poke around. Maybe I can find something." Princess Achara had taken off, but I wanted some time with that rabbit.

"Well, I should—" He cut himself off. A couple had stood up from the chair area. They had a small brown dog on a leash and were watching him as eagerly as puppies themselves. "I should report this, you know. To Mrs. Franklin. But I'm rather backed up."

"See these people, Doc. It looks like they've been waiting." I knew how the widow Louise would react from the first time she thought I'd taken her pet, and I really didn't need Creighton involved in this. "We'll talk after."

He nodded, the decision made, and gestured to the couple with the puppy. I tried to catch Pammy's eye, hoping to fell her with a glare. She, wisely, kept her face averted, and so once the coast was clear, I returned to the cat room. I wanted to find that brush, and I was also ready to interrogate a bunny.

The brush was my first priority. As I recalled, I had left it on the table, and it made sense that it might have been cleared away. But a thorough search through the shelves didn't show anything like it. Down on my knees, I found more dust—but no brush. Nor did any of the other cages show a grooming brush. I took a breath. I wasn't going to panic. It had probably been filed someplace. Put aside when the table was needed first thing in the morning. There was no reason to believe that whoever had taken the cat had taken the brush, I told myself. I knew I was lying.

There was nothing for it, though, but to move on. The cat might be gone, but I had a witness. In a way, I was in luck. The rabbit in the opposite cage was an older bunny, an altered male, which made him less excitable than many of his peers. Rabbits are tougher than most realize. Some will even cohabit with cats, which is probably why Doc Sharpe had placed the beast in this room. Still, the strange surroundings and that basic bunny fearfulness do not make for calm. The brown-faced creature I found huddled into his shavings was quivering more with fear than curiosity.

"Hey." I stopped a few feet from the cage and spoke just loud enough to be heard. "Thank you for the warning." That's what I had picked up, I was sure of it. "Can you tell me what happened?"

"Oh dear, oh dear, oh dear." The little nose sniffed the air, and I waited. Robin's outburst had shaken the tender creature. *"Oh, dear."* At the very least, that woman was not cut out for animal care. She was worse than Pammy. I sent out calming thoughts—sunny hillsides. Ripening grasses. A prey animal like this would know the world by scent as much as anything. I had the sense that he was getting my mental images, but also that he was taking my measure. I could only hope I didn't smell too much of Wallis.

"Big, scary...." Oh great, he must be getting a mental image of my tabby. I tried to clear my mind. *"Dark."*

I waited, doing my damnedest not to think of Wallis' sleek stripes. Instead, I focused on the rabbit. His ears, in proportion with his body, were long and sensitive, and I knew he would have clearly heard whatever had happened on the other side of that screen. The question was, would he tell me?

"Scared, scared, quickly. Hide!" The command came quietly, but it was still a command. *"Run away."*

I looked at the little animal. "Are you warning me? Telling me to run away?"

"No, no, no. Too confusing." The velvet nose quivered. *"Watch out. Soft, but not soft. She bites."*

"Are you talking about the Persian?" I didn't understand. "Or are you quoting someone?" The rabbit hadn't been here when the cat had lashed out at me. Still, he might have overheard someone talking. "Is that what you're saying?" I pictured the missing feline, and immediately realized my mistake.

"I trusted you. I did." The bunny was shivering, and I fought the urge to reach for him. If I tried to comfort this small animal, I could shock him into a heart attack.

"Sorry. I'm sorry." In my softest voice, I tried to make my regret felt. "Poor bunny."

"It's Tadeus, please. And I'm a rabbit." Dark liquid eyes peered up into mine. *"I heard it, you know. I heard it all. I was wrong. I'm sorry. I bite."*

"Wait, are you saying *you* bite?" This was hopeless. Wallis was right. I couldn't expect any assistance from a rodent. "Or that you heard—" I was in mid-question when the door opened and Doc Sharpe came in.

"Any luck?" He wasn't expecting an answer, not really, and turned from me to the rabbit cage. "The latest trend. House trained, if you can believe it."

"Why's he here?" Usually, we get the rabbits later in the spring. Easter bunnies, once the novelty has worn off.

"Wiring."

I looked up. Was I missing something? The rabbit hadn't seemed crazy.

"He chewed through some wires in his family's living room," Doc explained. "The family caught it just in time. It could have started a fire."

"Poor little loser. So that's what you meant about biting." I reached through the bars of the cage, drawn by the soft brown fur. The bunny jumped back, startled. Prey animal. All he cared about was security. All he'd want would be a safe place, a haven. His warren. "Did you realize what you were messing up when you gnawed away?"

One hop. Two. Slowly the rabbit approached. I held still and felt the first tentative touch of leather as the trembling nose came up and sniffed my fingertip. "Little fool." Doc Sharpe was looking at me. I addressed him as much as the bunny. "He couldn't help it. It's what he does."

"Just like you."

I recoiled.

"We are who we are."

"Did he bite you?" Doc Sharpe looked over.

"No." I eyed the rabbit. "It just occurred to me what little pests these guys are."

Chapter Thirty-six

Despite Doc Sharpe's Yankee reserve, it was clear that I was still in the hot seat. Didn't matter that Robin wanted that cat as much as I did. Didn't matter that I had no more means of spiriting a cat away than she did. Didn't matter that I'd reported the loss. I had access to the shelter and, as the good doc pointed out, I had motive.

As I did a quick clean up of the cage room, he had reiterated his suspicions—and his responsibility to act on them—and I had to think fast. I really didn't want him to call Louise Franklin. The woman already thought I was a nag, at best. And my reputation as the local cat lady wouldn't help either. The idea of him calling Jim Creighton didn't make me feel any better. Jim liked me, sure. But he was a cop.

"Look, Doc, can you give me some time on this?" I said as I wiped down the table. I was still wearing my funeral finery, but it seemed prudent to be useful. "I'm sure there's a simple explanation." I wasn't, not by a long shot, but I needed a little room to figure it out. "It's not like Mrs. Franklin is going to come by for a visit."

He opened his mouth to complain. And shut it. I was guessing that he had realized the negative impact of the news. Shelter directors are not supposed to lose animals. Especially not animals that supposedly have commercial value.

"Forty-eight hours?" I was near to begging. If I couldn't find her in that time, I'd think of something else. The deadline did it, however. Mumbling something about Monday by closing, Doc Sharpe retreated, leaving me along again in the cage room.

"I'll want to examine that cat," Jim Creighton had said—was it only three days ago? Had he been serious? I'd read the news reports, the ones that talked about using pet DNA to convict home invaders. I'd never heard of anyone checking the pet herself. Not that it mattered. At this rate, there would be nothing left for him to inspect. For a half a second, I thought of calling him. Maybe he could fingerprint the cage.

No, I shook my head. For one thing, Doc Sharpe's cooperation was based partly on the tacit promise to keep this quiet. For another, if I were to bring him in on this, I'd have to confess to stealing the brush. I was in too deep to call for professional aid now.

Besides, I wanted to get home. My broken pump had me walking with a limp, and if the snow had continued—back here, it was hard to tell—my shoes would be beyond salvaging soon.

I looked back at the rabbit—Tadeus—but all I saw was that dappled back. *"Stay warm, dig deep..."* Images like waking dreams floated by. A dark place. Safety. The quiet of solitude. I turned away with a twinge of guilt; the little creature had given me what he could. *"Search out a burrow, a place to hide."*

◇◇◇

Pammy was gone by the time I emerged. The waiting room, deserted. Doc Sharpe was still in back—I could see the light— but I made sure the door locked behind me anyway. Not that I thought any other animals would go missing, but if any did, I didn't want the blame. And then I stepped out into the maelstrom.

Snow in the valley isn't like in the city. Without the packed-in buildings, it has fewer borders. Even here, on a commercial street, I could see waves of the white stuff, swells of it blowing down the street. Trying not to think about my poor shoes, I bent my head against the wintry blast and made my way to my car. I'd dealt with storms all winter, enough so I was used to it again. But I didn't have to like it.

It took a few minutes for the heat to kick in, and I used those to scrape off the windows. At least the road looked empty as I pulled out of the parking lot and headed toward the highway. I didn't want to prolong this drive. With this weather, with any luck, I'd not see another car till I got back to Beauville no matter what my route. Barefoot—the soggy pump was worse than useless—I tapped gingerly on my brakes. A little skid, not bad. It was all a question of knowing what you were dealing with.

By the time I got to the highway, I was almost enjoying myself. My big old car didn't have four-wheel drive, but it had heft. Besides, the radio worked, and with no traffic, I could take my time. Tom would have laughed at me, driving like this. Tom could go to hell. As the wind picked up, shaking the car and dashing more of the white stuff at me, I did find myself wishing for one slow truck. If I could have followed some taillights all the way home, I wouldn't have to think.

So when I saw the headlights coming up behind me, I gave a little cheer. Not a truck, but something big. Probably something with four-wheel drive and newer tires than I had, anyway. We were the only vehicles on the road, and I waited for it to pass. If it didn't go too fast, I'd fall in behind, taking advantage of the slipstream as well as the lights.

Only the car didn't pass. Another burst of wind shook my GTO, and I realized those lights were still behind me. Great, another genius with the same idea. We were at the point where the road turned, curving a little to deal with a steeper grade, and I slowed in response. Not enough, I realized, as my rear tires fishtailed on the icy road. Rather than braking again, I lifted my foot from the gas. Too much, and I'd lose control. I only wanted to slow it down.

The car behind me didn't notice. Instead, the lights crept up through the snow until they filled my rearview mirror. Squinting, I gave the old car a bit more gas.

And the lights came up again. In the reflection, I couldn't see the car, couldn't see a driver. He had to see me, though. I was in front of him. I was—

The first bump left me gasping and confused. I gripped the wheel, expecting to feel the sidewind of a blowout. Had I hit a pothole or a branch blown into the road? My GTO steadied, and I whispered thanks to American steel. Lights or no lights, I'd keep my eye on the pavement, what I could see of it, the rest of the way home. Behind me, the car had dropped back, leaving me in sudden darkness, except for the cones of illumination directly in front of me.

That was fine. The road was straightening out here. No more distractions—just a simple shot to Beauville. While the wind buffeted my car again, I settled in. I'd faced down crackhead muggers and urban rats that swarmed up from flooded subway tracks. I could handle this.

Those lights, though. This guy was getting annoying. I didn't want to stop, not on a road like this. I wanted to give him a message, and it wasn't peace and love. I clicked on my directional. Let him think I was pulling over. There wasn't much of a shoulder. We were back on what was more or less a straightaway, but the raised road bed tumbled into a ditch before it hit trees. As the lights came up, I sidled to the right.

"Pass me, asshole." The lights came closer. "Come on..."

For a moment, I relaxed. That driver was cutting it close. I had an impression of a big black town car, a silver bumper shining in its own reflected light, creeping up on my left. "Pass, damn it." Where was that uninhibited acceleration now?

I pulled over slightly more. Felt the rumble of uneven ground. Any further and I'd be off the pavement. "Pass!"

And then I felt the screech and crunch of metal as the big car moved into mine, forcing me into the ditch and into a roll and then into a blackness as heavy and unyielding as that car.

Chapter Thirty-seven

My mother always said I had a hard head. I couldn't have been out for more than a few seconds when I woke up, my mouth filled with blood. The engine was still ticking, I was still warm, and the snow was still melting to star-shaped slush on a windshield that leaned at a crazy angle to the world outside.

I spit out the blood, and gasped against a wave of nausea as the movement jarred my right arm. Twisted somehow behind me, it made itself known with a throbbing howling pain that could have put me back under, if I weren't so angry and, I'll admit it, scared.

The car was right side up, more or less. But it was leaning so far over that I knew there'd be no driving back out of the ditch. Nothing for it then. Bracing myself for the pain, I reached over with my left hand to hit the safety belt catch and cried out loud as it released and I automatically caught myself with my right. It was my wrist, hot and burning, though I noted with some pleasure that it still seemed to work. Still, I used my other hand to grab my bag and root around for my cell.

For a moment, I hesitated about who to call. My mother. Lew. They were gone and the momentary flash—Wallis was my closest contact—had me barking out a laugh that set my wrist throbbing like a beacon. As much as I didn't want a fuss, Mack and Tom were out of the question. Not if I wanted to be sure I got out of here. No, it was Creighton. At least I had his private line, which was a little better than dialing 911.

"Where are you?" He was all business, and to my horror, I started to cry.

"About five miles out of town, heading west." I worked to keep the quaver out of my voice. "I hurt my arm."

Twenty minutes later, I was in an ambulance, and protesting less than I would have if they hadn't given me something very nice to smooth out the pain.

"Hang on." I was lying on a stretcher, making noise about getting a ride home, when Creighton climbed in. "Give us a minute." The EMT left.

"Okay, what happened?"

I smiled. It was the drugs. "You care." I was joking, but it came out softer than I meant.

He wasn't having any of it. "This isn't funny, Pru. You haven't been back that long. This is still winter. People die on the roads in winter." He had his stern face on, those light blue eyes as cold as steel.

Through the haze of painkillers, I remembered something. "It wasn't my fault. Really. Someone drove me off the road."

His brows went up at that and he crouched by my side. "Tell."

I did. Not that he bought any of it.

"Saturday night. Maybe they'd been partying at Happy's."

Thoughts like trapped flies buzzed around my head. "Wrong direction. I was heading into town." Besides, I knew I'd never seen a car like that in the lot behind the bar.

"Well, I wouldn't make too much of it. Night like this, someone gets a little careless…" He gave me that look again, like his eyes could fix me to the floor. "You've got to be more careful."

"It wasn't my fault, Jim. Really." The drugs were pulling me under, keeping me from making my case. "It was a late model sedan, black or dark blue, and it rammed me. Twice."

"Why don't you leave this to me, Pru." He was patting my hand, looking up at the EMT. "I'll look into it, and see if there's anything to it." And then he was gone.

I woke to a nurse who was talking to me like I'd talk to a goldfish.

"Now, we're just going to bandage you up and get you comfy, all right?"

"No." She looked at me, a little confused. I could see her measuring my next dose. "Is it broken?" I lifted my arm cautiously.

"Why don't we wait till morning—"

"I'm not going to." Frustration was making me angry, and anger cleared my head. "I need to go home." I didn't add the obvious—that I had a cat to feed. I knew this kind of place. That would make them keep me in longer.

"It's sprained. Badly." The baby talk was gone, and I could see how thrilled she was. Recalcitrant patient. Saturday night wreck. I had to hope she wasn't going to draw blood anytime soon. "You're to be under observation."

I kept my mouth shut. Once she had me in a room, I'd make a break for it. My wrist ached, with a grinding throb that made me think of dentists and Nazis. As long as it wasn't broken, though, I could take care of myself. Clothes might be a problem; the EMT had cut away my shirt and coat with what seemed a bit too much glee. And a ride…

Blame the drugs. Jim Creighton was one step ahead of me, waiting as I was wheeled into a room. "I bet you think you're leaving." He nodded to the nurse. They'd had some kind of agreement.

"Damn straight," I said, careful to hold my arm against my belly as I levered my legs off the table. "You have no reason to hold me."

"Not even for your own safety?"

That blindsided me, as did the sudden dizziness that threatened to put me back down again. "I thought you didn't believe me?" I fought against it, focusing on the hem of the curtain. Anything rather than his tight-mouthed frown.

"I said, I'd look into it." He was enunciating every word slowly and I managed to turn toward him. The hour—or tension—had aged him. The short-cropped blonde hair was still boyish, but there was a set to his face, lines around his mouth, that I didn't remember from our last time together.

That startled me, and I realized how drugged I must have been. He'd heard what I'd said. He'd been trying to play me. The thought warmed me, rather to my surprise. Not that he cared, but that he had the wits to try to outsmart me.

"What are you smiling at now?" Despite his tone, his face had relaxed a little.

"Nothing, officer. Nothing at all. But I'll make you a deal. If you get me home tonight, I promise I'll stay out of it. Leave it to you and go about my business. You know I'm fine, and I've got Wallis. She's probably worried stiff."

I meant it as a joke and was rewarded by the ghost of a smile. When he didn't respond beyond that, I had a moment of worry—and tried to think of alternatives. But then he spirited a parka out of somewhere, and I realized he'd been prepared for this. That was okay. He knew me well enough by then to know that I had no intention of keeping my word.

Chapter Thirty-eight

"Stupid, stupid *human*. I can't believe…" If I expected sympathy, I got none. Instead, I had Wallis pacing the kitchen floor, her tail lashing furiously as she muttered under her breath.

"What?" I'd shooed Creighton off with a promise to call in the morning and come in to fix myself a drink. The pain pills had begun wearing off while we were still getting me dressed, and I'd refused more, preferring an anesthetic I knew. Besides, the smooth warmth of the whiskey reminded me that I was an adult. More and more, around Wallis, I felt like an idiot child. Or, perhaps, a kitten. "It wasn't my fault. Is this because I lost the cat?"

"When I hunt, do I walk up to my prey and announce myself? Do I?" Her ears were halfway back. This was serious.

"No…" I didn't really see what she was getting at. That could have been the last of the pain meds, though. It might officially be Sunday already, but I really needed to get back to bed.

"You can't just go about getting yourself in trouble. You can't."

I nodded, leaning back against the counter. Bed. Sleep. I felt the soft pressure of her head as she rubbed against me. I reached down to pick her up with my good arm. It was awkward, but she was purring. *"You* can't."

"I need you, Pru." With my face buried in her lustrous fur, I found my way upstairs and lay down, still holding her soft body. Her purr was the last thing I heard.

When I woke, however, it was her words that echoed through my head. Announce? Who had I told—and what?

I'd have asked Wallis, but she was nowhere to be found. I understood. Neither of us is good after displays of unguarded emotion. And while I was intensely curious to follow up on what she'd said, I was relieved by her major point. Unlike Creighton, my tabby had believed that I'd been targeted. She wasn't buying the whole "Saturday night drunk" crap.

Then again, I acknowledged as I made my creaky way into the kitchen, she was a cat, and cats don't have to deal with cars. I did, and as the coffee was brewing, I made some calls. Creighton wasn't a bad guy. He'd had my GTO towed into town. Someone would be looking at it. I was tempted to leave it at that. It was Sunday, I had no clients, and the longer I was awake, the more my various bruises made themselves felt. My wrist might not be broken, but the simple act of dialing the phone had set it throbbing again. Maybe Creighton wasn't so clueless. Maybe I could leave it all to him.

Then it hit me. He didn't know the half of it. Thanks to my urging, neither I nor Doc Sharpe had told him the Persian was missing. He didn't know about the missing brush—or the hair I had found on the brush. And, I realized with what felt like a physical blow, I couldn't tell him. Not without implicating myself in petty theft at the very least—and a lot more complicated matters if I went on.

I'd already searched the shelter; the Persian was gone. But she was out there somewhere. Doc Sharpe had given her a deadline of Monday. Someone else had intervened with what might be a more pressing threat. An animal in my care had been taken and was in danger. And nothing gets me moving more than a good head of steam.

A few calls and the offer to mortgage my first born got me a rental car: a four-door sedan better suited to my grandmother. The roads were a mess, the early spring snow settling into a wet slush that had lighter cars hydroplaning on the curves, and the Ace bandage on my wrist didn't help, but I managed. The rental's new-enough tires had some traction, though I could tell my wrist would be screaming by day's end. Well, by day's end maybe I'd have some answers. First stop was the auto shop.

I knew Mikey G from the old days. We'd never been close, but we'd been part of a crowd that hung out together, sharing beer and weed, so he'd only muttered a little when I called him at home. He met me at the shop where his father held court, looking so much like his departed dad I did a double take as he ushered me in.

"Axle," he said, pointing. My baby blue baby was up on the lift. I had a vague memory of family members—other mechanics—working here, but today he was alone. "Front right." With his father's girth, he'd adopted his speech patterns—or lack of them.

I nodded and swallowed. It wasn't like I had a choice. "Did you notice anything unusual—anything on the back bumper?"

It was a long shot, and it didn't pay off. He only looked at me. I told myself that the storm and the mud from the ditch would have obscured any trace of the other car. In truth, I knew that among all the dents and dings, one more would be hard to pick out.

"Never mind. When can you have it up and running?"

Another pause. The way he rubbed his chin made me think of the beard he'd grown in high school, back when he'd cracked the occasional joke. "If I still had my cousin Red helping out," he started, then stopped himself with a shake of his head. "Tuesday?"

My wrist was in for a workout. As I ducked under the garage door, though, another thought hit me. "With this weather, you must be getting lots of work."

My car might not show a dent, but the car that had hit me had been gleaming, bright and new. He shook his head. "Not really." For a moment, he looked fuddled and I dared to hope. "Maybe I can get it back to you tomorrow." He coughed up the sentence like it was penance. "Late. If I have the parts."

I nodded. That hadn't been my point, but I'd take it. I had another lead to follow.

◇◇◇

The sedan drove like a truck, and my wrist felt like a fireball by the time I reached the cop shop. If I were lucky, Albert would be in his office and I could cadge some aspirin—or something stronger—from his desk. If I were really lucky, he'd have brought in Frank, and I'd have a shot at intelligent conversation. First, though, I had to try out an idea. Telling myself the pain would keep me sharp, I pushed open the big glass door that led to the police station. Just another accident victim looking to file a report.

Creighton looked happy to see me. Once I started talking, that changed.

"Someone really was trying to drive me off the road, you know. That wasn't an accident."

"Good morning. And how are you today?" He motioned to the seat in front of his desk. I took it, but could barely sit. "Feeling better?"

"I'm fine." He looked down at my bandaged wrist, so I kept talking. "I'm here about last night. It wasn't just someone trying to pass, Jim. That other car rammed me—two or three times. *Then* they tried to drive me off from the side. I can't tell if you were just trying to humor me last night or not by saying you'd investigate, but that's the truth. Someone wanted me off the road. Someone wanted me—" I paused, the word sticking in my throat—"dead."

"And why would anyone want that?" His words stopped me. In truth, I hadn't thought much about it. I was looking into a suspicious death, two suspicious deaths. And I'd lost a cat. I'd also stolen and then lost a grooming tool. I hadn't told Creighton about the brush. Right now, it seemed like small potatoes.

"Who the hell knows?" I believe in a good offense. "All I know is that it wasn't an accident."

"I believe you, Pru." He said, his voice quiet. "I wanted to get you out of there, and I was hoping you'd stay in the hospital or at least at home, in bed, where you'd be safe." He cleared a sudden roughness from his throat and refused to meet my eye. "I'm not a fool."

"I know," I whispered. "I just—"

"You just want to be in control of everything." There was an edge now, and he was looking straight at me. "But I wish you'd let me do my job. I've made some calls. I've got people checking, and there haven't been any late model sedans brought into body shops in the five-town area. Not overnight, not this morning."

"That doesn't mean—" Anything, I wanted to say. He didn't let me finish.

"I know how to investigate a crime, Pru, but you're not the only person in this town. I've got responsibilities, and if you keep getting yourself into trouble." He paused to clear his throat again. "Look, maybe it was an accident. Or maybe someone just wanted to scare you. You can be a pain sometimes. You know that, don't you? So, for me, can you just let it be for a while? Just lay low? I'll stay on it. I promise."

I nodded. Everything he'd said was true. But even as I moved my head, I was making my own plans. He'd stay on it, sure. That meant he'd call around again on Monday, maybe on Tuesday. Or he'd deputize some underling who didn't see the importance of locating a dented fender from an accident during a spring storm. And he'd said "five towns," which meant Beauville to Amherst. We were only a short drive from Albany, and I didn't know if his jurisdiction meant he could compel information from body shops in another state. No, I'd have to look into this myself. I would simply have to lay low enough to stay off Jim Creighton's radar.

Chapter Thirty-nine

I wasn't expecting answers as I made my way out of the cop shop. I wouldn't have minded a consult, though, and was disappointed to find the adjoining office locked up tight. What else did Albert have to do on a Sunday? I toyed with the idea of dropping by his house. It wasn't the bearded animal control officer I wanted to consult with, it was his ferret, Frank. But the idea of encouraging any intimacy—or of entering his living quarters—made me vaguely ill. No, I had other sources. Didn't I?

Princess Achara. The Siamese had tried to tell me something yesterday. She may have even engineered her visit to the animal hospital in order to reach me. Sitting inside the big rental car, I called her person to arrange a visit.

"Nancy? This is Pru. I wanted to touch base about Princess—Pickles." I caught myself quickly, but I heard her chuckle.

"Princess Pickles. I like that. And what a sweetheart you are!"

I liked the cat. I did. That wasn't why I was calling. "Would you like me to stop by? Sometimes, an injury or an accident can be traumatic for an animal."

Princess Achara had more poise than most people I knew. I wanted to talk to her.

"Oh, we're just fine. Thanks anyway."

"You're fine?" I was stalling. It paid off.

"Completely. It was the darnedest thing." Nancy Pinkerton's voice sounded more proud than confused. Knowing her cat, I could understand that. "I felt like she just *had* to get into the garage. Just had to go for a ride, and that was before she started playing with the ribbon, too. But it all worked out, didn't it? We even got home before the storm, so don't you worry about us. We're all tucked in and cozy."

"Well, see you on Wednesday." Her words had only confirmed my suspicion: the Siamese had been trying to tell me something. What that was, though, would have to wait.

The car was toasty warm by then, the car's oversize engine purring like Wallis. Driving this beast might be difficult, but it was certainly powerful. And the body, well, if anyone else tried to ram me, at least this baby had airbags.

That's when it hit me. I needed to retrace my steps. Go back to the accident site and look around. I shivered despite the warmth. Then, I thought, back to the county shelter. I'd been pretty panicked when I'd been looking around yesterday, and the crowd hadn't helped. Maybe on a quiet Sunday, I'd be able to find out something new. Maybe the brush would turn up. Maybe the Persian would, too.

As I cruised along the state highway, I had another thought. Perhaps I'd been looking at the wrong crime. Nobody would kill to cover up a catnapping, would they? No, this had to tie in with something bigger. Tom hadn't told me all he knew. He'd been afraid to. And his buddy, Bill as he'd called himself? There was something going on with him.

The big car lacked road feel, but it did eat up the pavement as I replayed our conversation. Lew. My questions. Tom. None of it seemed inflammatory. I hadn't even had a chance to ask about Donal Franklin's will. In his own way, Tom's employer—that was the only way I could think of him—had almost seemed to like me. The image of his leering smile, his insinuating offer, came back, making me shudder. The feeling wasn't mutual.

I don't like feeling intimidated. I like being sneered at even less, and, besides, this big car was eating up gas. I pulled over into a service station and before I filled up, I looked through the numbers that had called me recently. Only one had a New York area code: Tom.

"Hey, Pru." I'd caught him off guard. I could tell by the laugh. "What's up?"

"Your friend." From the silence, I assumed he was with a woman. I didn't care. "From the funeral? Bill?"

"Oh, yeah, Bill." He was stalling. It was too early for him to be drunk, and he wasn't usually slow. "What about him?"

"I need to speak with him. Now."

"Pru, that's not a great idea." I had his attention now. "You don't know—

"Tell him I'm a client. A potential client. He gives credit to ladies, didn't he say that?"

Silence. I had no patience for that trick today. "Tom."

A sigh and what sounded like a muffled curse. "I'll call you back."

Nice thing about mobile phones, they're mobile. So I filled my tank and set off down the road. Ten minutes later, I was cruising a stretch of highway, looking for something that might identify where I'd gone off the pavement. Trouble was, I couldn't tell. Bare trees, still black with moisture. Patches of snow on dead leaves. I was slowing to check out one spot—something about that stand of birch seemed right—when the phone rang. If I'd been in a smaller car, I might have driven into the ditch again. Instead, I pulled over and reached for the phone, cursing under my breath.

"Tom." I wasn't in the mood for any more delay tactics.

"Sorry, honey." Bill's voice sounded obscenely close to my ear, the endearment as chilling as glass. "You got me instead."

I swallowed. I hate starting off with a disadvantage. "Can we talk?"

"Sure, how about lunch?" He named a restaurant near the shelter, and for a moment I had a creepy feeling he was watching me. "I know you do some work with the animal hospital near there."

The explanation didn't help, but I agreed. I looked out at the cold and sodden woods. I wasn't going to find anything here anyway. We picked a time, and he hung up, leaving me with more questions than before.

"What if…" How could I forget? Although my senses were too dull to pick up anything, I wasn't alone out here. Far from it. Parking on the verge, I got out and tried to acclimate myself. That turn, those birches. No, it was no use. So instead of looking for clues, I tried to clear my mind. I had been here—or somewhere near—only the night before. There had been violence, a disruption.

"*Flee! Flee!*" The alarm call made me jump, and I spun around in time to see the shadow of a hawk. "*Quick!*"

Something scurried under the leaves. I took a breath and tried to settle. Thought back to the storm, the snow—and the awful thudding route my car had taken down into the ditch.

"*Watch it, watch it, watch it. No!*" I looked up, but no. Some other small tragedy had just occurred. Nature was taking care of its own. My misadventure was nothing to these creatures, last night an eternity ago. With that thought in mind, I got back into the big car and made my lumbering way toward lunch.

At least, I thought as I waited for the hostess, I'd be early. I wasn't sure what I wanted to ask Bill. I didn't think he'd confess to anything, no matter how charmed he pretended to be. Watching him, though, that might be something.

"Were you meeting a gentleman?" The hostess was looking at me expectantly. Sure enough, Bill was already there, rising to greet me, that big grin firmly in place.

"Miss Marlowe. How lovely." I nodded and took my seat, afraid for a moment that he would kiss my hand if I offered it. "Oh dear, you've had an accident."

The damned Ace bandage. Then again, that might be my in. "I wouldn't necessarily call it an accident." I wanted the acid in my voice to cut through the grease in his. "Someone tried to run me off the road last night."

He raised his eyebrows. He didn't look surprised. "And you'd like my assistance with something?"

This was an interesting development. "You do that kind of thing?"

"I—" he waved his hand, as if the words were too unpleasant. "I can often provide services. Introduce people."

"You're awfully candid." I found myself smiling. It isn't often that a gangster comes right out with a menu.

"Tom said I could trust you." The smile was back. "Not that I necessarily trust Tom."

I laughed. I was warming to the old guy. "Tom is Tom."

"He also said that you would say that." At that point the waitress showed up and we ordered. A burger for me, a Cobb salad and a glass of burgundy for Bill. "Wine?"

"No, thanks." This was becoming one of the stranger meals I could remember.

"So," he linked long fingers together and leaned forward, over them and closer to me. "How may I help you, Miss Marlowe?"

"It's Pru." His eyes were clear and grey. For a moment, I thought about that hawk. "I'm trying to find out what's going on." Lew, Donal. They both flashed through my mind, along with the missing Persian—and my own car crash. Leads on any of these would be interesting. And useful, and I realized that not choosing was the best strategy of all.

He was watching me still. Then he nodded, just once, as if I had confirmed something he already knew. "Your gentleman friend."

I nodded.

"So silly." He sighed. I thought of the wind in a graveyard. "It's manners, really. You look like a young lady who understands manners."

I understood something about predators. My burger arrived, but I kept my eyes on him. "In my line, you understand, there is an emphasis on discretion." He paused to look at his salad, then speared a piece of cheese and ate it. The burger smelled fantastic, but I didn't want to miss anything. "Particularly when introductions have been made, when allowances have been made."

He gestured with his fork and looked over at my plate. "Is anything wrong with your burger?"

"Not at all." I picked it up and took a bite without tasting it. "What do you mean, 'discretion'?"

"Please, we're all adults here." He was eating with relish, but he paused to dismiss my question with another wave of his fork. "Would you like something else? A steak?"

I shook my head and tried again. "Well, tell me about the introduction, then."

"Your friend and I had some things in common." He smiled, unaware of the lettuce that had stuck to his right front incisor. It didn't make him look any less lethal. "We are both soft touches for beautiful ladies."

Will power kept me in my seat. Will power and curiosity. "Did Lew introduce you to Louise Franklin? Robin Gensler?"

He shook his head slowly, as if reprimanding a child. "Please, Pru. I'm a gentleman. What message would that send to a lovely lady such as yourself?"

"But you provided a service?" I was fishing.

He knew it, shaking his head. "I am happy to do favors, particularly for friends and for"—his smile widened, showing more teeth—"beautiful ladies. But, please, I, too, am a man of honor."

Donal. I'd forgotten that he knew him, also. Not that it did any good. Forty minutes later, I'd given up. Bill had said all he intended, becoming the master of evasion when I pushed. At Donal's name, he only shook his had, his smile turning a bit sad. When I asked how he knew Tom, he shrugged. His own business was dismissed as "a bit of this and that." Even his home base was vague. "I'm partial to the city, of course. But this area has some lovely vistas."

Exhausted, finally, I dressed my burger properly and ate, letting him grill me about my life. I figured, he'd have been able to get it all from Tom anyway. To my surprise, he asked me several questions about my work with animals.

"Most of it is pretty basic." I was finishing the fries by then. "Simply try to put yourself in their place. See what they see, figure out what they want."

"Try to think like them, huh?" Those gray eyes sought mine.

I swallowed hard. He had put me off my guard. "Something like that."

"Fascinating." I held my breath, but he only turned to signal the waitress. "Allow me," he said when she arrived with the check. "This has been a most wonderful lunch."

I was still reeling a little as he helped me on with my coat, but I had the foresight to excuse myself before he could see me out. Ducking into the ladies room, I watched him walk out the front door, and I quickly made my way to the foyer window. True to form, he paused once he descended the steps, turning first left and then right like a wild creature on the lookout for predators—or prey. Then he pulled a ring of keys from his pocket and walked into the parking lot. I strained to see. I still wouldn't know why, but if he got into big black car, especially a car with a dented front grill, I would know who. I would know the enemy.

I saw him duck down and cursed my luck. I'd have thought him too old for a Maserati, but the smile that spread across his face—much wider and more relaxed than any he'd shown me—made him look years younger as he got into the cherry-red sports car and drove away.

Chapter Forty

Unlike Albert, Doc Sharpe took his work to heart. His Sunday hours were shorter, and the county shelter quieter, but the door was unlocked when I arrived a little before three.

"Doc?" It wasn't that I was nervous. That lunch had been confusing, to say the least, but I'd gotten the distinct—strange, but distinct—impression that Bill had liked me. I'd also pretty much decided that he hadn't been the one who had tried to drive me off the road. Still, I found myself breathing a little easier when the vet's bespectacled face peered out from the office door.

"Pru." That one syllable told me I was still in the dog house, so to speak. I needed to get back some leeway.

"Thought I'd drop by. See if you could use a hand." I'd put on my brightest smile, but he was looking at my arm. "I still have one."

He made a noise somewhere between a bark and a grunt and retreated. I followed. I would work around to asking about the brush. First, I went into the cat room—to Tadeus' cage. The little fellow had been hard at work; the wood shavings piled by the back had softened the hard contours, making it look almost cozy. There was something too still about it though, too silent.

"Tadeus?" I kept my voice low, my thoughts on the brown and white bunny. Nothing.

I unlatched the cage and reached in. The wood shavings were indeed soft, but they were cool and still. No living creature had been in here in quite a while.

"He's gone." The voice behind me made me jump, and as I turned, I knew my horror must have shown clearly on my face. "The rabbit."

"Gone?" The soft, little bunny.

"Oh, no. No." Doc Sharpe had the grace to look abashed. "Adopted. The mother of the family came by earlier. He was box trained, and they know about the wiring issue. I don't destroy healthy, well socialized animals."

"Well socialized." Did that take biting into account? But as soon as the words were out of my mouth, I felt the vet's eyes on me. He still thought I'd taken the Persian. Asking about the grooming brush would only make him more suspicious. "Hey, want me to clean this up for you?" I nodded toward the cage. Pammy wouldn't be in until tomorrow, and chores like this one tended to get put off as long as she dared. "It's not exactly heavy lifting."

"If you think you can." He eyed my wrapped arm. I smiled and nodded, and he left the room.

In case he came back, I started with the cage. It felt wrong to dump all those shavings. Tadeus had arranged them so neatly, and as I scooped them into the garbage, I noticed how he had hidden a burrow in the corner, concealed by the food dish and another mound of shavings. The smell of cedar, warm and fresh, rose to greet me. He was a neat animal, and had piled his droppings in the far corner, behind his self-made nest. It made me think of a house, actually, with the trash placed around back.

I was still thinking of that as I got the disinfectant—a bleach mixture—to finish the job. Something about the arrangement was sticking with me, like a reminder of something I'd forgotten. I was alone in the cat room: even the black-and-white had been taken home, so I didn't think I was picking up on anything. No, it was a tickle in the back of my own mind. Something to do with bunnies, with burrows or cleanliness.

The room was so quiet that I jumped a bit as my phone rang. And cursed after. I didn't want to think that the crash—I couldn't call it an accident—had shaken me that much.

"Hello?" My voice was steady. I could do that.

"Hey, darlin'." Mack. I relaxed against the examining table and tried not to feel pleased. Last time I'd seen him, he'd been with another woman. I hadn't been polite. "What's up?"

"Nothing much." He might be regretting Saturday night; he might need money. I was on my guard.

"Oh, don't be so cold, Pru. You know you're my girl." There was no answer for that. "In fact, I've been thinking a lot about you. About us."

"Uh huh." I put the phone on speaker and reached for the bleach bottle with my good hand. I was curious why he had called, but this wasn't worth wasting my time.

"It's been a while, Pru. I mean, it's not like you haven't had other interests."

"Not a good tack, Mack." I poured some of the liquid onto the floor of the cage and grabbed a handful of paper towels. "Not right now."

"Oh yeah, right. Sorry. But, hey, maybe I can help cheer you up."

I waited for the inevitable: an invitation to Happy's. In truth, I wasn't sure what I'd say. Creighton was a little too close for comfort, and he was a little too much of a cop for me right now. Tom was, well, Tom was involved in something. Mack had the advantage of simplicity. I knew what I was getting with Mack.

"Maybe." Mack and his women sparked a thought. One of those women was Robin. "Hey, do you know a foreign guy, older, who's been hanging around? Bill he calls himself."

"Doesn't sound familiar." I wasn't surprised.

"That—ah—might not be his name." I described the short, tough-looking man. "Pointy chin. Smile like a shark. Big yellow teeth?"

I could almost hear him gasp. "Him."

I waited.

"You don't want to be involved with him, Pru. Believe me."

"Oh, this sounds interesting."

"It's not, Pru. Trust me. Look, I'm busy tonight, but tomorrow? We can talk. I mean, I could give you a lift to the garage, at least."

I could have choked on my unspoken words. Could have choked him, easily. Somewhere in the back of my mind, I heard my mother's voice: something about lying down with dogs and getting up with fleas. Wallis would have sniggered at the phrasing. But before I could lash into him—or even follow up with more questions—he had hung up. The smell of bleach was strong, making my eyes tear. Whatever I'd been thinking before the phone rang was gone now, wiped as clean as any traces of Tadeus. But in addition to making my nose sting, the sharp tang was also waking me up. I'd been missing too much. Reacting instead of acting. What was Mack really up to, and what was Tom's—hell, what was Robin's—involvement in all of this?

And how the hell, I asked the empty cage as I threw the wadded paper towels away, did Mack know that my car was in the shop?

Chapter Forty-one

I could have called Mack back. I knew him well enough to pressure him. Only until I had a better sense of what exactly was going on, I didn't want him or Tom or even Creighton knowing what I knew, or what I didn't know. If push came to shove, I didn't trust anyone but Wallis.

I pictured her then. How her whiskers would arch up, just a little, at that compliment. Her eyes would narrow and her front paws flex as she kneaded in an involuntary reaction to pleasure. Wallis had admitted it, just last night. She needed me. Well, I realized, staring at that empty rabbit cage: I needed her, too.

It was time for me to make a last search of the place, and then go home to my cat.

I wasn't sanguine about finding the brush. I'd looked pretty carefully only the day before. Still, I went through the cat room, looking into and behind all the empty cages. I had no better luck with the stock room, though I did make a note for Pammy about the shortage of disposable litter pans. Spring kitten season was around the corner. Before I left, I knew I should ask Doc Sharpe, but I hesitated. He already suspected me of taking the cat. Why would I be asking about a brush?

Wallis, of course. I could say I'd brought in Wallis' brush and left it behind by accident. It was a lame excuse. After all, why would I have brought Wallis' brush into the shelter? Could I get away with saying it was new? I tried to remember what it looked like, fresh from the garbage behind Louise Franklin's house.

And it hit me. What Tadeus' neat housekeeping had reminded me of. What Princess Achara had been trying to tell me, as she manipulated her person into bringing her in. The trash had been around the side of the carriage house. A carriage house that hadn't been converted into a condo or apartment. A carriage house that still served its original purpose, after a fashion. If someone had a car, a damaged car, that she didn't want seen, what would be more obvious?

I wanted to go home and confer with Wallis. I had to go look in that garage.

"Doc? I'm going to head out." I called down the hallway. "Doc?"

The door to the small room he used as an office opened and he stepped out. "Before you do, would you come speak with me for a moment?"

"Sure." I tried to make my voice lighter than I felt. I really didn't need the lecture—or his suspicions. And I really wanted to make it to the Franklins' place before the last of the tenuous daylight disappeared.

"Have a seat, Pru." Avoiding my eye, he'd walked back behind his desk and took his own seat. "Please."

The "please" boded well, so I did.

"Pru, I know something about working with animals."

I nodded. And waited. He seemed to be having more problems with words than Wallis with a recalcitrant furball.

"I understand the attachment one feels."

"If this is about Donal Franklin's Persian—" I needed to get ahead of this.

"It's not. Or not only." He looked at his desk blotter for a script. Not finding one, he finally met my eyes. "It's also about Nancy Pinkerton's cat and other clients' pets."

"You have a gift, Pru. I've seen that. That's why I've been happy to recommend your services, despite your lack of a formal degree."

I swallowed. I'd put off the good doctor for months now with the idea that I was completing my degree. He didn't need to know that I'd compiled all the practicum hours necessary to be certified even before I left the city. "Thanks." The word came out, despite the dryness of my throat.

"But I wouldn't be a good boss, I wouldn't be a good *friend* if I didn't speak out."

He saw my look of confusion.

"Pru, you live alone. You talk to animals. You need, well, you need to get out more."

It took all my self control not to laugh in his face. Poor Doc Sharpe. He wanted me to get professional help. Or, at least, get laid. But his Yankee reserve would only let him go so far. "I'm going to see a friend now, Doc. Thanks."

I flashed him my biggest smile and stood up. He stood, too, clearly embarrassed by his daring foray into my personal life. This was my chance. "You haven't seen a grooming brush, have you? I left one in the cat room by mistake."

"What? No." He seemed a little flustered by my abrupt about-face. "This friend you're going to see, she wouldn't be a cat, would she?"

Chapter Forty-two

I was able to promise Doc Sharpe that I was off to visit a human friend, and I was only partly lying. Louise Franklin was no friend of mine. If what I suspected was true, she was up there with my worst enemies. Still, better to know what you're dealing with, I figured, as I drove.

Someone had wanted me hurt or killed. Someone had wanted me gone. I didn't think I ranked high enough in any man's scheme of things for jealousy to be an issue, and nobody hates the dog-walker enough for work to be the cause. Mack had known about my accident, and I was going to catch up with him later. But there could have been a few ways that tidbit had come to him. He might have seen my car in the shop. He might have been drinking with Mikey G at Happy's. Or maybe a little bird told him.

That's what I was putting my money on, assuming the bird was a Robin. Their relationship was still a mystery to me. Not that I cared, except that she was in this a lot deeper than I knew. The Donal connection—the cat. Bill. It was all a bit much.

First things first: the only person I knew who had negative feelings toward me—okay, who I had antagonized—and who had a garage was Louise Franklin. And with that, I took the turnoff for her place, letting the sedan glide quietly onto the shoulder, under a stand of pines. I stepped out of the car and into shadow. The afternoon had quickly faded into dusk, and I stood for a moment, wondering what I should do next. On one hand, the dying light meant more cover for my snooping. On the other, it made it harder for me to see. Add in that my wrist had started aching anew from the drive, and I almost climbed back in. A bourbon and the company of Wallis just seemed so much more inviting.

Maybe it was Doc Sharpe's words—that comment about my friend being a cat—that stopped me. I didn't care who thought I was a recluse. But I was not going quietly into whatever self-imposed darkness awaited me. Someone had tried to kill me, and I wasn't running away.

Careful to stay close to the hedges, I snuck around the side of Louise Franklin's house. It was dark enough that I could see light inside, but not so late that she had drawn her curtains. The light was warm, almost yellow, and I wondered if a fire had been lit against the evening chill. I remembered a floor lamp, its cover of shaded glass. Antique probably, its light golden and soft. Standing by a yew, I thought of how cozy it looked. Then I remembered the man who had been killed there. Nice property wasn't all it was cracked up to be.

I was still watching, mesmerized, when a movement caught my eye. Over by the trash. *"Quick! Quick!"* A young raccoon, male, was foraging. Out on his own for the first time, probably, he should have been looking for a nest of his own. Finding a safe place that he could defend from his peers. But the scent of last night's dinner had lured him. He was hungry, I got that. He'd learned to be cautious. I got that, too, and as he scurried away, I took the lesson to heart.

Crouching below the level of that window, I made my own way past the trash cans, the middle one with its lid still ajar. The carriage house was just beyond, at the end of a curved driveway. As I waited, the shadows grew longer, the house threw its shade over the little building, and my way was clear. On my toes, careful not to lean on my right hand for balance, I could see into the window of one of the wide double doors. Sure enough, I made out a car. A large car. Could have been black—could have been dark blue or green. The lack of light made it hard to tell.

I strained to see in the dying light, and realized with a burst of disappointment that I was looking at the trunk. The front end was shrouded in shadow.

A quick circumnavigation of the outbuilding revealed one other door—and it was locked—and so with a quiet caution that that raccoon would have appreciated, I reached for the main handle. It didn't turn, and I cursed silently. Of course, the carriage house exterior might be vintage, but the door itself was probably on some kind of automatic opener. It might be locked, but it might also simply not function without the remote. Unless I wanted to break a window, and risk alerting whoever was home, I'd wasted my time.

That was my cue to leave. Unlike that raccoon, I did have a nest of my own, even if it wasn't quite as nicely furnished as the Franklin place. In the deepening dark, the light looked brighter now, and I could see the interior of the room clearly. That lamp, as I remembered it, and then Louise Franklin moved in front, gesturing with both hands.

I couldn't resist and moved closer, confident that I would not be visible in the gloom. The window was thick enough to muffle the sound, but I could hear her voice, loud and agitated. She was yelling at someone, and once again I found myself wondering who this woman was: the pedigreed spouse of a wealthy man. The unbalanced shrew who had accused me of stealing her pet—and yet insisted that that same cat was responsible for her husband's death. The heartless woman who only saw the Persian as a pricey gift, or the mourning widow, all soft and courteous. None of us were simple, I knew that as well as anyone. This woman, though, seemed to embody more contradictions than most.

I was mulling that over when she turned toward the window. I ducked, slightly, and held my breath as she came up to the sill. She was reaching for the window, I was caught. But no, there must have been an end table below it, because she retreated holding a lump of light, and in that moment I remembered the ashtray Mack and I had found in the trash. It must have been part of a set, and this was its unbroken mate. She walked out of my range and I stood up to follow her movements. She stopped again to light a cigarette, holding it in her left hand and gesturing dramatically, as if its glowing end could better punctuate her words. If only I could make them out...

A row of bricks defined a plant border, giving me just enough height to peek above the sill. Using my left hand, I pulled myself close to the window and turned my head to listen. The window was thick, and despite her gestures, Louise Franklin was now keeping her voice under control. This close I could make out words—popping words—"promises?" "Payment?" It was no use. Sunday night, odds were it was social rather than business. I wondered about that pretty boy she'd first shown up with. Odds were, my fervid imagination was creating a drama out of pissed off woman yelling at the TV. Letting myself back down, I started to walk away.

That's when I saw her. At first, I thought it was a reflection. That dark brown hair, smoothed to shoulder length. A cream-colored sweater that spoke of money. But Louise, the Louise holding the cigarette, was wearing navy: a twin set augmented by pearls. And Louise was still there, facing her. Still talking.

Either the other woman had guts that I could only begin to envy, or something very strange was going on here. Because before my eyes, I could see two women who I thought hated each other. And Louise Franklin might be angry, but there she was, shaking another of those slim, gold cigarettes out of its pack and reaching for her lighter. The lighter was a piece of work: crystal, like the ashtray, with works of a richer gold than the cigarette. The person holding it out to her was her younger rival, Robin Gensler.

I stepped back—and off the brick, tumbling onto the wet ground. By instinct, I reached behind me with my right hand to catch myself, and before I could stop let out a cry of pain.

Almost immediately, a figure appeared at the window and I froze, counting on the darkness to hide me. Like an animal, prey in the night, I hardly dared breathe. Up close, dark against the light, I could make out the silhouette of a woman. The soft lamplight highlighted dark hair, picking out red in the brown. But pressed as she was against the window, I couldn't see her eyes, and I was struck again by how similar Robin and Louise looked. Mirror images, really, as Robin had taken the lighter with her right hand. Poor Donal, what a fool he must have been, going for the same woman twice.

And then I heard it. Soft, almost inaudible. *"Help. Help me. Please."*

The figure stepped away from the window, and in a flash, I was back, my throbbing arm forgotten. The women were both sitting, facing each other like territorial cats on two sides of a herring. The room was silent and still, the only movement the slow trail of smoke drifting up from Louise's cigarette.

"I'm here," I whispered as loudly as I dared. Neither woman moved and I repeated myself, trying to open my mind to any further calls. "I'm here to help." Silence.

That voice, that sound—had it even come from the window? I'd been so focused that perhaps I had assumed too much. I stepped back. The side of the house was dark, the upstairs windows still and black. "Hello?" I dared a wave. Nothing, the night was still.

I whirled around. Ran back to the garage.

"Are you there? Hello?" No response. "Do you need help?"

Despair seeped into me, like the dampness through my jeans. Someone—something—had called out to me, and I could do nothing. I was too late. I turned toward the woods and thought about the young raccoon, hungry and alone. Perhaps the cry had nothing to do with me. Perhaps I had simply heard a plea from the woods. Nature, taking its harsh course.

With a heavy heart, I slunk back to my car. My jeans were wet through. I was cold, and my wrist throbbed like a jackhammer. None of that would have mattered, though, if I could have found the source of that voice and saved it. Maybe Doc Sharpe was right. I was becoming sentimental in my old age. Wallis would never let me hear the end of it.

Chapter Forty-three

Wallis, it turned out, was nowhere to be seen as I limped into my house about forty-five minutes later. I called for her as I came in, and looked around as I headed for the kitchen, swallowing two aspirin dry and then pouring myself a water glass of bourbon to wash the taste down.

"Wallis?" The bourbon helped, but some company would have been nice. I made my way back to the living room, switching on the radio as I did. Western Mass has as many colleges as it does squirrels, and my favorite had a jazz DJ who kept it hard bop and bluesy most nights. Feet up, I waited for the combo to work its magic. In addition to my sore wrist, that headache had started up again and, with it, the threat of some kind of virus. I didn't want to think about that. Didn't want to think about the last time I'd gotten sick, and what had happened then. I'd go to sleep, or at least get a good buzz, and chase that thought away. Another healthy swallow and I closed my eyes, willing the music to whisk me into dreamland.

"Huh." A little snort, and a thud on the sofa by my feet let me know I'd been joined by the cat. I smiled, my eyes still closed. Maybe I was coming down with something. At least I could still hear Wallis.

"Thinking of ourselves a lot, aren't we?" Wallis began kneading the cushion by my shins.

"What?" I sat up. She continued to make her seat comfortable. Only after settling into the familiar sphinx pose did she deign to answer. Even then, she was cryptic.

"And you care?"

"Yeah, I do, Wallis. I've had a hard day."

That little snort again. *"You've had a hard day."* She closed her eyes.

"Do you want to tell me about it?" I'd never really known Wallis to confide. Still, there's always a first time. I roused myself into a sitting position, pulling my jeans leg from under her tail.

"Watch it." I tucked my feet under me, and she relaxed again. *"And I have no interest in confiding in you."*

"Sorry, I just thought—"

That snort again. *"Why would I want to confide in you anyway, when you're such a trustworthy champion of the four-footed?"*

She was pissed off, I could tell. If I'd been more awake, I'd have noticed the way her ears tilted ever so slightly backward. The relaxed pose was just that: Wallis was spoiling for a fight.

"What did I do?" I was too tired for this. "I didn't even see any animals today."

"See." The way she said it, I knew it meant something.

"Wallis, come on. I'm too tired." Nothing. "Please, just tell me."

"Just tell you, like if I did, you'd listen. You'd hear."

"Wallis." Now I was getting worried. Had I been missing things? Not hearing some animal correctly?

"There is nothing wrong with your senses." She looked over, and the look in her green eyes was not friendly. *"Your receptors, if you will, are working perfectly."*

"So, I'm what? Misinterpreting?"

"That would involve actually listening. Actually paying attention to what anyone is trying to tell you." With that, she tucked her nose into her tail and fell asleep. Leaving me alone with the music, wide awake and puzzled.

The bourbon did its job eventually, and I woke on the sofa, sans cat and aching. Stretching helped some of the stiffness, but my unease about the previous night only became stronger the more my brain woke up. The only message I had not been able to respond to yesterday was that soft plea. Had I misinterpreted it? I reached out with my right hand and caught myself. No reason to set that wrist throbbing again. Yes, I had. Probably. Unable to find whoever had called out to me, I had decided that the cry had come from the woods, beyond my help. It had seemed a reasonable supposition at the time, one I thought that Wallis as a hunter would understand.

Life with a cat could be difficult.

If that had been my failing, however, I wasn't sure how to remedy it. I could go back, though returning in broad daylight would expose me to discovery. Or, I could get help—of another sort. My back creaked as I stood and stretched some more. Fatigue and pain were aging me, and I wondered if I was actually considering this. But as I made my way into the kitchen, I realized that I was serious. I was thinking of calling Jim Creighton, or better yet, dropping by, and enlisting the aid of the law.

"Wallis, you win." I called up the stairs as I ascended, mug in hand, a few minutes later. "I'm calling in the cavalry."

I was headed straight for the shower. If I was going to do this, there was no point in stalling. She wasn't there when I got out, and it did give me pause. Maybe I wasn't supposed to solicit human help. Maybe I was supposed to go back to the Franklins myself—or the shelter. If the Persian had been found, today might be her last.

Great. Mondays were busy even in normal weeks, and I had to walk Growler before doing anything else. Lucy, too. Maybe I should take a lesson from Lucy and be more willing to play on my feminine wiles. Maybe the little dog would have some advice, I thought as loudly as I could. Wallis, if she heard me, declined to respond. Between the cat and Creighton, I was being squeezed. Either that, or I was developing scruples, which at this point in life, would be a real bitch.

Chapter Forty-four

"I don't know what's gotten into him." Tracy Horlick paused to inhale, then breathed out a cloud of pale smoke. "Bitsy was such a good little dog, before you came along."

I was standing on her front step. Since she was in the doorway, one step up, the smoke hit me right in my face. I forced myself not to blink as I tried to figure out what was going on.

"Before I came along?" It wasn't the best line, but it beat blurting out "what the hell?"

"Before." She stopped to pick a stray tobacco leaf from her lip. "Such a sweet little thing."

I waited. The Bitsy I knew—aka Growler—was a macho little fellow, despite his size. I found it hard to imagine he'd ever been anything but.

"If you've noticed any changes in his behavior, the first step would be to get a full veterinary work up." The spiel I was giving her was standard. It was also designed to dissuade her. I doubted she'd spend money on a vet if Growler were foaming at the mouth. "Often such changes are signs of an underlying illness."

Growler had not appeared ill to me in any way, nor had he complained of any aches or pains. Nothing except his mistress, Tracy Horlick.

"He's not sick." She squinted through the smoke. "I'm just wondering if you're a bad influence on him."

"What's he doing?" I didn't want to get into it with her. I really didn't. Still, this was part of the gig.

"He's been irritable all morning." She started—and I started to tune her out. Then her next words got me. "He was jumping around, almost like he was dancing."

I could have burst out laughing. "Was he wagging his tail?"

"Yeah, he was." She squinted, looking suspicious.

"He's a happy dog, Mrs. Horlick. That's all." Her eyes were still screwed up—and focused on me. It went against the grain, but I owed the bichon. "He was letting you know he loves you."

"Huh." She took a drag. "Seemed like some sicko thing, you ask me."

I was right at my boiling point. If I didn't need the money, I'd have walked a while ago. As it was, I locked my jaw. Responding wasn't going to help. And I was rewarded by a short, sharp bark, the sound of scratching, and a series of dull thuds. Tracy Horlick had locked the bichon in the basement again, and Growler was doing his best to call for help.

"I think someone wants his walkies." I forced a smile and silently prayed that the little dog would forgive me. "Bitsy? Are you there?"

Unable to score any more points—or unwilling to have her dog foul her basement—Tracy Horlick turned with a heavy sigh. Three seconds later, the little white fluffball came barreling out. I managed to snap on his lead while barely breaking his stride. "Back soon!" I called over my shoulder.

"*Women.*" Growler's thoughts packed venom. I didn't contradict him, and instead let him vent on the duplicitous nature of the so-called fair sex all the way to the corner. I couldn't say I didn't understand. "*Duplicitous, conniving…women!*"

"She lock you up all night?" I had questions of my own, but the white dog deserved a chance to vent. Besides, I was curious.

"*What?*" His button eyes looked up at me. "*You mean old smoke teeth?*"

I had to smile. "Yeah, old smoke teeth."

"Nothing new there." We had reached a particularly popular stump, and I waited while Growler made his olfactory reckoning of the day's other visitors. *"Pack behavior…when they get together."*

"Growler?" This worried me. He might have been talking about old Horlick's bridge club: that would fit with his being locked downstairs. But if dogs—or any other animals—were joining up, it could mean trouble for smaller creatures like my charge. "What's going on?"

"You tell me." He didn't even bother to look up. *"Huh, Duke's kidneys are acting up again. Okay, walker lady, next stop."* I had no choice but to follow.

Two blocks on, and I'd still not come up with a response. It wasn't that I didn't want to. Growler might not like women much. Considering the person he was stuck living with, who could blame him? It was more that I was becoming concerned about my own behavior. Tracy Horlick was full of crap. Growler was as healthy as a horse, and, despite the alpha male inside the fluffy white package, as cute as button. Still, I couldn't entirely discredit what she had said. From what I could tell, I was the first human to address the little dog by what he considered his true name. I knew about his sexuality and let him indulge his interest in the intact male dogs of Beauville, or, at least, in their scents. Once you see someone as an individual, it is just too difficult to tuck that knowledge away, and it was quite possible that my behavior had changed his. Maybe, in some way, I was encouraging the bichon's butch behavior. Maybe my acceptance had freed him to act out.

"Forget about it." The little dog was trotting ahead of me, and I nearly stopped short in my astonishment. *"You're not that important."*

"Sorry, Growler." I had to smile. "I just didn't want to get you into any more trouble. And I didn't realize you could hear my thoughts so clearly."

"Women." If a dog could mutter, Growler did, accompanying himself with a guttural sound deep in his throat. *"What do you expect, anyway?"*

I was quiet for the rest of the walk, and the bichon focused on the neighborhood news, as delivered by scent. We both felt more relaxed by the time I followed him up Tracy Horlick's concrete walk. I was even ready to smile.

"Here you go, Mrs. Horlick." I stood well back from her cigarette this time, and reached to hand her the lead from the bottom step. She raised one eyebrow, but didn't deign to remove the cigarette from her mouth. I only made my smile wider. "I think we all just needed to let off a little steam."

Growler wagged his tiny tail, turned back to me and barked once. *"Tell Lucy, thanks."* Another short bark. *"For nothing."* Then, with a look back up to me that said more about caution and perseverance than any words could, he ascended the stairs and gamely went inside.

"Poor dog," I said to no one in particular as I walked back to my car.

"Poor dog?" A squirrel had begun chittering in the tree by the curb. *"Poor dog? Why do you say 'poor dog'?"*

"You wouldn't understand." I unlocked my door. "He's trapped in that house. Hell, he's trapped in that little body, and everyone looks at him like he's some kind of a toy or something."

"Poor dog, she says." I heard the branches rattle, a few remaining leaves scrape each other as the gray creature climbed. *"He's running himself ragged, trying to communicate with you, and you say, 'poor dog.'"*

"What?" I stood back up. This wasn't the kind of interspecies communication I was used to. Disrespect from my tabby, I got. From a squirrel? I shook my head to clear it, and realized that I'd missed the point. "What do you mean, 'running himself ragged'?"

More chittering. I got an impression of Growler at the street corner, picking up the scent of his compadres. Maybe there was no point. There certainly was no "running" going on in the image the squirrel was replaying for me.

"Silly, silly. Running…working." The branches above my head shook, and one of last year's leaves, brown and folded, came

drifting down. I looked up and thought I could make out intense black eyes and a twitching nose. *"So silly."*

"Speak for yourself." It was rude, I knew it. But I'd lived with Wallis too long to take a rodent seriously. Besides, this little creature wasn't making sense.

"Cat here?"

"Sorry." I tried to blank my mind. "It's just me. But, hey, aren't squirrels afraid of dogs, too?"

"There's a lot out there to fear." The answer came back soft, but still clear. *"But I can tell what's going on, as long as I stay up here…"* And that was it.

◇◇◇

"Sorry, Lucy. Your routine doesn't work for everyone." I'd left the Genslers only a few minutes before. Eve Gensler had been almost reluctant to let me take the poodle. She'd been brushing the short, curly coat while Lucy had stared at her with what I assumed was supposed to be love. "At least, not for Growler."

The tawny toy turned those big eyes on me. *"What is 'routine'?"*

"Don't play act with me." I was a little riled. My wrist was hurting. My head throbbed. "Your 'girly' act."

"Huh." That little chuff was accompanied by a few of what I thought of as her dance steps. *"Well, what do you expect?"*

"What *I* expect?" It was my sinuses. It had to be.

"We must always act appropriately." She trotted up ahead of me, the better to cast a longing look over her shoulder. *"Appropriate to who we are."*

"To who we are," I repeated. "And you are Emily Post?"

"I am Lucy the poodle. The loved and pampered poodle." Another backward glance. A tentative wag of the short tail. *"River?"*

Chapter Forty-five

Wallis. She could help. If I could only be sure that she would, I would have driven straight home to ask her. After a quick walk along the river, I'd been more confused than ever. Frankly, Lucy was getting under my skin. I'm not girly. It had never stood in my way before. Hell, from what I could see, Louise Franklin was a tough broad herself, and she hadn't done too badly. At least, until a week ago.

I was wasting time and energy. What I should be doing was trying to figure out who had taken the cat. And why the Persian hadn't said anything. But what were my clues—the words of a rabbit? A squirrel? There would be no living with Wallis if I brought them up.

Wallis, however, wasn't my only ally. Frank wasn't a rodent, no matter what Wallis might say, and our recent communication issues had been disheartening. But he might be able to interpret some of the signals I'd been getting from the smaller animals in the community. At least, he might be willing to try.

I was in luck. It was nearly ten by the time I pulled into the lot, but Albert was just getting out of his pickup. And unless he was undertaking some new form of grooming, he was talking to something burrowed into his down parka. Squelching the thought of fleas, I concentrated on the latter and bounded out of my car with a jaunty spirit that I hoped would mislead the bearded officer.

"Hey, Albert! What's shaking?" I tried for guileless, focusing on the grin.

It didn't work. He stopped short, panic in his staring eyes. But a movement inside his parka, right behind the duct-taped spot, let me know someone had heard, and in a moment a small brown and white head had poked out, its pink nose twitching as Frank took the measure of the air.

"And you brought Frank, too."

"Yeah, he gets, I don't know, nervy sometimes. Like I have to take him."

I pondered that as the masked ferret climbed up on Albert's shoulder, and as the human fussed with the lock, I made eye contact with his diminutive colleague. Frank was trying to tell me something, I could sense that. Whether he was waiting for privacy, or our lines of communication had broken once again, I would just have to wait and see.

"So, what's up, Pru? I hear you've been having some problems over at County." Once Albert had let us both in, he'd left me for the small shelter office. I could hear him rummaging in the mini-fridge, a bear waking from hibernation.

"Nothing major," I called over. This was as good a time to peruse the papers on his desk as any. "Why, what did you hear?"

"Something about a cat."

I listened with half an ear. Pushed a report on raccoon relocation out of the way. Another, on a possible Eastern gray wolf sighting, gave me pause. Somehow, I'd have to find a way to talk to Wallis. "Oh?"

"Yeah, some cat was giving you trouble or something." Albert raised his voice to compete with the faucet. "That Persian?"

The clank of a spoon and a muttered curse. Albert was making instant coffee with hot tap water again. Too hot. I dropped the wolf alert back on the pile, ready to step back. It slid to the floor, and I reached for it—just in time to see Albert walking back.

"Looking for something?" He sounded curious, rather than miffed.

"Not really." I shrugged and watched as he put his mug down. Undissolved grains floated on top, circling like little ants. Frank had emerged from his coat by then, but even his usual curiosity didn't extend to Albert's drink. "Dolly's was closed?"

"They raised their prices." He sipped and jerked back, spilling the coffee on his desktop. Frank squealed and dived into an open drawer. "Damn."

"Here, let me." I started grabbing up papers. That's when I saw it: Sheriff's Department, Town of Beauville. "What's this?"

"That's official." He reached for it. "Came in yesterday."

"You were here?" I'd thought the shelter was locked up tight.

"As a town official, I'm always on call."

I nodded. He'd dropped by for something—probably the beer he kept in the fridge—and Creighton had cornered him. "Well, if I can help in any way."

"Maybe." He sipped again, more carefully. "Maybe not."

I leaned over the desk. Albert intimidated easily. "Albert?"

"Look, Pru. I'll get in trouble. Okay? Why don't you talk to your boyfriend?"

"Frank?" I was stalling, but as if on cue, the little creature stuck his head out. His rounded ears were straight up and his whiskered nose quivering. There was something going on and I tried to clear my mind. I would have given anything for ten minutes alone with him.

"Ha, ha." Albert made a point of neatening the papers. Frank took a few steps toward me. I reached out my hand—to him, but Albert responded, jerking the papers back. "Pru, I can't!"

"I wasn't talking to you." I focused in on the small brown creature, ignoring the puzzled look on Albert's face. I tried to keep my mind blank, to ignore the fat man behind the desk. "I just wanted to greet this little fellow."

Frank stood on his hind legs, stretching his slim body up toward me. I reached forward, slowly, and let him sniff my fingers. I thought of all the animals I had spoken with recently. Taddeus the rabbit. That squirrel. Even the white Persian.

"Shiny." Like a spark, the word flit through my mind. *"Sparkly."* Frank liked pretty things. Had a tendency to steal them, truth be told, and I pulled back, automatically. I don't wear jewelry. It's not my style, but I reached for my keys, the change in my pocket, before I realized what I was doing.

"Sorry," I whispered. It was too little too late.

"Gone." That was it. All I felt was the ticklish touch of whiskers. Watching me, Albert shook his head. "You're getting as crazy as they say." At least his voice had some sadness in it. "Maybe you did do it."

"What?" It had all started with the Persian. She had blocked me out, and now I couldn't hear any animal. Frank was still staring, but all I could see was that flat, white face.

"Stole the cat, Pru. That's what the report is about."

Chapter Forty-six

Stole the cat? There was only one animal Albert could be talking about. The report, which he had reshuffled into the coffee-stained pile, had to refer to the white Persian. My head reeled as I tried to piece together what could have happened.

Doc Sharpe. He was the obvious leak. A valuable, if not exactly valued, animal goes missing from the county facility where he is in charge, and he must have alerted the authorities, if for no other reason than to save his own butt. But, no. Doc Sharpe had said he'd give me time. And for all his flaws, the good vet was a straight shooter. That, like his circumspect way of talking, was an essential part of his Yankee nature.

Pammy? She worked at the shelter, too, and I knew nothing of her code of ethics, including whether she had one. She was responsible for leaving the back door unlocked, but that just might make her more eager to place blame. No, I couldn't see her going to the trouble. Not on a Saturday night.

Louise Franklin fit Pammy's description of the woman who had gone back to the cage room, but I dismissed her out of hand. For starters, she had every right to take the cat. I'd been hoping she would from the get go. She was the only one who placed any value on the silky white beast.

The only one besides Robin Gensler. Robin had wanted that cat. Robin had heard that she was going to be euthanized. No, the timing was all wrong. The cat had disappeared before

Robin had heard the news—and besides, I had seen her. She was the only logical possibility, she'd gotten to the shelter before me, and yet—

"Pru. Glad I caught you." Creighton was coming toward me, his face grim.

"I didn't do it." Behind me, I heard a muffled grunt from Albert. It might have been a laugh. I turned and he ducked down, suddenly finding something in his lower desk drawer very interesting. Frank, however, stood staring at me, his eyes dark and unblinking.

"I didn't mean…" Behind me, Creighton cleared his throat. "Pru, can we talk?"

I looked at the ferret. The ferret looked at me. Albert, of course, stayed down. I had thought of trying to recruit Creighton to find the Persian—or to search Louise Franklin's house, but I hadn't come up with a strategy or an explanation. And now I had no choice, and no adviser I could trust, either two- or four-footed. But as I reached for my coat, I thought, just for a moment, that Frank shook his head. It was a very human gesture, and so slight as to be imaginary. It could have been excitement—that little hopping dance ferrets do when aroused. Still, I couldn't help but wonder: *"No,"* he seemed to be telling me. *"No."*

"No, what?" Don't go? Don't confide? It isn't Robin?

"Pru?"

"Sorry." I had to focus. "I was thinking of something else. Shall we?" He nodded and turned toward the exit. Glancing back, I couldn't help but notice that for once Albert and Frank seemed to be on the same page: confused and a little worried. I smiled, for both of them, and followed Creighton out the door.

"What's going on, Pru?" He had led me to his private office and started in as soon as he closed the door. "I thought you were going to stay out of trouble for a while."

"I'm only doing my job, Jim." I leaned back and put my feet up on his desk. He scowled, which helped a bit. This was a role I was accustomed to. "Why did you want to talk to me? You know, I didn't take the animal."

"It's not the cat, Pru. I talked to the vet over there, Doc Sharpe, after that report was filed, but he assured me that the animal had simply been isolated for some tests."

I nodded. Good ol' Doc Sharpe.

Creighton wasn't buying it. "However, I still need to examine that cat."

"I thought you'd decided that the shooting was an accident?" I should have been gratified. I wasn't.

"It probably was, okay? All the evidence points toward an accident, but considering the odd provenance of the gun…" He paused. I knew he regretted telling me what he had. Funny, Lucy's wiles might have come in handy about now. I just waited. "The case is still open, Pru. I mean, the coroner has ruled it death by misadventure, but I've got jurisdiction here."

"And why are you telling me this, Jim? I'm not an insurance agent. Or," I paused to consider, "a gun collector."

"No, but you've been seen in the company of some folks who are. And if I just ask you to mind your manners, I know what will happen." He slumped against the wall. It didn't make him look any less starched, but I had to fight the urge to go to him. Instead, I smiled, and took my feet off his desk.

"Look, Pru," he continued. "This is serious. I need you to stay out of it. And that means no Tom and no Benazi."

"Benazi?" He had my attention now.

"Wrinkled little guy? Face like a hatchet?"

I nodded. "His first name isn't Bill, is it?"

"Not lately." He suppressed a grin. "Try Gregor."

The accent, that Old World graciousness that smoothed over the underlying threat. Of course. "Gregor Benazi." I tried it out. And as I did, the other questions that had been percolating in my mind finally came together. Questions that didn't seem to be on Creighton's radar at all. It was a nice piece of luck that cleared my way to investigate. "Okay, Jim, I will."

He narrowed his eyes. He knew me too well to think I'd capitulate that easily. "Pru?"

I was heading toward the door, though. I had other things on my mind beside a suspect gun—or a suspect gun dealer. Benazi—"Bill"—had actually been charming, in his way, but I'd had enough of sleazy older men to last me at least till fall. I had a cat to locate before Creighton ran out of patience. That was trouble enough.

Chapter Forty-seven

I walked to the car with more swagger than I felt, sure that Albert, at least, was checking me out. My wrist had started aching again, and I was due at the Chinese restaurant. But I was sick of this car. I wanted my wheels back. And then I wanted the answers to some questions.

On my way to the garage, I tried to piece together what I'd seen with what Creighton had told me. If I could only reconcile the timeline, I'd have bet that Robin had taken the cat out of sentiment. Snuck it out of the shelter illegally, to give it a good home. What I didn't see was how she had done it—or when. And the visit to Louise Franklin? Could that have been an attempt to justify her feline thievery? To make peace or bury the hatchet with her lover's widow?

As I drove, I tried to recall their faces. Neither had looked happy. Louise's gestures and her chainsmoking both signaled annoyance, if not anger. Could Robin have been threatening the older woman? With what—animal abuse? From what I'd seen, Louise Franklin wouldn't care. And it still left the basic problem unsolved: how would Robin have smuggled the cat out—and why would she have reacted so strongly when we found her gone?

Louise Franklin could have taken the cat. But why sneak out with what was legally hers? And why then report the animal as stolen?

And then it hit me: Because I would suspect Robin. Everyone would. It would be a perfect, if petty, bit of revenge. It might also, I was beginning to think, be the first step in a larger frame, for a crime much bigger than catnapping.

There was no point in going to County. I had to warn Robin. Whatever else was going on, if she thought she'd made peace, she was in for trouble. First, I needed my car.

For a Monday, the garage was busy. The threatening weather had everyone hustling to get errands done, but I saw my blue baby parked right out front. Mikey nodded to me when he saw me, and waved me over to the tiny office to settle up. Through the glass door I could see a woman in a mohair coat occupying the one plastic chair, her face buried in a catalog, and so I opted to poke around instead. Mikey was talking to someone—new money, by the looks of him—and had a Beemer up on the lift. The little sportster looked cute, but I couldn't see it surviving our potholes. From the way Mikey was gesturing, it hadn't. They had some more words, before he left. A woman in the larger version—more the size of my sedan—had been waiting in the lot. From what I'd heard of her husband's temper, I didn't blame her.

Miss Mohair would be next, and so I made my way around back. The garage was built up against the rock wall, and I used a stick to trace the water trickling down its side. In a few years, or centuries, that water would wear all this down, and Beauville would slide into the valley. For now, though, it was kind of pretty: the touch of nature shielded by the dirty garage.

"Hey, Pru! There you are." Mikey had found me. I looked up, surprised. "You beat the storm."

"Thought you had another client." I could see the mohair coat, getting into a late model import.

He shook his head. "That's my cousin, Robin. She just dropped by, but she really liked your car."

"Robin?" Of course. "Mikey G—you're Eve Gensler's son?"

"Yeah, you walk her dog, right?" I nodded. "She was talking about you—you and Red, I mean, Robin."

"Robin said—wait, you called her Red?"

"Yeah." He smiled and shook his head. "Growing up, we called her Carrot Top. Can you believe she wanted to come work with me? She's doing a lot better now though. Hang on, okay?"

He turned back toward his tool case, and I ducked out, just in time to see Robin pulling out of the lot. Through the rear window, I saw her sleek brown 'do, so similar to Louise's. And it hit me. The clothes, the makeup. Robin—"Red"—hadn't been born looking like Louise Franklin. She'd remade herself in the older woman's image. Trying for class, or maybe to keep the interest of her older lover. Maybe Donal had suggested the change, or maybe Louise had somehow masterminded the metamorphosis, bringing the younger woman one step closer to being her double. To being her fall guy.

◇◇◇

I didn't know what was going on, but I did know Robin was in deep. I had to warn her. Yelling something at Mickey—he knew where I lived—I raced toward my GTO. The keys were on the mat, and my baby woke with a roar. I took off after Robin, leaving Mikey waving in my rear view mirror. Hell, he had the sedan in his lot as collateral. Mickey must have done something besides bodywork, though, or else two days with the big sedan had made me heavy footed. The GTO jumped beneath me, and I fishtailed as I swung onto the state highway.

Robin had a good head start—and no reason to know anyone wanted her to stop. I could only hope she was heading someplace local. Glanced up at the sky, I thought of Saturday's storm. The clouds had thickened again, the light growing gray. I should head back to the garage, but a bird in the hand...Wallis, I knew, would understand.

I could barely keep her in sight. That initial burst of speed seemed to be wavering, my GTO not responding as it should, and I cursed whoever had driven me off the road. Something was still wrong with my car. The accelerator had a mind of its own, one that made me ride it carefully—titrating the pressure with every sputter and start. This wasn't going to be fun, especially if the sky opened up. I was concentrating so much on my car that I almost missed the turnoff. At the last moment, the sight of Robin's little sportster registered, and with a squeal of wheels, I followed, powering my car into a turn that made something grind in the front end.

"Great." Mickey said he'd replaced my axle. What else could it be? I like to drive. But it's the speed, not the mechanics, and I was bemoaning my limited knowledge when Robin turned again. Hell, growing up in that family, she probably knew more about my engine than I did. It wasn't a happy thought—and my mindset didn't improve as I realized where we were. Coming from the garage, I hadn't recognized the road. Now I did. We were heading toward Louise Franklin's house.

Chapter Forty-eight

I slowed down as she entered the driveway and let my rumbling ride idle behind the hedge as she parked beside the outbuilding. Through the branches, I could see Robin approach the house. Did she suspect that Louise had the cat? That she might be setting her up for murder? Or did she simply want to clear her name? I waited until Louise Franklin's head popped out, and the two began talking.

I'd left the car running—the way it sounded, I didn't trust it to turn over again. But over the low rumble, I couldn't hear anything. From what I saw, the heated discussion of the other night was being continued on the front stoop. It all seemed rather public, and my curiosity was getting the better of me, when Robin reached into her bag.

I realized I was holding my breath. I didn't know what I expected—money. A bundle of love letters. In the growing dusk, I couldn't see—only that Louise retreated, backing into the house, and Robin followed. I waited, curious how this strange little drama would play out.

Less than a minute later, the door opened again. This time, Robin stepped out first, holding a set of car keys, and I saw the garage doors swing open. In her other hand she held, by the thick scruff of her neck, the white Persian.

That was no way to hold a cat, an adult cat. I started to get out of the car, to complain, when it hit me. I'd been blind. Or, worse, as deaf as I'd thought that cat. For all Robin's complaints about being denied ownership of the white Persian, she had never once asked if she could visit her. Never asked if she could see the animal she supposedly cared so much about until that last time—when I had forced the issue. Even then, something had been off. I remembered her reaction to Tadeus, recoiling from a cute little bunny. Robin Gensler was no animal lover. I'd read her wrong from the start.

Wallis, Frank…they'd all tried to tell me. I was insisting on hearing what animals *saw*, rather than what they sensed. Lucy had been quite clear that Robin was smart, manipulative as well as pretty. And Tadeus, the rabbit, had his own message, letting me know that even the most innocent-seeming creatures could bite.

I still didn't understand why Louise Franklin, the legal owner, had felt the need to sneak her cat out of the shelter. But I was beginning to understand that she feared the younger woman. Feared her with reason.

"Wait." It was too late, I knew that, but I was out of the car, yelling above the rising wind. "Robin!"

She turned toward me, but the dusk made it impossible to tell what she saw—or if she had even heard me. The cat, however, did. Although her body hung down, tail limp, the wide white face turned slightly.

"Help me." That voice again. It was the Persian. She was on her last legs, and I was her only hope.

Leaving my car running behind me, I crashed through the underbrush in time to see Robin toss the animal into the trunk of Louise's black sedan. I stepped onto the driveway, but she was already behind the wheel, and I found myself jumping backward to avoid being hit as she reversed down the drive at breakneck speed.

"What the hell…" I had landed in more bushes—on both hands. I ignored the shooting pain in my wrist as I ran back to the GTO. She had Louise's car in drive now, and tore past me, fast and reckless, and I cursed as I grabbed the wheel by instinct with my right hand. This time, the pain blindsided me—sweeping over me with a wave of nausea. I fought it off, gasping back tears, and couldn't have lost more than five seconds, but it was enough. She was nearly out of sight by the time I got going—and she had gone by too fast for me to see what shape the bumper was in.

It didn't matter. All I could feel was a white-hot fury in the shape of a cat. I didn't know why that animal hadn't spoken to me before. I didn't understand what was going on. I did know animal cruelty when I saw it—and this time, tears weren't going to buy me off.

The snow started in earnest about five miles down the county highway. By the tenth mile, I was hunched forward, cradling my useless arm against my body and straining to see through the windshield. Robin was driving without any regard to the weather, heading uphill into the blast, the big sedan solid in the storm. Between the howling wind and my misfiring engine, I felt like I was riding a bucking bronco, and each jolt sent fresh stabs of pain up my arm. If I could only catch her, I wouldn't care.

Somewhere beyond the turnoff for Bransville, my heater died. Whatever Mickey had done to my car, it wasn't good. I kept going. The road started turning here, snaking its way up the spine of the mountains. My breath was fogging the windshield, and I used my bad arm to wipe it. The pain was useful now: it kept me focused as we raced through the empty miles. At least the storm had forced Robin to turn her lights on. With every turn, I feared I'd lost her, but then I'd see her taillights: red and glowing and just a little too far ahead.

I caught a break about fifteen minutes later. We'd turned into a pass, where the overhanging peaks sheltered us from the wind, and I could see the big sedan not that far ahead. It was an odd choice—a hairpin road that climbed up to a scenic overlook. In summer, tourists clogged the road, stripping their gears in both directions, just to look at a bigger version of their world, or down into the abyss. Dark evergreens still lined the road, shielding us from more of the storm, but the road peaked above the treeline. There were no exits that I knew of—not till the top, and I gunned the engine, desperate to catch her. To make her pull over. To make her stop.

I leaned in, desperate for the chase. My GTO might be old, but it had the power, taking the turns like a pro. One mile. Two. Five. The distance began to close, and then I heard it. A hiccup. A knock, and suddenly the engine went dead. I had a flash of memory—of sliding sideways across the road. *Not again*, I found myself screaming. But I'd been on the straightaway as the power went out, and my tires held. There was no curb, but I drifted to the side. My car sputtered and was still.

It was hard finding my phone. My bag had slid under the seat in the rush, and my right arm was worse than useless. By the time I had dug it out, I had almost decided who to call. Mikey G owed me, that was for sure. Though when I thought back to the garage, I remembered who else had been there. Mikey's cousin, "Red," who knew cars as well as he did.

Creighton would come for me. He'd smile and shake his head, tell me I'd gone off half-cocked again. Maybe it was time to tell him everything.

I flipped the phone on and waited for a signal. This deep in the hills, it could be iffy. I tried to remember how far back the last town had been. That diner, the one up by the last turn—it was closed this time of year, wasn't it?

It didn't matter. Ahead, in the snow, I saw taillights. Someone had stopped for me. No, I saw with something like disbelief. Robin Gensler had stopped for me. Had backed up along the highway and was now walking toward my car.

"Robin!" I got out and waved with my good hand. "Over here." Torn between fury and relief, I wasn't sure what to say.

"Give me the phone." Her voice was grim.

"Excuse me?" I leaned in, sure that the wind had stolen the sense of her words.

"Give me the phone." She moved closer, her face strangely still even as her hair tossed in the wind.

I looked up at her, trying to understand. The rounded face, the soft lips. They were still the same. Then she gestured with her hand and I looked down. I knew, then, why Louise had handed over her car keys. Had handed over her cat. In her hand, Robin Gensler held a gun.

"Here." I fumbled it, the growing numbness in my other wrist making the effort almost natural. Wincing, I held it out to her—and cradled my hurt arm back against my body. The move wasn't just for effect, although I had almost lost feeling along the outside of the arm. In my pocket I had my knife. It was only a switchblade, but I knew how to use it. I willed my fingers to close around the handle, to fight the shooting pain, the growing numbness. If she came close enough...

She stepped forward. I made my move. But my hand was too numb, too weak, and we both watched as the knife clattered on the pavement.

"Cute." She stopped where she was and cocked the gun. It was not, I noted, an antique. "Toss the phone." She motioned across the highway, moving the gun as little as necessary. "Now."

I looked at her. I looked down at the gun. There was a similarity, the little gun was as dark and glossy as the woman. As cold. Taking the phone in my left hand, I tossed it awkwardly, overhand across the highway. It landed on the pavement, and I suppressed a smile. As soon as she took off, I'd retrieve it.

"Good. Stay here." She backed toward her car. I took a step toward her, and she raised the gun. It was small, but I didn't want to get any closer to it. Not out here. With a beep, she released the trunk and in a moment I saw her plan.

"Don't get out!" I yelled the words out loud, concentrating as hard as I could on my memory of the cat. "It's not safe. Stay!"

I tried not to think of how terrified that poor cat probably was. She would probably leap out at the first chance, desperate to escape from that noisy bumpy ride. From the woman who had thrown her back there. I got a strong image of the Persian cowering in the back of the trunk, white fur against gray utility carpeting. I hoped it wasn't just wishful thinking.

It didn't matter. Keeping the gun raised, Louise rooted around in the trunk. I heard a howl and a muffled curse. Those gloves could only do so much, and in a moment she was stepping toward the side of the road—the cat once again suspended from her hand.

"So sorry to meet and run." She turned toward me again, her smile colder than the sheen of the gun barrel. She saw me looking. "Oh, don't worry. I can't risk another gun 'accident.' Don't think I'll have to, really. That old car, the weather…. They're predicting another hard freeze."

She walked over to the verge. The cat was struggling, but Robin held her tight. "Isn't it awful what happens to animals out here?" She was smiling. I could hear it in her voice. "That's nature, I guess." And with that she tossed the cat into the woods and ran back to her car.

Chapter Forty-nine

Wallis was right. I was getting soft. Maybe fatally so. I should have run after Robin. Tackled her to the ground as she stooped to enter her car. I should have grabbed the gun—and then got my phone. Instead, I went after the cat. It wasn't the smart move, but smarts didn't play into it. A small voice calling for help was all I heard.

"Kitty! Don't run!" Even with her white fur, I wouldn't be able to find her if she dashed into the woods. "Kitty!" Hell, with that fur even if she survived the storm, she'd be easy prey out here. I thought of the coyotes. The hawk.

Out on the highway, I heard the tires of Louise's fancy sedan squeal, as Robin turned and sped away. I thought briefly about tire tracks—about evidence—and realized that everything would point to Louise, would implicate us both. It would be my word against hers, and she'd done her best to turn the gossips of Beauville against me. I could only hope Robin would skid on her way back to civilization. At least under the trees, I had some shelter from the snow. "Kitty?"

"Here." Huddled against a fallen tree, I made out a spot of white. Melted snow, but no. *"I'm here."*

Heedless of the pain in my wrist, I scooped up the soft white creature and buried my face in her fur. She smelled like talcum powder, like warm cat.

"Kitty." I murmured into that white softness. "Why didn't you tell me?"

"I called to you. Twice." Her voice, now that I heard it, was clear but soft. The same voice I had heard twice before. *"You people…None of you…"*

I didn't really need the images that now flashed through my head. Cages. Other animals, lots of them. The comfort of another, a mother, taken away too soon. Hands, strangers. More cages. Not the shelter—a cattery, overcrowded, and factory-like. And here I was, assuming a pedigreed animal had a soft life. Louise had rescued her and given her—to Robin? Yes, but Robin was the intermediary, the gift-bearer. It was Donal who had taken her into his heart. Donal who had loved her, and he was gone. Nobody else mattered. Life no longer mattered. The grief, the overwhelming sadness that I had expected from the widow, I now felt—in Donal Franklin's cat.

"You don't trust any of us, do you?"

"I did. It was my fault."

"It wasn't." I thought of the gun. "It couldn't have been."

In response, all I saw was Donal. His face, his hands. And an overwhelming flood of grief, of self-recrimination. She should never have warmed to anyone else. Never trusted anyone else. Especially not the woman who had at first seemed so kind. The woman who had betrayed them both.

"Is that why you won't talk to me?" I paused, thinking back on all our interactions. "Is that why you won't tell me your name? Why—wait!"

The animal twisted in my arms, every muscle tensed.

"What is it?" Shadows had closed in, and I knew my senses were no match for the cat's. "Did Louise—"

"Dog. Large dog." I felt her claws dig into me. *"Wolf."*

"I don't think we have wolves here anymore." As I said it, I remembered the notice on Albert's desk. I'd dismissed it. Still, alone, in the dark, a pack of coyotes or feral dogs would be just as dangerous. Besides, now that the initial shock had worn off, I was freezing. The thick canopy could not protect us from the worst of the storm. "Time for us to go."

Holding the cat as much for warmth as for her protection, I hiked back up toward the road. Already, a layer of white covered the asphalt, melting to slushy ice where the tire treads had left their mark. The phone—I smiled remembering my own bad toss. It had to be near where she had stopped. And it was: beneath the tire treads. Through luck or malice, Robin had run over the little device, shattering its plastic case and leaving its insides open to the elements. Luck? I could have laughed. Robin had this figured from the start.

The cat was straining in my arms at this point, and I longed to let her down. My arm ached and I knew she wanted freedom of movement. I couldn't risk it, though. If she were spooked—or decided not to trust me—she could head out to where I couldn't help her. We might not have wolves, but something was out there. Instead, I returned to my car.

"Here we go." I deposited her on the passenger seat, where she immediately began to groom.

"Heat, please."

I couldn't help smiling. This Persian might not have had the easiest life, but she was used to certain standards. "I'll do my best."

I'd left the key in the ignition, and with a small wordless prayer reached for it. No, my wrist was too badly hurt. I couldn't grasp it to turn. Next to me, the cat stopped bathing to watch, as I reached awkwardly around with my left hand and turned the key.

A click, a rumble. I tapped on the gas. Nothing. I made myself pause before trying again, knowing that a flooded engine would have less chance of turning over. Tried the key. A click, no rumble. One more time, and even the click was gone. Robin at the garage. I remembered my other "accident." Saturday night—after Doc Sharpe had accused me of taking the cat. She couldn't have known anything, not for sure, but she wasn't the sort to take chances. I guessed I should be grateful that this time I had simply drifted to the side of the road.

In the fading light, the Persian's white fur looked luminous, a warm counterpoint to the falling snow.

"I'm afraid we're stuck here for a bit, kitty." Her blue eyes looked up at me. "Could we use the time to get acquainted?"

Just then, a blast of wind came roaring down from the hillside, startling us both. Funneled by the highway, it rattled the car, blowing wet snow up in clumps against the glass. In a car of this vintage, the doors and windows never completely close, and the wind whistled at the cracks, howling and moaning like a hungry animal, eager to get in. I longed to reach for the cat. Instead, I turned toward her, and she to me. I thought of a fireside, of warm blankets, of light. She blinked and slowly began to let me in. I sensed fur, a velvet pillow. The way paws could sink into deep down as they kneaded a duvet. Together we created an image of safety that helped stave off panic. I could not guess what dark fears remained behind those blue eyes, but I let myself believe in our shared vision of comfort until the unearthly cry died down.

Then I took a breath. It was time to make a move. To plan how exactly I, the human in the equation, was going to get us out of an untenable situation. And then we heard it: an answering howl. Louder and more wild. This time, it came from outside the car. It came from the woods.

Chapter Fifty

"This is not the time to panic." The blue eyes looked up at me, blank and once again mute. "Or to withdraw."

Through my own fear, I sensed what was happening. Humans had betrayed this cat too often. My failure to protect her, to get us out of the storm, was another failure, and she had retreated into some distant feline space.

"Please, work with me." I licked my lips. They'd gone dry, chapped in the cold. "I need your help."

That wind again, rattling the window. I saw the Persian hunch back, as if she could sink into the seat, but I fought the urge to stroke her. To this cat, such contact would not suggest comfort.

"You were betrayed." I kept my voice low and even. "We're not all like that. Your person wasn't, was he?"

For a moment, I thought I'd touched her, so strong was the impression of hand on fur, long silky fur. That wasn't my hand, though. I saw a man's long fingers and felt a warmth the Persian had never shared with me. "Donal."

As soon as I said his name, the cat recoiled. Of course, the shooting. "I'm sorry, kitty. But it wasn't your fault." I reached for her. It was an awkward move, marred by pain. Still, the way the cat drew back, hissing, startled me. "What?"

Nothing.

"Come on." My head was throbbing in time with my wrist. "I thought we'd gotten past this."

I reached out again, and, again, the Persian drew back. She raised one paw as if to smack at me. The injured paw. I got a flash of a hand, reaching just like I had. Only this hand was tipped with nail polish, not dirt.

"Here, kitty, kitty. Come here, Fluffy." A woman's voice, matching the hand, soft and beckoning. For a moment, I was confused. This wasn't right. I wasn't hearing the animal. I was hearing something in her head. A memory.

There was something creepy about it all. The hand, the voice that called to me, soft and sweet. I felt the pull. Loyalty, trust… the desire to be loved. "Here, kitty."

The hand drew closer. A pretty hand, outstretched in welcome. It smelled like soap, and yet…

Trust.

Quick as a slap, the image changed. Hands, hands around me. Grabbing pulling. I struggled. Screamed and spit. And the image in my mind changed. I saw the one I loved. The one I trusted. His face, a kind face, was frozen. Hatred. Fear. Then a deafening blast, like an explosion, knocked us both back. And I heard no more.

Back in the car, alone with the cat, I blinked to clear my head. The struggle, the blast. It explained the deafness, just as I'd first suspected. It wasn't just the sound, though. This cat had finally found love. Had opened up, only to have her beloved— and herself—betrayed. And she had shut down somehow. Had turned people—had turned *me*—off.

Some of it was grief. I now understood what Lucy had been trying to tell me. She mourns. Maybe, even she withdraws. But some of it was guilt, too. I could see that now. She had warmed toward Robin, had let her in. Robin had used her to get close to Donal. Too late, the cat had responded by lashing out with rage. Deafening rage.

The blue eyes held me, cold with hate. Had I done the same thing? Those frightening moments when I couldn't hear—didn't want to hear, perhaps…

I didn't have time for my own issues now. I needed to get the Persian back. "I get it, kitty. I do." We sat, looking at each other long enough for something else to sink in. "I have issues with trust, too." The cat shifted on the car seat beside me, glancing up with cool eyes. I almost smiled. "Yeah, ridiculous, I know."

There wasn't time to get into it. Not that I wanted to. "Can we go back, kitty? Can we just try?" I needed to have a name for this cat. A way to reach her.

"No. Never again." She had turned toward the passenger side door, leaving me with only the view of her snow-white back. At least I heard that. I looked at the cat. We were talking, weren't we?

"If we must." She shuffled in her seat. *"Felicity."*

My confusion must have shown on my face.

"You keep asking."

"Ah, I get it. Well, thank you, Felicity. I'm Pru."

"No shit."

The human expression, coming as it did from the pristine white cat, made me smile, despite everything. In response, the white cat—Felicity—hunched up tighter. Cats cannot stand being laughed at.

"I'm sorry, Felicity." I held my hands up in surrender. "It's just—well, that's a very human expression."

"I've been hearing a lot, lately."

That sobered me up. "I believe it, and I'm sorry."

"At least you helped. Finally." She shuffled in the seat. *"At least someone did."*

"It wasn't your fault, whatever happened." I thought about that beckoning hand. I'd felt its appeal, despite everything. It was pretty. It smelled welcoming.

From the start, I'd suspected something was off about the shooting. Cats may be able to fire a weapon, but it was damned unlikely—and if I had my suspicions, then law enforcement would, too. Louise had always seemed like the strongest suspect.

The unhappy younger wife of a wealthy man, Louise had an alibi, but people would wonder. People would question. And

Robin—Robin had seemed weak and soft. But she'd been the one with teeth.

◇◇◇

The wind howled. I hugged myself, ignoring the pain. If only I could gather the large white cat into my arms. Our truce seemed too new, though, too tentative. "So what was Robin doing—trying to get you out of the shelter?"

"This." A one-word answer. Nothing else was necessary.

"And Louise?" Silence, but I realized I knew. Creighton had told her he needed the cat. He'd told her that there might be evidence. Louise knew she was being framed—and that the cat was her last defense.

"So why didn't she just spring you? Take you back?"

"Huh." The cat chuffed, not deigning to answer. Wallis. Tadeus. All the animals, they'd tried to tell me. Fear. Robin was a predator, and Louise had been trying to stay out of her line of sight. *"She burned the rags. Burned my blanket."* The cat curled in on herself. *"I could smell it. I could—"*

I felt it then, the fear behind the anger. The helplessness behind the guilt. She had been with Robin—left with Donal—by a wife who wanted something, but not this. The Persian hadn't cared. Had welcomed the visit. I heard soft words. I felt hands, trusted and warm, until they grabbed her paw. Forcing her— *"No!"*

"I'm sorry." I gathered the cat to me now, her compact body heaving with emotion. Cats don't cry, and that was a pity. This poor creature had been forced to do the unthinkable. To hurt the one person who had shown her real kindness.

Gently, with my good hand, I stroked her head and back. Softly, I murmured to her. Nonsense words for the most part. The kind of thing my mother probably once did for me. Outside, the storm began to die down. The wind to quiet. Eventually, the Persian stopped trembling.

And in the quiet, an inkling of an idea was forming. Crazy as it seemed, it was possible. DNA. The news report Creighton had told me about. "Robin wanted you gone. She was afraid there would be something on you—something that would prove what she did, didn't she? But why not—"

I caught myself. Why not kill the cat? One thing was obvious: if Robin pretended she valued the pretty Persian, she was in a better position to set Louise up as the bad guy if the accident theory was discredited. I'd fallen for it; others would, too. After all, what good is the perfect cats' paw if the cat is no longer around to wield it?

The open window. "She wanted you to run away, didn't she? She was hoping you'd end up in the woods. That you'd disappear on your own. The theory of the crime would still hold, and she could wail about losing you. And when you didn't..." She'd been pushing for possession of the Persian from day one.

The wind had nearly died down, but outside the car, deep in the woods, something howled. "Coyotes." I was talking to myself, but the cat hunkered down into the seat, and I shivered. "We don't have wolves anymore. Not here."

The cat was silent.

"She wanted you to run off into the woods." My mind kept circling around this. It was a horrible fate, devised by a cruel woman. But then, if I was right, Robin had arranged to kill Donal in cold blood, and set up his pet as the cause. Outside, the wolf howled.

Chapter Fifty-one

I slept, I must have, because at some point I started up, stiff and aching. The Persian—Felicity—was still on my lap, lying across my right leg. That was the only part of me that was warm, and I stretched my good arm to get some feeling back. Outside, I could see the sky turning gray. We might not have sun, but dawn was on its way. And so, I figured, we should be too.

"Want to hoof it back to town?" The cat stretched and looked up at me, blinking those blue eyes. "Are we not talking again?" Without coffee, I was not in the mood.

"Why should I?" She'd been dreaming, I got that now. Dreaming of Donal. A corduroy lap and the faint smell of pipe tobacco. No wonder she hated waking up.

"I'm sorry, Felicity. Really." I arched my back, the movement sending bolts of pain down my bad arm. "Look, we can't stay here. I'm going to head out. My wrist is messed up and I'm getting sick, and it could be another week before anyone comes by here. You can stay in the car, if you want, until I come back for you. Maybe it will be the best thing."

"No, no cage." She was on her feet.

"All right." I looked outside. The sky was lighter, streaks of yellow showing through the gray. But the woods were still black, the inky shadows stretching halfway across the road. "I'll carry you."

Rather to my surprise, she let me, waiting by the open door until I could turn and scoop her up in my left hand. Bidding a silent goodbye to my blue baby, I hoisted the Persian onto my shoulder and turned toward the road. It was easier than I expected. The cat was light, lighter than Wallis, and as I turned to start down the mountain, I wondered about her captivity. Felicity had only been in Louise's house for about twenty-four hours, but I suspected those hours had been in a locked closet or a basement. Louise might not be a killer, but she had no love for this cat. I didn't know if she'd been eating at the shelter, either. Doc Sharpe had been busy. Pammy—less than diligent. I kicked myself. "I should have checked to make sure you ate when you were fed."

"Fed. That's it." The voice came as a rumble against my cheek, warm as I picked my way down the road.

"I'm sorry. I don't have anything on me." Nor did I want to start foraging in the woods. I wasn't sure what we'd heard last night. I didn't want to take the chance that it might still be hungry.

"No, no." Claws dug into my shoulder with impatience. *"She wanted to be fed."*

"Louise?" I remembered the steak bones. The Bordeaux.

"No!" The claws again. I thought of Robin, plump and pretty. Mack had said she'd grown up poor, but she didn't look like she'd missed any meals lately. I could have used a hot dish right then. Something with bacon. Meat. I could almost smell the coffee when the prick of claws brought me back. I'd been falling asleep on my feet. I had also, I realized, made the mistake of listening to an animal on human terms.

"Fed? You mean, she was hungry?" Nothing, and I could almost feel the Persian's impatience growing. "She wanted something. Of course."

"To be fed." What would Robin want? Money, probably. A share of the spoils.

There'd been talk at the funeral, and I remembered Llewellyn scoffing at his friend. Something about how he didn't want to spend money on women anymore. Not women who already had enough. Creighton had said that, too—the will isn't a potential motive, he'd told me. So what did Robin have? What gave her a hold over the widow? "Was Donal going to change his will?"

Felicity was silent. Cats don't deal with details, and I sighed as we turned the bend. The sun was rising, the sky growing lighter by the second. People were just as predictable, weren't they?

All except for Jim Creighton. The thought of my sometime beau warmed me. Creighton didn't blindly follow the clues. He'd had every chance to close this case, and he had refused to follow the obvious trail. He'd tried to keep me out of it, sure. He hadn't let go, though. He had kept investigating.

"He kept the case open." I stopped so short, the cat shifted and I reached for her with my right arm. Mistake. I let her down, and we walked side by side. I no longer worried about her bolting. I no longer had the energy to worry. Instead, I thought about Creighton and hoped Felicity would understand. "He was still working it, see? That must have been why Robin hadn't been paid. That's why they were fighting. If the case was open, Louise might not have access to any joint assets."

With the sun, the wind had picked up, and I shivered. Maybe I could carry the Persian again soon. "But that's not a big deal. All she had to do was wait it out." Assuming she inherited, that is. A stray memory began to surface. Something I'd heard. "Unless—"

I stopped. Off to our left, there had been a noise, an animal sound—not a bark, more like a "chuff." Frozen in place, we both turned. Nothing was visible under those trees, but my sensitivity or an instinct older still told me something was there. Watching. The skin on the back of my neck rose. I stared into the blackness, trying to see, to understand. And jumped back as a crow went flying, cawing his displeasure loud into the sky.

No, not displeasure. Something louder. Fear.

Even on the wing, the crow was afraid, broadcasting his warning near and far. There was a predator on the hunt. A wolf.

I grabbed the cat and ran, heedless of the pain in my arm, of the rough road. Of anything but getting through this barren land and back into territory where humans held sway.

Chapter Fifty-two

A half hour, maybe more. We'd turned one corner and still the road stretched out, as vague and endless as my sense of time.

I was running a fever, I could tell. The cold, the flu, whatever bug had been wearing at me all week long. My wrist. Together, they'd broken down my resistance. Not my will to live. I had a good head of steam, and I was going to get us out of these woods. Without it killing either one of us.

Will can only take you so far, though, and the morning sun gave more light than warmth, glaring off a cold mist that lurked beneath the trees. Before long, Felicity had squirmed to be let down again, and I'd lowered her to the road. Ten minutes later—or was it twenty?—I could tell she was regretting it.

"You okay?" The Persian was limping, and as I looked over, I stepped on something—a rock, a pinecone—and stumbled to the ground, catching myself by habit on my hands. The pain that shot up my arm was electric, bringing a wave of nausea that had me choking. I rolled onto my back, cradling my bad arm to my chest. Tears leaked out through my clenched eyes, and I could hear the sound I was making—an animal noise. I lay there on the smooth blacktop. The cold seeped through to my back and I waited for it to get to my arm, to stop the throbbing. To stop the pain. Only then did I feel the soft touch of whiskers on my face, the slight snuffling breath of the cat.

That was it. I wasn't giving up. I don't give up. For a moment, though, I needed to catch my breath. Felicity needed to rest.

We both needed to take stock of the fact that we were stuck on a scenic route in stick season, freezing and vulnerable. Whether we'd heard a wolf or not was going to be immaterial in a few hours. The cold would be enough.

I didn't want to think about it. I wanted to lay back down, to go to sleep on the cool, cool road. Those whiskers, though. The breath they carried was warm. Alive. I sat up. I made it to the roadside and sat on a boulder. Felicity jumped into my lap, and I rested my bad hand on her soft body as I stared through the trees. A mist was rising, blurring the ground, but the bare trunks were stark and black. Between their trunks, I could see the fog rolling in, obscuring the bend in the road. I squinted against the haze, and tried to make out the road, the further curve. The one below that. If only I could let myself fall forward and roll, like the rock I was seated on, down through the trees. Then I could get us down there, back to a land of color and warmth.

I slumped forward, stopping only when the cat in my lap shifted. We were beyond words by this point, both wrung out. I felt my head nod. The mist rose. It stung my eyes and they closed. I thought I was dreaming when I heard it: the whine of an engine, somewhere above us. I blinked, sat up. Peered up through the mist to see a flash of color. Red. The color of a cardinal, or of blood. The whine grew louder, changing in frequency like a shift in gears. And then, through the trees, on the stretch of road we'd walked down only moments before, I saw it. Coming down from nowhere. A cherry-red sports car, going through its paces as it made its way down the slope.

I should have stood. I should have yelled and waved. As still as we were, that car could have driven right by us. Someone had sharp eyes, however, and as the red sportster came around the curve, it slowed to a stop, idling before me in the road.

A Maserati, in mint condition. Gregor "Bill" Benazi leaned over to open the passenger-side door.

"May I offer you a lift?"

I was too tired to question. Almost too tired to stand, but Felicity sank her claws in, just enough to wake me up, and I did both, carrying her over to place her on the empty seat. The leather felt welcoming, almost warm to my touch, and I wondered who else had been sitting in it recently. And what strange fate had brought this man down from a wilderness overlook at dawn in the middle of March.

"What?" It was all I could manage.

"I needed to drop off a package." Bill leaned over as if to confide a secret. "Happy to be able to oblige a lady on the way back."

There was something chilling in his voice, but I was too dazed with pain and cold. I'd run out of options. Felicity shuffled over. I got in the car.

As I warmed up, I felt myself getting sleepy. I didn't want to relax. The leather upholstery was soft, though, and the cat warm in my lap, and my eyes kept closing. To keep myself awake, I sat up and made myself focus on the big, unanswered questions: What hold did Robin have on Louise? Why had they fallen out?

I wished I could figure what Creighton had been doing. He'd been investigating, I got that. But had he let Robin know? Was he applying pressure that way? No, it didn't make sense. A woman cool enough to commit murder wasn't likely to crack. Was she?

I leaned back into the leather. It smelled new, like money. I yawned and stretched my good arm, looked around. A Maserati doesn't have a backseat per se. It does have a slight storage area, just big enough for groceries. Against the black leather, the tan stood out like a flag. Just a corner, peaking out from under the abbreviated rear seat. It reminded me of something. A good leather purse. A girl's first.

All of a sudden, sleep was the farthest thing from my mind. What had Mack said? Robin was broke. She couldn't pay him. Who knew whom else she couldn't pay.

I looked over at our driver, his angular face silhouetted against the morning light. Gregor "Bill" Benazi. Gentleman gangster. Creighton had warned me. Nobody had warned Robin. Had she owed for the pistol? For other favors? Or was it simply that murder had not been on the menu, and Robin had carried things a bit too far?

"He was a man of honor," Benazi had told me that day in the cemetery, fresh from Donal Franklin's funeral. "I, too, am a man of honor," he had said over salad and a glass of red wine.

As if on cue, Benazi turned and smiled at me. A lupine smile, full of teeth. A wolf.

I grabbed the Persian as I recoiled, pushing myself as far away as I could. The smile only broadened. "Good morning," he said. "You—"

To my surprise, the cat pushed back against my embrace. "Kitty," I leaned down and whispered into her fur. "Stay away from this one. He's dangerous."

"No, he's strong." My bad arm hurt too much. She squeezed herself out of my embrace and jumped over the gearshift to lean against Benazi's side. *"He will keep his word."*

"Lovely animal." He reached down to stroke her as he drove. "Is she Himalayan?" And as I looked on in horror, she began to purr.

Chapter Fifty-three

When I asked to be dropped at the Beauville police station, Benazi only chuckled. He did lean over Felicity as he stopped, as if to whisper in the Persian's velvet ear. I reached over and grabbed the cat, startling them both, and stumbled out of the car.

"*No!*" The Persian's angry howl conveyed her sentiments to us both, and Benazi nodded. I wondered what he'd said—and how much the white cat had understood. I didn't have time for questions. I raced into the glass foyer and the police station beyond. And there, I gather, I fainted dead away.

When I came to, Creighton was leaning over me, and for a moment I thought we were still in the station. Then I realized I was warm and clean—and my arm was in a cast.

"Well, if it isn't little red riding hood." Creighton smiled. "Welcome back. How was Grandma's?"

"Robin Gensler killed Donal Franklin," I said. "And Benazi— I think he may have killed Robin." At least, that's what I tried to say. My mouth was too dry to work properly, and whatever sounds I made had Creighton looking around for a nurse. "No, no." I shook my head and raised my good hand. "Water?"

That he understood and in a moment was holding a plastic straw to my chapped lips. "Thanks," I managed to rasp. He nodded. So I repeated, "Robin killed Donal. She used the Persian and she was trying to set up Louise."

"The original cat's paw, huh?" Great minds think alike.

"Not news?" I sipped some more, pleased by our tacit understanding.

"We've had our suspicions."

"The shopping trip? Too obvious?"

He nodded. "For starters. Yeah, she and Louise were planning something. Louise wanted out of the marriage, but she was supposed to catch her husband cheating—not witness his murder."

The makeover, the cat. Throwing Donal and Robin together. Those had been Louise's ideas, only they had given Robin a hold over Louise, the proofs of a setup the younger woman could threaten to reveal. If the accident theory fell through, she could frame the widow. Her benefactor, her friend. "The cuckoo." That was all that came out. "You raise them in your nest, but they take over."

He didn't ask. "But Robin didn't know the whole story." He paused, playing for effect. "The will. Anything other than a natural death—with doctor's certificates, you name it—and it all went to charity. Seems our Donal Franklin had a history. And, yeah, his wife had been informed."

Robin hadn't. Instead, she'd gotten greedy. Rather than be the wife's paid accomplice, she thought she could set herself up for life. Kill Donal, and blackmail Louise for everything. Only she hadn't bothered to check the details. Wallis had tried to tell me. They all had. I found myself sinking back into sleep and jerked forward with a start. "The cat!"

"She's fine. Back at the hospital, a little worse for wear, but she'll be all right now."

I nodded, suddenly very tired. "There's something on the cat. On the brush." I'd never figured out exactly what. Felicity hadn't been able to decipher human evil.

"I'd told you I wanted to examine that cat, Pru. You thought I was bluffing."

I waited. This was Creighton's show.

"There was more powder on the cat. Even with all she'd been through. And not just on her paw, but around her middle, deep under the fur. As if someone had held her."

"Is that enough?"

He snorted with laughter. "Hardly. But we found a brush, too, wedged under the spare in Louise Franklin's trunk. That had prints on it—prints made with fulminate of mercury..."

◇◇◇

When I next woke up, he was glancing around the room.

"You okay?" I tried to sit up. Mistake.

"I'm not here." He closed the door by leaning back on it. That's when I saw what he held in his arms.

"Wallis!" The big tabby leaped onto the bed, and I felt my eyes tear up as she nuzzled me with no other sound but her loud, rumbling purr. I didn't care. So, I'd been sick again. Maybe this is how it went.

"This is so against regulations." Creighton spoke softly and picked a dark hair from his shirt. Wallis', not mine.

"Boy Scout." My voice sounded soft, even to me. Imagine my surprise, then, when another, more acerbic, chimed in.

"Watch it, Pru. He's not as stupid as he seems."

"Wallis?" I murmured into her fur. "I thought..."

"Sometimes you think too much, Pru." It took me a moment to realize the voice, clear in my head, didn't carry to the man beside the bed. *"Try not to be so...human."*

I didn't have a response to that. Instead, I kept my face in my soft pet's fur until the fear of tears had passed. When I looked up, Creighton was still there.

"So how long have I been here?"

"Since Tuesday morning."

I gave him a look.

"It's Thursday. Two days. You've had pneumonia—as well as a broken wrist. Anyway, I've been going by to feed your friend here, and today she followed me out. Jumped in the car. I swear she knew I was coming over to visit you."

Neither Wallis nor I had to respond to that.

"Sometimes, Pru, I wonder..." He shook his head. I closed my eyes and enjoyed the smell of warm, clean cat.

He smuggled her out a little later, with a promise to spring me as well. When I next woke up, I found Doc Sharpe leaning over me, a worried frown on his usually placid face.

"Doc!" Even through my drugged haze, he'd startled me.

"Pru, you're awake." I nodded. He always did have a firm grip on the obvious. "I'm so glad. We were, well, they tell me you had quite an ordeal."

Through the haze of sleep and drugs, a thought began to bubble up to the surface.

"It was worth it, for the cat."

He cleared his throat, and I realized how little of the story he knew.

"I didn't steal her, Doc. I rescued her." I didn't have energy for anything more.

"So I gather, so I gather." He reached over and patted my hand. "Officer Creighton has been telling me quite a tale."

I nodded, fatigue getting the better of me. It helped to know I might still have a gig. Another thought was nagging, however.

"How's Felic—I mean, the white Persian. Fluffy. How's she doing?" I had to catch myself.

"Strangest thing. She's had a total turnaround in her behavior, and then a foreign gentleman came in to ask if he could adopt her. Bengazi?"

"And you let him?" I was awake now.

"After Officer Creighton examined her, Mrs. Franklin called. Said she didn't want to fuss anymore. So I saw no reason not to put her in the adoption area. This gentleman seemed to have been waiting for just such an opportunity. He went right to the Persian, and she began purring. When we took her out of the cage, she was actually kneading his shirt. With everything I've heard, I would say this is the best possible outcome."

I lay back on the pillow and closed my eyes. Let him think it was the flu.

Chapter Fifty-four

It took me longer to get back on my feet than I'd have liked. Spring was in full blast by the time I was completely back to normal, April's showers washing away the rest of the snow to reveal a gaggle of daffodils in my front yard. My mother's last project.

Doc Sharpe had commandeered Pammy, making sure she took over my regular gigs for those few weeks. She was only too happy to give up the early morning dog walks after that, though I suspected from some comments that Tracy Horlick made that my substitute had been more forthcoming with the gossip.

No matter, I was grateful to get back to the routine. Maybe it was me, maybe it was that spring had finally sprung—I sensed a new mellowness in the air. Growler still hadn't succeeded in winning his person over, but he didn't seem to resent our entire gender anymore. Once I could have sworn he wagged his tail when he saw me. I knew better than to mention it, though.

Lucy seemed to take it all in stride. "*Yup!*" She had barked, when I heard that my job—the walking, as well as the training—had come to an end. "*Training, done!*"

I had come by for our last walk. The woman who handed me her lead could not have looked more different.

"Here you go," said Eve Gensler—an Eve Gensler who had pink in her cheeks and something akin to a bounce in her stride. "Give you a chance to say your farewells. But don't worry, Pru. I'm sure I'll be calling you again when the weather gets bad."

I smiled, but I wasn't going to count on it. Even as we headed out, I saw the old lady lacing up new pink walking shoes. Something had turned her around.

"Something?" The little toy at my side looked up through her long lashes. *"Or some dog?"*

"Don't tell me your tricks made all this happen." I'd seen her dancing around her person as Eve Gensler had opened the door. I'd seen the look of pleasure on the old lady's face, too.

The poodle shook herself in a kind of canine disclaimer. *"A little sweetness, it never hurts."* The tawny dog stopped for a moment to hold me in her large, dark eyes. *"Sometimes, we get more with a little sugar, non?"*

"Oui." I couldn't begrudge her this small victory. She was a small dog.

"Out!" She barked, and I followed. For one more walk, anyway.

◇◇◇

Louise Franklin's sedan had been found near an Albany bus station. The DA was working on the theory that Robin Gensler had left the car there, Creighton told me. Disappeared into the hinterlands. I knew she'd disappeared all right. I didn't think she'd show up in Iowa with a new hair color any time soon.

Creighton and I had begun seeing each other again—occasionally. Warily. As cautious as two animals in the woods. As a measure of how things had shifted, I'd told him what I suspected about Benazi and Robin: an appointment to settle a debt, a more commensurate payment exacted. He wasn't surprised. However, without evidence, he didn't have anything to go on, and the DA wanted to keep it simple. When the county decided to prosecute the widow, Creighton had to go along. Maybe he thought she deserved some of the blame, too.

It wasn't a bad case, and it dragged on through the summer, as cases will. Especially when there's money. What physical evidence the county had was attacked. All that time in the shelter, and both Doc Sharpe and Pammy were called to the stand. Experts in antiquities discussed the gun. Even Louise Franklin's pretty escort had been found, working as a house boy in the Adirondacks. He had been an assistant of sorts, it seems, in that he'd been paid to step out with her, and that was all. No wonder Donal Franklin hadn't cared. When things got tense, he'd split. I figured that explained Louise Franklin's moodiness. She'd lost her latest toy.

At my request—and with Creighton running interference—I was barely a part of it. The way I saw it, I'd played my part. Not only had I rescued Felicity, but my presence had distracted Robin. I was pretty sure she'd meant to dump the brush, too. Only I'd been there. In the way. Maybe that was worth a broken wrist.

The DA seemed to believe that he could make a case without my testimony, at least for conspiracy. Llewellyn's paperwork had included the Franklin's pre-nup. It was ironclad against any kind of frivolous divorce. No matter that he'd started giving money away. No matter that he'd wanted her to cut back—have a little less "fun"—Louise had to have "cause" to get out, at least if she wanted to get out with anything. That's what I'd misheard that day at the cemetery. Now it was clear: she had taken the younger woman in, paid for her hair and the new wardrobe. Put her in the house with her husband, alone. But she hadn't told her about the will.

For a while there, things started to look bad for the widow. Nobody believed that Louise wouldn't challenge the will, once the husband was disposed of. Money is a big motivator, and my original theory—that Louise had used Robin—kept coming up. Louise didn't do herself any favors. She started off playing innocent. It had all been the younger woman's idea. Every bit of it. And since Robin Gensler wasn't there to defend herself, it might have worked. If Mack knew anything, he wasn't talking. And Lew? Well, I had a feeling Lew would have stuck up for the younger woman, if he'd been there. Maybe he already had.

Not that I had much time for theorizing. Not when the county DA told me that, yes, I would have to take the stand, and so I did, describing what I had seen—and what Robin Gensler had put me through on that lonely mountain road. I don't know, maybe it did me good to go through all that again. I didn't like it. I was so afraid that I'd let something slip, something about the Persian or how we had gotten through the night, that I knew I sounded jittery. Girlish. Lost. The DA loved it, though. Said I sounded vulnerable. I bit my tongue to keep from responding.

Hearing how all the parts played out must have been the final straw for Louise Franklin. Soon after that, the widow cracked. She confessed that she'd brought Robin into their lives. That she'd groomed Robin to appeal to Donal in the hope of catching him in a compromising position, of forcing him to make a better settlement. Only as she took credit, I began to see more of Robin's manipulation at work—how she eased her way into the household, all the while dreaming up a bigger crime and a lifelong source of blackmail.

Sure enough, the phone setup had been Robin's idea—Louise was supposed to catch them alone together, to raise a fuss with the shopkeeper as a witness. Then Robin would break down and play her part, the aggrieved mistress—and be paid off. Only Robin had other plans—played on the trust she had seduced from both Franklins and their cat. The rest was history.

The fact that she'd wanted a divorce, not a murder didn't make Louise Franklin much more sympathetic. She was convicted of being an accessory to the murder, ultimately, but her lawyers got a light sentence in return for her revised, and much more complete, testimony. Five to seven in minimum security, minus time served. She'd be out in two.

The funny part, Louise confessed, was that Donal hadn't fallen for her mean-spirited ruse. Despite his wife's apparent infidelities—her moodiness, even her dislike of his adored pet—he had remained true. A man of honor.

◇◇◇

The fate of the dueling pistol was a little more subdued. Between one thing and another, the bulk of the estate was liquidated, the proceeds to be distributed to various charities. The pistol went immediately to one of the more discreet New York auction houses. The listing was innocuous: *Wogden & Barton, c.*

1808, scent-bottle, chased silver. V. good. Still, it brought less than expected, perhaps because it had been fired. Rumors did circulate that interested parties had been warned off bidding, but the auction house could turn up no evidence of malfeasance. Consistent with the house policy, the buyer, who worked through intermediaries, was not disclosed.

◇◇◇

Robin was listed as a fugitive, her name and face sent out on the wires. And the only loose end was Felicity. She had disappeared with Benazi, and he may as well never have existed. I worried about the white Persian, and at the risk of offending, brought it up to Wallis one night.

"He's a gangster, Wallis." I said, my mind traveling back to that lonely open road. "A killer."

"Oh, please." She closed her eyes in disdain, stretching in the warmth of the fire. It was September by then. Still early for frost, but I'd piled the logs high.

"What?" I shifted. My wrist ached, especially on these chilly nights. "I know she likes him. But she's a show cat. A pedigree. She might not always have had it easy, but what does she know of danger? Of revenge?"

I thought of Robin. Of wolves.

"Why do you think she chose him, anyway?" Wallis twisted to face me. Slits of green peering out. *"Don't you know, we're predators, too?"*

Acknowledgments

Antique gun buffs are a generous lot, and I owe many thanks to the various forums and dealers who steered me toward my murder weapon. Al Grindley of vintageweaponry.com and Richard Reich at James H. Cohen Antiques, New Orleans, were most helpful. Clyde W. Howard of Texas, in particular, found my dueling pistol for me and repeatedly explained its workings, always with great patience. All errors are mine and none his. Deep thanks to my readers—Chris Mesarch, Jon S. Garelick, Tee Jay Henner, Karen Schlosberg, Naomi Yang, Brett Milano, and the indefatigable Lisa Susser. Without you guys, I'd be sunk. Of course, the eagle eyes of my wonderful agent Colleen Mohyde of the Doe Coover Agency and editor Annette Rogers contributed greatly, as did my dear friends including Vicki Croke and Caroline Leavitt, who provided encouragement and inspiration, and Sophie Garelick, Lisa Jones, and Frank Garelick, my most loyal fans. Most of all, thanks to Jon for putting up with deadline insanity and revision temper. You're the best, sweetie. I owe it all to you.

To receive a free catalog of Poisoned Pen Press titles, please contact us in one of the following ways:

Phone: 1-800-421-3976
Facsimile: 1-480-949-1707
Email: info@poisonedpenpress.com
Website: www.poisonedpenpress.com

Poisoned Pen Press
6962 E. First Ave. Ste 103
Scottsdale, AZ 85251